BLOOD
FOR
BLOOD

BLOOD
FOR
BLOOD

ZIBA MACKENZIE BOOK ONE

VICTORIA
SELMAN

THOMAS & MERCER

Text copyright © 2019 by Victoria Selman

Published by Thomas & Mercer, Seattle

www.apub.com

Amazon, the Amazon logo, and Thomas & Mercer are trademarks of Amazon.com, Inc., or its affiliates.

ISBN-13: 9781542040525 (hardcover)
ISBN-10: 1542040523 (hardcover)
ISBN-13: 9781503905054 (paperback)
ISBN-10: 1503905055(paperback)

Cover design by Mark Swan

Printed in the United States of America

For Tim, the wind in my sail

Men never do evil so completely and cheerfully as when they do it from religious conviction.

Blaise Pascal

PROLOGUE

The boy has the face of an angel. A radiance of golden curls. Botticelli lips. Baby-wide eyes. Only the marks around his neck spoil the effect. A dark stain on white wings. The Devil alone knows what he's done – and undone.

CHAPTER 1

It happened at 17.27 on a Thursday evening in mid-autumn. The weather was unsettled and I was out and about for the first time in weeks.

'*The train now approaching Platform 1 is the northbound Thameslink service via King's Cross St Pancras. Please remain behind the yellow line at all times for your safety.*'

I stood well back. The edge of the platform has an allure I can't trust.

People jostled for position as the engine tore down the line, fighting their way to the front before it had a chance to stop. Rush hour doesn't bring out the best in anyone. We've all got places to be.

The doors hissed open. The crowd surged forward.

The carriage was jammed but I managed to spot a vacant rear-facing seat by the window and plonked myself down before someone else nabbed it. I inhaled deeply and focused on my breathing. It didn't work; my chest was tight, the edges were closing in.

Embrace the suck and get a bloody grip, I thought. Today's supposed to be special.

'*This train is ready to depart. Please stand clear of the doors. Mind the closing doors.*'

There was a strong smell in the carriage, like steamy refuse or gone-off fruit. Wrinkling my nose I looked around, trying to get my bearings and ground myself. A coping strategy, my old therapist called it.

A guy standing in the aisle a few feet away was looking at me. He had a buzz-cut, pleats down his shirtsleeves so sharp you could have cut yourself on them, and a tie knotted tight. So, highly strung and clearly agitated, I thought, observing his twitching facial muscles and rapid blinking.

In the row adjacent to mine, a man with cystic acne, hollow cheeks and rotten teeth was swatting his arms and picking at his skin. All the physical characteristics and behavioural tells of a methamphetamine addict. He caught my eye then turned away quickly.

Narcotics aren't my field, but I picked up a bit from Duncan when he moved to Vice, or SCD9 as it's called these days. Most meth-heads have a criminal record. And the profile's nearly always the same – paranoia, violence, insomnia, hallucinations. Though when they're not high, users can actually be quite lucid.

Across from me, a lady in her late sixties wearing a small gold cru-cifix and a rosary bracelet was reading the *Metro*, biting her fingernails and jiggling her leg up and down. Nervous then. Or perhaps what she's reading is making her uncomfortable, I thought, glancing at the head-line at the top of the page spread open on her lap. Without thinking I gave her the once-over.

Crucifix. Rosary. So a Catholic – a believer in redemption and hell. Blouse buttoned all the way to the top. Handbag small and unbranded with stiff handles and a snap clasp. A person indifferent to status, some-one closed off from those around her. And beige clothes, a neutral tone often linked to feelings of loneliness and isolation. I looked down. My jacket was the same colour.

This was a woman who shut herself off from the world. Possibly someone she'd trusted had let her down. Maybe she thought she was safer keeping herself to herself or perhaps she just didn't like people.

We stopped at a signal point. I leaned against the wall of the carriage, resting my head on the window. There was a drill going behind my left eye, the beginning of a migraine. The cool glass was soothing.

Outside, the scene was as grey as the sky. High walls spray-painted with obscenities. Tunnels and metal bridge supports. Rail huts and lines of wires. All covered in a thick film of soot.

A freight train trundled past on the neighbouring tracks. A maroon-and-yellow locomotive pulling thirty corrugated metal containers tagged with graffiti. And at the back of the line, eight silver cylinders with the Shell logo printed on the side.

'We apologise for the wait. We'll be moving shortly.'

I yawned, opened the copy of the *Metro* I'd picked up at the station and began to flick through it.

Five pages in, there was an article about the anniversary of Samuel Catlin's murder. An illustrated double-page spread with the photo of him in his school uniform that made all the papers when I was a kid.

There was also one of him waving goodbye to his parents with his baseball cap on back to front and a rucksack covered in dinosaur stickers. It had been taken as he walked to the bus stop, the first time he'd ever travelled to school on his own.

He was ten years old and he never made it home that night.

Parents' Plea to Catch Son's Killer

Twenty-five years ago today, Samuel Catlin, 10, was kidnapped and murdered on his way home from school. His body was later found on a canal towpath by Camden Lock in North London, his head resting on a folded anorak. Despite a massive national investigation and widespread interest in the case, the person responsible has never been caught.

Yesterday, his parents issued a renewed appeal to the public for help catching their son's killer.

'Samuel had this gorgeous blond hair and a smile that'd melt your heart. He wanted to be a helicopter pilot when he grew up. He loved chocolate-chip cookies and pancakes – anything sweet.

'Our lives will never be the same without him. We won't stop looking until we find who took him from us,' said his mother, Anne, 59.

'Someone out there knows something. They may think it's too small to be significant but every detail matters. If you know anything at all, please contact the police. We need your help to catch Samuel's killer so the person who did this to our son can finally be punished.'

Fighting back tears, Samuel's father said the devastation his family felt was made all the worse because his child's murderer had never been brought to justice.

Anyone with information is asked to call Crimestoppers on 0800 555 111.

The woman opposite me shut her eyes and sighed. Her thumb was tap-tapping the handle of her bag. The corner of her mouth was twitching like she was trying not to cry. She'd been reading the Samuel Catlin article too.

She whispered something so quietly that if it weren't for my ability to lip-read I may have missed it.

They never caught him.

She sighed again making the sign of the cross.

I sighed too. I shared her sentiments but I also knew from experience that unsolved child homicide cases always remain open. Perhaps the Catlins' appeal will produce fresh evidence, I thought. Though given the amount of time that had passed it was pretty unlikely.

My eyes wandered again. The paper wasn't holding my attention. I'd been reading the same line over and over, unable to concentrate. I'd slept the night before but it had been a cursed sleep: light and fitful and filled with nightmares so that when I'd woken in the morning it was as if I'd never slept at all. And it looked like I wasn't the only one.

There was a guy across the aisle with bags under his eyes, felt-tip on his shirt cuffs and a white splotch on the shoulder of his pinstriped suit jacket. A father, then, with a new baby and a toddler at home; a little girl probably, given the glittery pink ink stain. And a formula-fed baby, judging by the chalky colour of the spit-up.

The woman next to him – blonde hair, little skirt, lots of cleavage – was applying lip gloss. The badly concealed shadows under her eyes told me she hadn't had much sleep either but going by the smile hovering at the corners of her mouth and the love bite on her neck, it was for a different reason.

And what about the woman absently stroking her barely-there stomach and looking off into the middle distance? Well, she may not have been yawning just then but if I was right about her she'd know all about sleep deprivation in less than nine months' time.

'We will shortly be arriving at Kentish Town. Please ensure you take all personal belongings when departing the train.'

The Catholic woman opposite me folded up her newspaper and popped it in her bag, checking the seat for forgotten items before getting up and making her way to the doors.

I glanced at my watch as we emerged from a tunnel, shooting out into the semi-daylight.

17.27.

The air was warm, the train's rhythm soothing. I was just closing my eyes, head against the glass, hugging my bag to my chest, when the train jolted. There was an ear-rupturing screech and the shriek of steel grinding on steel, as the engine fought to decelerate.

My eyes shot open. There, lying on their sides across the parallel track, were three cylindrical Shell containers – the word FLAMMABLE painted in red across the centre.

CHAPTER 2

Time distorted. There was only a split second between that moment and the next but it seemed longer to me. An illusion, of course. The brain's emotional centre becoming more active.

My scalp tingled. My body tensed. My stomach slipped a rung.

The evening rush hour was at its peak. We were trapped in a metal tube, hundreds of commuters packed in tight. Men, women and children. Workers reading the paper and thinking about what to have for dinner. School kids loaded up with homework and games kits.

Across the aisle, the pregnant woman was holding her belly, mouth open. The lip-gloss girl was hovering her make-up brush over a compact. The tired father's eyes were stretched wide.

I raised my arms to shield my face, an instinctive reaction. There was no time to adopt the brace position or get down on the floor. No time to take cover beneath a seat or even shout a warning to the other passengers.

We'd been travelling at 65 mph, at least. At that speed and with the distance we were from the wagons, despite the massive deceleration, braking wouldn't be enough.

There was a boom – thunder-loud – a body blow and hard recoil as we smashed into the derailed petrol container.

For a moment the carriage became airborne, thrown upwards by the impact of the collision, before crashing to the ground.

I was pressed back into my seat, pinned by an invisible hand. The passengers across from me were hurled forwards, the force of the impact catapulting them out of their seats as though somersaulting, their necks twisting as their heads slammed into the people and objects opposite.

A second later, an explosion. A cannonball of fire and air. Windows popping. Glass shattering. Flying debris.

The air was thick with dust and smoke. The smell of diesel was so strong I could taste it, bitter and acrid in my mouth. Fuel dispersed and ignited by the collision.

There was screaming, moaning, a baby crying. And from far away a mobile phone ringing, 'Tubular Bells'. The sounds were muffled though, as if heard through foam; temporary hearing loss caused by the blast.

My mouth was parched, my skin drenched in sweat. We could have been in a furnace the heat was so intense.

Too far away to reach, I saw a man engulfed in flames visible only in hazy outline through the black smoke. Everywhere small fires licked the scorched carcass of the train.

The stench of diesel gave way to the sickly-sweet smell of singed flesh. Nearby someone started to cough.

My whole body trembled, but this wasn't about fight or flight, not any more. Now it was about something primal. It was about survival.

CHAPTER 3

Post-explosion protocol was part of my basic training. I knew what to do and how to stay alive.

I kept my mouth open and took small breaths. Most people think the deadliest part of a blast is the heat or shrapnel. It's not. It's overpressure from the shock wave.

We instinctively hold our breath when we're scared but this just turns our lungs into high-pressure balloons. After a confined explosion, the shock waves puncture and rupture them, causing internal bleeding and severe chest pain. Only around 6 per cent of victims die from burns and shrapnel injuries. The rest die from the effect of burst lungs.

I touched my hand to my face and torso, assessing the damage – cheek badly cut, bruises but no broken ribs, and no stomach, back or chest pains. The sensation of having cotton wool in my ears was receding so my hearing was intact. My eyes stung from the smoke but they weren't burning and my vision wasn't blurred. I could breathe and, getting to my feet, I found I could walk – just about. My right leg wasn't wounded but it wouldn't work properly. I fell forward into the debris.

Fuck this, I thought, struggling back up. I staggered over to the wall of the train, put my palms on it and managed to support myself in a semi-upright position. I scanned the carriage, getting a read.

'Stay low. Cover your mouths,' I shouted. My voice was muted and I started to cough as I inhaled a lungful of dust.

The carriage was stifling and black with smoke; a widow's veil. At first I could only make out shapes. People trapped where they'd been sitting. Others on the floor beneath rubble and broken glass, thrown from seats that had been yanked away from the side of the train in the explosion.

But as the smoke began to clear through the gaping chasms of blown-out windows and doors and my eyes started to adjust to the darkness, I saw more. The father in the pinstriped suit with no face. Another person badly burned and spreadeagled under a heap of metal. The motionless body of a young woman; eyes wide open, sockets empty.

There was a crater in the middle of the carriage, broken glass and bodies torn apart. The bodies of husbands, fathers and grandfathers. Wives, mothers and grandmothers. Sons and daughters. Brothers and sisters. People who'd raced to catch the train. People whose families would never see them again.

I took a breath and looked around again, this time with a different eye, an appraising one. Where to start?

Everywhere people were screaming and calling out for help.

The spreadeagled man was leaking tears of pain. His torso was crushed by the weight of the metal on top of him. His face was black with blood and dust. His hands were swollen and pierced with shrapnel. I wanted to go to him but there was a ravine between us. I'd never make it over there with my sodding leg acting out the way it was and even if I did, I mightn't get back to help anyone else. Better to stay here and tend to the wounded I could reach more easily.

The lip-gloss girl from before was lying nearby. She was pale, her clothes were torn and she wasn't moving.

I put my cheek to her nose and mouth to see if I could detect any breathing. Nothing. I thought of her secret smile earlier. Smoothing away her hair I pressed my fingers to her neck checking for a pulse in her carotid artery, willing her to be alive. I wasn't sure at first but then I felt it. A faint beat. A sign she wasn't ready to give up.

I placed the heel of my hand on the centre of her chest, put the other on top and pushed down.

'One, two, three . . .'

Thirty compressions. Two rescue breaths. Repeat.

Come on.

I blew air into her lungs. Her mouth and throat filled with blood. It was over.

'Help me,' said a trembling female voice. It wasn't coming from far away but I was suddenly exhausted. Moving even a few metres felt like a feat.

Limping, I picked my way through the debris towards her. The pain seemed to stab through my ribs with each step. My throat stung. My eyes hurt.

'Help me,' she whimpered as I reached her. It was the woman who'd been stroking her belly before the crash. Her hair was matted with gore. A pool of dark blood was soaking through the seat of her jeans.

'I've lost it, haven't I?'

Her eyes filled with tears.

'You need a tourniquet,' I said, though I knew she wasn't referring to her leg.

There was a deep rip along the femur. A large shard of metal was sticking out of it and blood was oozing over her fingers, which were instinctively pressing down on the wound. I took off my cardigan and tied it round her thigh. It wasn't ideal and it certainly wasn't what Duncan would have called 'wash', but it was all I had and with any luck it would stop her bleeding to death.

'What's your name?' she asked as I pressed down.

'I'm Ziba. Ziba MacKenzie.'

'My name's Liz Cartwright. You've got to let my husband know what's happened to me. Will you do that? Please. Will you let him know?'

'You're going to get out of here and you're going to tell him yourself. Do you hear me?'

She nodded and I pulled the knot tight.

'Now, put your hand here and keep the pressure on it,' I said, looking around the carriage for the next candidate.

That's when I saw her, the Catholic woman, collapsed on the floor. I hobbled over.

'Hey there,' I said, putting a hand on her shoulder. 'How are you doing?'

It was a stupid question. Looking at her, I could see exactly how she was doing. She had no external wounds but her eyelids were fluttering. There was a large plum-coloured ecchymosis on her neck and a massive swelling in her thigh. Internal injuries. There was nothing I could do for her.

Sighing, I surveyed the carriage – triage based on instinct. But the Catholic woman had other ideas.

She grabbed my arm, gripping hard; her face drained white, her eyes stretched wide. She wasn't looking at me though. Something else had drawn her attention.

I might have shaken her off had she not turned to me then. Her eyes were Duncan's eyes. That same mixture of grey and green that used to make me think of mountain lakes. I knelt down and cradled her head.

Staying was against all the guidelines. There were others for whom my help might have made a difference. But I didn't care. I wasn't with the special forces any more and I wasn't leaving this woman to die alone.

Every now and then her body jerked as an invisible current passed through it.

'It's okay,' I said. 'I'm here.'

I wanted her to hear my voice. I knew it didn't matter what I said so long as I said something. So long as she knew someone was with her.

She tried to speak.

'He—'

She stopped, struggled, then opened her mouth again. Whispering something unintelligible. But determined to get the words out.

'I don't understand,' I said, leaning in to hear her better. 'What are you trying to say?'

She looked right at me and, clutching my arm, took a deep breath, the way you might if you were about to dive underwater.

'He did it. You have to tell someone.'

'Who's *he*?' I said. 'What did he do?'

'Please,' she gasped as the final breath rattled out of her body.

She'd lived just long enough to pass on her message. But I had absolutely no idea what it meant.

CHAPTER 4

By the time the first emergency-response teams arrived on the scene in their hard hats and high-vis vests, I was loosening the charred clothing of a teenage girl with third-degree burns to reduce further damage caused by swelling. The skin on her hands was waxy, red raw and covered in blisters.

'We need gauze and cold compresses over here,' I shouted, waving my arms to attract attention.

Outside, railway workers were guiding passengers up the embankment. While on-board, survivors able to move were helping each other climb over seats and out of the carriage through gaps in blown-out windows. A few metres away from me, a man in a suit turned grey with dust was bashing at a door with a metal pole – a handrail ripped loose in the crash.

'If you can walk, make your way over here,' called a rescue worker, shining a torch into the carriage.

Stumbling, survivors made their way through the scorched wreckage towards him. Some supported themselves against the wall of the train, some supported each other.

The rescue worker stretched an arm into the carriage to help them down. They dropped, one by one, and began moving, dazed, along the track to the other side where more rescuers were handing out blankets and coffee.

'You're not going to leave me, are you?' The girl's voice rose in panic.

'I'm not leaving you. Try to relax. You're going to be okay.'

'We're not going to be okay!' screamed an elderly woman trapped in her seat beneath heavy shrapnel. 'We're all going to die.'

'No one's going to die.' I spoke with as much authority as my voice would convey, as well as some irritation. Hysteria wasn't going to help anyone.

'You should get off the train,' an EMT said to me as he checked the girl for airway involvement. He nodded at the gash on my face. 'Go get yourself seen to.'

'I promised I'd stay. What can I do to help?'

He shrugged.

'Keep her calm,' he whispered. 'Chat to her.'

Small talk's not my bag and I was never much good at interacting with teenage girls, even when I was one myself.

'So, what music are you into?' I asked.

It seemed like a safe topic.

'Classical, mainly,' she said, wincing in pain. 'Piano's my life. I'm auditioning for Juilliard in February.'

'You must be very talented.' I looked away, not wanting my expression to tell her what she hadn't yet realised.

'What next?' I said to the paramedic when he'd loaded her on to a makeshift stretcher.

My arms were quivering. I felt drained, but the pain in my leg was subsiding and I could put weight on it which meant I could make myself useful.

'We need to clear a path to get the wounded out.'

'Copy that,' I said, rolling up my sleeves.

It was only later when I was outside, standing by the mangled train and its fifty-foot plume of pungent smoke, that the scale of the accident hit me.

How had this happened? How had an everyday journey turned into an apocalyptic nightmare? How had I gone from wondering if today would be the day I'd finally be able to drag myself off the sofa to thinking I was about to end up as canned ham?

I've seen plenty of body bags in my line of work, but this was different. And it'd had an effect on me too. As the smoke filled the carriage, the fog I'd been in for the last few weeks lifted. Helping those people on the train had reminded me what I do best. When the buildings burn, I don't run away. I charge right into the flames.

Looking around, I could see I wasn't the only one. Men and women who'd jostled to get on board earlier were now stepping up to help total strangers.

Rush hour may bring out the worst in people, but tragedy brings out the best.

The stories emerged later. Acts of heroism, complete strangers helping each other. A man pulling a girl out from under a pile of debris despite being severely injured himself. Another who escaped his carriage only to go into the wrecked remains of the one in front to try to help the survivors trapped there.

Right then, though, I just saw simple expressions of humanity; the sort the news channels would never remark on. A boy in a hoodie giving an old lady with a cut jaw a swig from his water bottle. A woman supporting a limping man along the tracks. The type of acts that make you think maybe the world isn't quite as messed up as you'd thought.

And through it all, a question nagged, refusing to let up.

Who was the Catholic woman? And what had she been trying to tell me?

CHAPTER 5

I folded my arms, sticking my hands into my armpits, hugging my jacket tight. The sweat was cooling on my back. There was a chill in the air. It had started to drizzle.

In the distance I could hear the wail of sirens and everywhere mobile phones were ringing. The news had got out. Relatives and friends were checking up on their loved ones.

I'd lost my bag on the train but my phone was still in my pocket. On instinct, I hit Duncan's name. The line clicked.

'This number is no longer in service.'

My hand started to tremble. The phone slipped between my fingers.

'Hey, sweetie. Are you alright?' said an elderly black woman with woolly grey hair and a deep cut above her eye; another survivor.

She picked up my phone and put an arm round me, holding me close. The human contact made my throat catch.

It was stupid, but then so is the way I reach across the bed for my husband every morning despite the fact he's been dead longer than we were married. And so too is how I'm momentarily startled by the cold patch where he should be lying every time I do. After all this time, I still expect him to be there, just like I expected him to answer his phone now.

His death has turned the world into an empty chasm; all that's left is dust and stone. Whoever said, 'It's better to have loved and lost than never to have loved at all,' was talking out of their ass. Not a second goes by that I don't feel the cold suck of his absence.

I wish I knew how to forget you, Duncan. I'd rather have never met you than exist alone in this abyss.

'That's it. I've got you,' the woolly haired woman said, my face pressed against her side; the warmth of her body reminding me of something from another life.

'They've set up a makeshift triage centre at a primary school. It's this way. Come on, we'll go together.'

'It's okay. I'm fine.'

She spun me round, her hands on my forearms, looking down at me. She wasn't tall but she beat me on height – most people do. Her face was drill-sergeant firm with the voice to match.

'You don't look fine to me. That's a nasty cut you've got there on your face. I'd say you're going to need stitches.'

What a lot of fuss about a bit of blood! In the desert we took care of this sort of thing ourselves. Superglue holds a laceration together just as well as sutures. We all carried UHU in our kit bags. Out in the field, you learn to make do with what you've got.

There was a time, a while back, when one of my oppos managed to get shot in the leg. For some reason he didn't have a first-aid kit or pressure dressing in his backpack. But he did at least have a clean pair of socks.

I un-balled them, folded them over and pressed them against his wound, then ripped my sleeve to secure the pad in place. I'm not a medic, but it did the trick.

I considered saying all this to the woman helping me, but I didn't have the energy for story-telling and frankly it wasn't worth the effort.

'You go on,' I said instead. 'I'll catch you up. I just need to make a call first.'

As she walked away, I took my phone out again. This time I clicked Jack Wolfe's number.

CHAPTER 6

It is 07.07 on the seventh of October. This moment is perfection. 777. A trinity of sevens.

The man who calls himself Raguel looks at the numbers on his digital alarm clock for just a moment before sitting up in bed, his legs cramped from the tight foetal ball he always sleeps in. He'd like to look at the clock for longer but he doesn't dare.

He only has sixty seconds before the numbers change and then it'll be too late. 07.08 is meaningless, messy even. 07.07 is different. It's blessed.

He resets the alarm then swings his legs over the side of the bed feeling for his slippers with his feet. They're soft and brown with hard plastic soles, not yellow foam like in the other place.

As he bends down, touching his toes to get the blood flowing, the voices start up inside his head.

'Hurry,' they say, their whispers like slithering snakes. 'Be quick, quick, quick, or you'll miss her.'

He intones the Lord's Prayer, keeping his voice low as he walks to the bathroom on the points of his feet. There's no reason to be quiet or walk like this but he does it anyway. Old habits grip tight.

He pisses and then turns on the tap. The water's freezing, turning his hands red. If he let it run a bit it'd warm up but there's no time for that. He needs to be ready to go in ten minutes – by 07.17 – and there's so much to do before then.

He holds his hands under the flow. Counts to seven. Turns them over. Counts to seven. Turns them over. Counts to seven. Again and again until each side has been rinsed for seven seconds, seven times. It's important to get things right. Everything will fall apart if he doesn't.

He walks back into the bedroom. He's been living here for a while now but privacy still feels like a luxury; something to be savoured.

'In everything give thanks, for this is God's will,' he says aloud, making the sign of the cross.

The whispering voices murmur their approval.

'Yes, good. Good. Very Good.'

The shadowy figure hiding in the corner stirs.

07.11. Tick tock. Raguel needs to hurry. He makes his bed, pulling out the top sheet and blanket then lining them up so they hang evenly on all sides before tucking the fabric under the mattress. 07.13. Four minutes left. But four and three make seven. He'll be alright.

'God willing,' he says quickly as the whispers become critical.

Counting, he takes off his stripy pyjama bottoms and folds them on his pillow. Then he removes his undershirt, taking care to fold it precisely before laying it on top of the trousers. Still counting, he puts on a pair of Y-fronts, white socks, navy chinos, a shirt and tie, never moving on to the next item before reaching the sacred number.

He looks in the mirror and smiles, pleased with his reflection. Most of the others don't wear ties but he likes to look smart. Manners make the man, his mother used to say. Clothes command respect.

He gives the ficus on the windowsill a drink with seven short sploshes from his green watering can, gobbles a banana in seven careful bites and brushes his teeth seven times; brush, rinse, spit, repeat. All the while his eye is on the clock.

7.17. He's done it. He's on track for the day.

The Lord will be pleased, just as he was when Raguel answered that first call and his new name was whispered to him while the moon glowed red.

Raguel. He'd sat there by the water counting the letters out on his long piano-player fingers, remembering the cipher his mother had taught him when he was little. Each letter has a numerical position in the alphabet, A=1, B=2 and so on, she'd said.

But the letters in 'Raguel' added up to sixty-four. Nothing to do with seven.

That can't be right, he'd thought, clawing at his skin. Agonising.

He'd had to dig deep to find the answer.

Sixty-four. Six and four. Six multiplied by four equals twenty-four. Twenty-four priests served in King David's temple. And, he'd thought getting excited, if you subtract one (God's number) from sixty-four you get sixty-three. Sixty-three divided by seven equals nine. Christ died at the ninth hour and appeared nine times after his resurrection. It was alright. The numbers worked.

Seven and nine. Sixty-four. Holy numerals bound together to create a name that would keep him safe.

And now with that thought more follow; thoughts he can't control. Memories of the past and of Katie leaving him. Raguel grips the side of his head, groaning.

He has pills to make him feel calmer but they give him tremors and make his vision blurry. He prefers to self-medicate, despite the doctor's warnings.

Of course, he'd get into serious trouble if anyone found out about his drug habit but some risks are worth taking. And besides, today's special; he needs to feel strong.

He dips the tip of his knife into the pouch and snorts the powdered crystals.

See, he thinks as he does another bump. He doesn't need Katie. He can look after himself. Then a second later: screw her for ditching him, and a second after that Katie is out of his mind.

His whole body rushes with euphoria. Forget Katie. Forget seven. Forget what he wanted to forget. He's invincible. He can do anything. He's king of the world.

The alarm clock beeps. Raguel puts the baggie back in the drawer and hurries to the door, stopping to reposition the fruit bowl so it's dead centre in the middle of the table.

And then he is gone.

CHAPTER 7

It's evening now. Raguel is back at the station twisting the loop of string inside his pocket, gnawing at his lower lip. He can see the woman he loves waiting on the platform; a newspaper in one hand, her bag in the other.

She always gets this train home. He always rides it with her. And although he never speaks to her, there's comfort in knowing they're together, breathing the same air.

'*The train now approaching Platform 1 is the northbound Thameslink service via King's Cross St Pancras. Please remain behind the yellow line at all times for your safety.*'

Raguel stands back, his arms hugged tight across his torso, as the crowd rushes forward. He doesn't like being touched; even the faintest brush makes him feel violated.

He slips through the sliding doors just before they slam shut and the packed train shoots out of the station.

He looks around. Where is she? Has she got on a different carriage? Why isn't she here?

His heart quakes. His mouth goes dry. Today of all days he needs to see her; the morning seems so long ago. It's not enough.

'Ssssstupid, ssssstupid,' say the whispering voices, echoing in his ears.

He feels a team of ants crawling up his forearm. He swats at them and scratches at his skin but there's nothing he can do to get rid of them.

'Ssssso stupid,' say the voices again.

Their commentary is constant, relentless.

He closes his eyes and says seven Hail Marys under his breath. O God of Mercy and Compassion, let it be enough.

When he opens them he spots her putting stuff on her lips. A leather-clad heathen wearing a skull necklace was blocking his view, but she's there, his angel.

It's been years since they last spoke but he makes sure he sees her every day. Shadowing her to and from work. Following her home from the station at night. Watching her through the windows from the street below as she moves around upstairs. This time of year's perfect for that. The lights go on early and it's easier to see in when the rooms are lit up.

They're meant to be together, him and her. Tracking her binds them; it makes him feel safe. But sometimes it's not enough.

Raguel knows she approves of what he did but even so he longs to explain himself to her. Is this another reason he tails her, because there is unfinished business between them?

A pressure builds in his throat; a pulse throbs hard in his neck.

His yearning for her to understand him is almost physical. Whenever he sees her, his breathing becomes shallow and his heart becomes a lion trapped in his chest. There are times he has to clamp down on his tongue to stop himself calling out to her.

'Tut-tut,' whisper the voices. 'Dear, dear. Not good enough.'

Raguel presses his palms against his ears and hums to drown them out, but the voices just get louder.

'Bear your cross,' they say. 'Your punishment.'

They're right. This is the price he must pay for breaking God's laws to do his Maker's work. He must live the life of a ghost, invisible to the only person he's ever truly loved.

He can't stop staring at her though. She looks up and for a moment seems to catch his eye, then lowers her head. A spider crawls down Raguel's spine.

Did she see him? Did she recognise him? It's been so many years, but maybe . . .

His vision blurs at the edges. He starts to sweat and sway. Did it really happen? Did she really look at him or was it just a hallucination? He gets them more when he's coming down.

He forces himself to slow his breathing. He inhales. Counts to seven. One elephant. Two elephants. Then exhaling, he counts backwards. Seven elephants. Six elephants. The elephants are important; they stop him rushing.

He inhales again. In for seven. Out for seven. Seven times. It's only when the driver announces they're approaching the next station that he speeds up. He'll have to start all over again if he doesn't finish before the train stops.

His finger taps the side of his trouser leg seven times. He licks his lips seven times. And he blinks seven times. 777. A shield against 666, a protection against the Devil.

He's come so far since the Evil One had a hold over him, he thinks. And with that thought more follow, slithering to the forefront of his consciousness, screaming inside his head, more terrifying than any illusion his mind can conceive.

He covers his eyes with his hands. He hears his heart in his ears. His body starts to shake.

The train lurches. There's a screaming noise as it brakes, a loud bang as it collides with something on the track.

And then an explosion rips the carriage.

CHAPTER 8

At first everything is black. When he comes to, Raguel is lying on the floor of the train in a cruciform position: his arms thrown wide of his body, his legs straight.

Later he'll think of this as a sign. Now he's just relieved to be alive, though at first, as he begins to regain consciousness, he wonders if he is in fact dead. The burning brightness, then the dark; this could have been the road to the afterlife.

There are fires everywhere. The heat is unbearable. People are screaming, calling out for help. Maybe this is Hell after all? The burning pits, the tortured souls. It's all here.

But no, his Maker would never consign him to the Underworld. Raguel is the Lord's servant; his place is beside his master in Heaven. The work he's done, the call he's answered, the Lord wouldn't condemn him to suffer Satan's torments.

He struggles to open his eyes. His lashes are matted with dust. Not thinking he wipes them with the tips of his long, white fingers. It's a mistake. His hands are grimy and now his eyes sting. He blinks away the dirt and the pain and then from his supine position he surveys the carriage.

It's dark and thick with smoke. Covering his nose with his shirt-sleeve, he squints into the blackness. At first he just sees shapes; bodies, some moving, others not. His eyes begin to adjust. The smoke starts to clear.

He pushes himself up, looking round frantically. Where is his angel, his darling? Is she hurt?

Despite the risk, Raguel searches for her. He stumbles over debris and people mad with worry, the usual repulsion at being touched stifled by his sense of urgency. He must find her. He must know she is safe.

The smoke renders everyone featureless; the carriage is a twisted wreck. There are people all over the place. People and stones and metal and broken glass. How will he find her in this mess?

He moves to his knees, about to pray, but finds that this new angle yields results. She's over there, and there's someone tending to her.

Raguel creeps closer. The wreckage is the perfect cover. He hasn't been this near her in years. A foot further and he'd be touching her. The thought sends a delicious frisson through his body.

The woman who was with her gets up and moves away. His angel is still. Her eyes are closed.

The excitement from before gives way to dread. It's a few moments before he dares bridge the gap and touch her.

Three, two, one, and then, taking a deep breath, Raguel leans in and places his middle and index fingers on his angel's throat. There's no pulse. Her skin isn't cold yet but he's been around death enough to recognise it.

There's a high-pitched noise, shrill and wailing. The E note on a violin. The sound of foxes at night and horny tomcats. It's coming from him, though he doesn't know he's screaming.

Raguel retches. His throat fills with bile. He starts to shake.

He lays his head on her chest, her bosom a still-warm pillow. He clings to her, pressing his fingers into her flesh, part of him not believing she's real.

After all the waiting and all the years of watching from afar, he's finally holding her, only it means nothing without her holding him back. The moment of reconciliation he's ached for has been stolen from him. He feels cheated, alone.

He howls; great racking sobs tear through his body and leave him gasping for air.

His angel has gone. He is forsaken.

Time contracts. His fingers close round a shard of metal. He grips it tight. The edges dig into his hand, piercing the skin. But Raguel doesn't feel it. All he feels is the razor-edged agony of his loss.

CHAPTER 9

'If you can walk, make your way over here,' calls a man outside the train, shining a torch into the carriage.

The words sound strangled to Raguel, like they're being spoken from far away. He hardly hears them. His mind is elsewhere.

The man reaches his hands through a window, guiding people towards him. Bodies shift and separate: the Red Sea parting.

In a daze, Raguel joins the throng, careful to keep his distance so as to avoid being touched. The man reaches out a hand to help him down from the train. Raguel flinches.

'I can manage,' he says, his head turned away. Eye contact is another thing he has a problem with.

He grips the side of the carriage to steady himself as he prepares to drop down on to the tracks. He thumb-taps the edge of the window seven times and steps one leg up. Then he stops.

There's a group of men in orange high-visibility jackets and white hard hats moving up the track towards the train. Raguel counts them. Six. Not seven. Should he wait?

His breathing quickens. His heart flutters. He chews the sore patch on his lower lip. Then he stops again and exhales slowly in relief. His breath shakes as it passes out through his mouth. A rattlesnake slithering through the grass.

It's okay. The man with the torch is a rescue worker too. That makes seven after all. So it's safe for Raguel to get down.

The air outside the train is smoky but it's cleaner than in the smog-filled carriage. Raguel tries to inhale but a monster grips his throat.

'You've lost her,' whisper the voices. 'Lost her. You're alone now. No one to keep you sssssssafe.'

Raguel starts to shake. The monster at his throat tightens his grasp.

'You alright, mate?' A man pauses beside him, putting a hand on his shoulder.

The contact sends a swell of nausea through Raguel.

'You're shaking,' the man says, leaning in so close Raguel can feel his breath on his face. 'Look at me; are you okay?'

Raguel's lungs expand to breaking point. His heart guns in his chest. And although he lost his sense of smell a long time ago his nostrils are suddenly filled with the stench of cigarettes and Eau Sauvage.

The voices are shouting loud in his head now, a muddle of echoing, sibilant sounds and expletives tumbling over each other. Goading and criticising. A hundred people all talking at once. The voices he hears every day. The voices that make him want to bang his head against a wall and yank his hair out.

'Ssssstuuuupid. Ssssstuuuupid. Guh guh guh. Go on, go on, do it, do it. Don't do it. Sssss. Duh duh duh. Look at you. Pointless. Worthless. Ssssstuuuupid.'

Raguel presses his hands to his ears and starts to hum but he can't block them out.

People crawl out of the walls, their mouths growing larger and larger until all that's left of their faces are tongues and teeth. The ground undulates with worms.

Raguel is shaking violently now. He can't breathe. His head pounds and his body tightens as though he's being dragged through a suction machine. He's no longer standing by the wrecked remains of the train. He's there again. Trapped and frightened. Vulnerable and exposed.

The pressure grows in his chest. He can't feel where his body starts and stops. He can't feel where the sides are.

Raguel starts to run, an uneasy gallop over the tracks and loose stones. He trips, stumbling over a rock, and falls to the ground.

He looks round, heart booming in his ears, lungs burning, the voices still shouting inside his head.

'Sssstupid. Yes, yes you are. So sssstupid.'

Over his shoulder he sees the Devil behind him, gaining ground. Only he's multiplied into hundreds of identical evil beings.

The passengers coming off the train, the rescue workers, the police in their bright yellow vests – they all have the same face. The Devil's face. The face from long ago.

As one, the fiends turn to face Raguel, their mouths open wide, their tongues lolling out, dripping gouts of saliva down their chins.

'Look at me,' they say, a chorus in perfect unison. 'Look at me.'

Raguel clasps his hands together, bringing the tips of his index fingers to his forehead.

'Our Father, who art in heaven, hallowed be thy Name,' he whispers, saying the Lord's Prayer over and over, not daring to look up until he's repeated it seven times.

The voices in his head change. There's just one speaker now; the voice deep, the words cogent.

'Resist the Devil. Cast out the sinners from the earth. The time has come for you to put on the armour of God. I am the Lord.'

CHAPTER 10

'Here, get this down you,' Jack said, handing me a coffee back at my flat. Black, double shot.

The mug was white and slightly chipped with *We Do Bad Things to Bad People* written in big letters on the side. A present from Duncan way back.

'I couldn't find anything with the SRR's motto,' he'd said at the time. 'This was as close as I could get.'

'It's pretty close,' I'd said with a grin.

No confirmable information exists about the activities of the Special Reconnaissance Regiment. Just as well, really. Joe Public might have a hard time getting his head round some of the things we got up to.

I grimaced as I took a sip of lifer juice so thick with sugar you could have floated a bullet in it. For the shock, Jack said.

Curling my feet under me on the sofa, I leaned back and held the hot mug to my forehead. My migraine wasn't getting any better, but the heat at least had a numbing effect.

The radio was on low in the background.

Hundreds of people have been injured, and more than a dozen killed in a train crash near Kentish Town in North London. The Thameslink train travelling from King's Cross collided with a derailed freight train carrying diesel and heating oil earlier this evening.

Our reporter Bob Martin is at the scene.

The voice changed to a different man speaking into a microphone in a dramatic voice.

Lost lives, twisted and mangled carriages; the wreckage of a rail disaster. Emergency teams have been working under flood-lights tonight among the tangled remains of the two trains.

This disaster was the result of a dreadful chain of events marked by misfortune and bad timing. Somehow a goods train derailed, blocking the railway line and the path of the oncoming commuter train.

Hours later, emergency teams are still taking away the injured, searching through the wreckage to find the bodies of those killed and free trapped survivors, many of whom are in a critical condition. While ambulances have been transporting passengers to nearby hospitals.

Twenty people were trapped in the front carriage at one stage. At least twelve people are now known to have died.

The level of devastation suggests the Thameslink was travelling at nearly seventy miles an hour, which is the maximum speed on this stretch of track.

Back to the newscaster.

There's an emergency phone number for anyone concerned for the safety of relatives or friends. The number is 020 7546 6778. That's 020 7546 6778.

Our next update is at ten o'clock.

Oy, my father would have said; a Yiddish expression despite his Middle Eastern roots. My mother hated what she called that 'guttural dialect'. She reckoned being a Persian Jew gave him an air of the exotic but any reference to his distant European ancestry was frankly embarrassing.

'You sound like a mongrel when you talk like that, Aria,' she said one time, poking her head round the door of his study where the two of us were sitting; him smoking 57s in his old leather armchair, me on the floor at his feet plaiting the tassels on the old Oriental rug.

'I'm a mongrel too, *Bâbâ*,' I said, climbing up on to his lap, aware even then I was a misfit. 'I'm half English and half Persian and half Jewish and half Protestant.'

Maths has never been my thing.

'You're wrong, Zibakam. You're not a mongrel, you're a *fereshte*. An angel.' He kissed the top of my head. 'Now, how about some poetry? Shall we carry on with the *Gulistan*?'

'*Oy*, yes.'

He laughed and kissed me again.

These days, the lingo I picked up in the SF comes more readily to me than my father's Yiddish expressions. And in this case there was only one word for what had happened. Clusterfuck.

Why did I force myself to go out just because it was Duncan's birthday? I thought, taking another slurp of coffee and screwing up my face. The sweetness made my teeth creep.

I wasn't brave dragging myself off the sofa, I was stupid. I should have stayed home. I should have stayed where I was safe.

It's been nearly two years since I kissed the Special Reconnaissance Regiment goodbye. After my husband's homicide, I no longer had the emotional detachment and self-control the special forces require. Or put another way, I was a complete bloody mess.

Duncan had gone and yet he was still everywhere. Everything recalled him to me. The wedge of Gruyère wrapped in wax paper at the back of the fridge. The black reading glasses and dog-eared Steinbeck on his bedside table. The worn bar of Dove soap on the dish in the shower.

I imagined I heard his voice in the chatter of people on the road outside. Wherever I looked I saw him. In the spot by the kitchen counter where he ate his Quaker Oats every morning. At the barber shop by the station where he'd pop in for a five-quid trim and the occasional wet shave. Outside Little Thai where we'd stop off to pick up takeaway on Thursday nights.

His ghost was all around but he was lost to me and if it hadn't been for his best friend, Jack Wolfe, I might have lost myself too.

Setting up as a freelance consultant was his idea and it did make sense. A profiler trained by the special forces with unique experience in surveillance offering her services to Scotland Yard and other interested parties, as he put it that night.

'It's a perfect fit given you already have a connection with the Yard through your work with the SRR,' he'd said.

'I could do with a fresh start,' I'd answered, tracing the rim of my wine glass with my index finger.

I was listening to Iranian pipe music and drowning in Merlot. He was chucking me a life ring.

'Well then,' he'd said with a raised eyebrow and a pointed look.

What he didn't add was that Duncan's old colleagues at the Yard feel like they owe me something. It's not true, of course. How could I blame the team for what happened to him? I'm not some bitchin' Betty and they don't owe me a damn thing. But it does help that they send so much work my way.

It also helps that Jack's a crime reporter with a major national and that I have some financial independence thanks to my husband's well-invested share portfolio courtesy, in turn, of his father – a Scottish shipping laird whom I haven't clapped eyes on once since Duncan was killed.

'Weird,' said Jack now, digging into the chocolate Hobnobs as I told him about the Catholic woman. 'He did it. You have to tell someone. What do you suppose it means?'

'I have absolutely no idea. Or how I'm going to find out.'

CHAPTER 11

I lay in bed after Jack left, wiped but unable to sleep. The day's images were zipping through my temporal lobe. The moment of impact. The dead and wounded. The chewed remains of the train.

And the Catholic woman. The way she'd looked at me, boring through my eyes with the intensity of her stare, as she'd uttered her final words.

He did it. You have to tell someone.

This wasn't some trite dying wish. It meant something. I didn't need to be a profiler to work that one out. But how could I do what she'd asked without knowing who *he* was or what he was supposed to have done?

Jeez, I didn't even know who *she* was.

I had no starting point. The task was about as hopeless as trying to score a bullseye without a bang-stick. A real bag of dicks, as my oppos would have said.

And yet I couldn't leave it alone. What had she been trying to tell me? How could I find out?

'Put the book down and get some sleep, Zeebs. It's the middle of the night,' Duncan used to say, adjusting his snore strip and rolling on to his other side as I sat up reading until stupid o'clock. His arm was always set at a perfect right angle against his pillow, his slippers always lined up in a perfect pair against the side of the bed.

A minute later he'd be back in the Land of Nod while I'd be awake for hours, unable to set my novel aside until I'd reached the denouement. I never was good with suspense. But this was different. It wasn't just a matter of staying up till I'd reached the conclusion.

'Cut your losses,' my old SF instructor used to tell us. 'Know when to quit. It's a sign of strength, not weakness. Someone might let the pen-pushers over at Westminster in on that one.'

But despite the impossibility of it all, I couldn't quit.

For weeks I'd been a prisoner to the black dog. Waking at oh silly hundred hours, the cursed red numbers on my clock glowing in the dark. Unable to eat anything more than the inside of a square of Marmite toast, the bread turning to ash on my tongue with each mouthful. Feeling lethargic, weepy, hopeless.

The black pit gaped wide, sucking me in deep.

Duncan's birthday had been looming. That had been the trigger, of course.

Personally, I hate any sort of fuss. Birthdays were never my thing. We didn't mark them when I was a kid – my mother didn't believe in them. Pagan nonsense, she used to say. But Duncan was different. He loved to celebrate – food, booze, friends, the more the better.

If he'd been alive we'd have had a big night. The quietness that should never have been was deafening.

It was Jack's idea to do something. I put up a fight at first saying I just wanted to be on my own, but in the end I relented.

When the train crashed, I'd been on my way to meet him for dinner.

'Somewhere fancy,' he'd said. 'We'll dress up and raise a glass to Dunc.'

The collision had put a stop to all that. I'd lost the night I'd planned to have but that didn't mean I had to lose the battle against the hound as well. My fug had lifted but I know how easily it can creep back.

To keep moving forward, to muzzle the damn dog, I needed a win. I needed to figure out what the Catholic woman had been trying to tell me. My sanity depended on me unlocking the mystery.

And to do that I needed to find out who she was.

CHAPTER 12

04.00. I was still awake, brain on speed, trying to figure out a way to get an ident on my mystery woman. I'd started the day pumped full of lead, now I was charged and gunning to go. I had a purpose, but where to start?

Even if I'd been on site leading the identification team, I'd have had my work cut out for me. I knew from experience that the scale of the tragedy would severely hinder the official ID process.

In many instances bodies would have been disfigured or ripped apart by the explosion. The team would be looking at corpses that'd suffered extensive trauma. They'd be dealing with body parts as well as torsos.

On top of that, a lot of people, myself included, had lost their wallets and other personal belongings. Things like driving licences, bus passes and credit cards that in normal situations can be used to work out who someone is would have been separated from the bodies. Plus, more often than not, the deceased's personal appearance would have changed after a photo was taken.

Because of all this, the process was going to take time. But I was impatient. The lethargy of the past few weeks had given way to a new energy that wouldn't be stilled; the train crash was a call to action. I couldn't just sit on my ass and wait.

I thought about going onto Facebook to try and identify my Jane Doe, but quickly kicked that idea into touch.

I didn't have any pictures of her. And I didn't know a single damn thing about her. It was a *fugazi* plan. Stupid.

What about a call to the hotline? I could describe her. Maybe I'd get a match.

But no, that wouldn't work either. She hadn't had any stand-out features – no tattoos as far as I'd seen, no facial scars or moles.

There was no way I could hope to get an ID based on the little I could say about her. And even if I had known more, it was still unlikely I'd get very far.

The identification commission's priority would to be to get things right. They'd have learned the mistakes from Spain where, in a recent similar situation, the team in charge there had got nearly 10 per cent of identifications wrong.

So where did that leave me?

I rolled over on to my right side then back again on to my left. On one side my back ached, on the other my leg felt stiff. I couldn't get comfortable however I lay.

How about sitting down with a sketch artist? I thought. There must be someone over at the Yard who could put me in touch with one.

I plumped my pillow and flipped on to my back.

Yes, that could work. I could get a photofit drawn up and place an advert in the papers appealing for information. It'd cost me a few beer tokens, but it might be the answer.

Excited, I flicked on the bedside lamp and fumbled in the drawer of my nightstand for a pad and pen. Then I began to make a list of everything I could remember about the Catholic woman's appearance while it was still fresh. In the morning I'd put a call in to the Yard, see if I could get the name of an artist.

Thoughts unloaded, solution in sight, my brain finally let go. I turned off the light and fell into a deep sleep.

Only moments later, it seemed, my ringing mobile cut through my dreams. I'd been under so deep it took me several beats to work out what it was.

I reached for the phone, groggy and semi-conscious. But when I registered the name on the screen I instantly snapped to. Detective Chief Inspector Falcon. There was only one reason he'd be calling this early.

'Ziba MacKenzie speaking,' I said, sitting up and pushing the hair out of my eyes. 'What do you need, sir?'

CHAPTER 13

'Good of you to get here so quickly, Mac,' Falcon said when he met me in the reception area at NSY, as the guys in the job call Scotland Yard. I've never known an organisation that loves its acronyms as much as the police do. Or to reinvent them so often.

'Given your voice on the phone, it didn't sound like there was much time to waste,' I said.

'We need you *now*,' he'd said, with heavy emphasis on the last word, an indication of panic beneath a contrived exterior of calm.

I shook his hand and forced a smile.

As I'd stepped into the entrance area and gone through the airport-grade security, I'd immediately felt the sharp whiplash of nostalgia I get every time I come here. It's a Pavlovian reaction, of course. A meringue response, Duncan would have called it. A silly private joke.

This is where I met him. I'd been seconded to the Yard to help profile suspected terrorists. He was in charge of the operation.

'The UK is facing a real threat from Al-Qaeda, its affiliates and so-called lone-wolves. On top of that we're also facing an ongoing and significant threat from Northern Ireland related terrorism.'

Duncan had been in the Round Table Room addressing the team. His voice was deep and gravelly with a Scottish lilt. He used his hands. He planted his feet. He commanded the room. I couldn't take my eyes off him. The guy snared me the moment he opened his mouth.

Less than two years later I was kneeling by his side as he lay dead on the pavement; a circular wound puncturing his forehead, an unmarked VW Crafter speeding away.

I closed my eyes for a moment and forced myself to slow my breathing. I had a job to do; slipping back into the pit wasn't going to help anyone.

Falcon's handshake was firm, his skin soft and warm, his fingers unusually puffy.

'You look like you've been in the wars. What happened to your face?' He nodded at the cut on my cheek.

'My stripes? Got them yesterday. I was caught up in that train crash from King's Cross.'

'Jesus, I'm so sorry. I had no idea. Two of my men were on it too. Horrific business.' He shook his head. 'Are you sure you're okay being here?'

'I'm fine, so long as you don't mind me looking like ten pounds of smashed dog shit in a five pound sack.'

He laughed and clapped me on the back.

'Well, given what we've got going on, I hope you'll understand if I don't try to persuade you to go home and put your feet up.'

'You still haven't told me what is going on,' I said, although I was willing to hazard a guess.

His tone on the phone. The time of the call. My area of specialism. I didn't need to be a genius to figure it out.

'Let's talk in my office,' he said, leading the way to the lifts.

I noted the stiffness in his gait. Gout must be playing up again, I thought, adding his puffy fingers to the mix.

'Been on the track recently?' I asked, making conversation.

I reckoned it'd go down better than, 'How're the swellings in your joint?' Falcon's a real petrol head. The guy should be presenting *Top Gear* rather than working in Homicide. He even looks a bit like Jeremy Clarkson.

He smiled all the way up to his eyes. His feet skipped. Either a recent win or else a new engine, I guessed.

'I'm taking our eldest rallying in my new motor this weekend. A Subaru Impreza. Three hundred odd horsepower, flies like shit off a shovel and makes a wonderful racket. Can't wait to give it a good belting.'

New engine it is.

'Let's talk in here, shall we?' He held open the door to a small office with a bird's eye view over the Broadway. A sign of his seniority. 'Have a seat.'

I pulled up a pew. 'So, what's the sitrep?'

He leaned forwards and clasped his hands together, tucking the thumbs away. An indication of negative emotions. I braced myself. Whatever was coming wasn't going to be good, but then I already knew that.

He glanced at the table and back at me.

'You've heard of the London Lacerator?' he said.

So that's what this was about.

CHAPTER 14

The name of the UK's most wanted serial killer wasn't quite what I was expecting to hear, though I was on the money with the subject matter.

I've been studying signature murderers for years. I know what drives them. I know what makes them tick. And I know that, like me, they're also profilers.

The only difference between us is that I hunt offenders to bring them to justice while they hunt people for prey. Our methods are the same, though. We both seek to understand our targets to achieve our goals.

A serial killer goes to his stalking ground – a shopping centre, a bar, a video arcade, wherever he'll find the type of victim he's after – and he'll zero in on the person who best matches his set of preferences and who strikes him as the most vulnerable.

To do that he reads body language. He checks out his would-be victim's behaviour and the way he or she is dressed. He notes the way they talk. He observes how they interact with other people. He watches to see if they're shy or outgoing, if they're confident or socially awkward.

And he does it all in a matter of seconds.

For my part, I look at the clues killers leave behind. The victims they choose, the nature of their crime, the risks they've taken.

Goethe put it well. He said, 'Behaviour is a mirror in which everyone displays his own image.' Or put another way, what a person does reflects their character.

If there were a profiling catchphrase, it would be 'behaviour mirrors personality'. Though admittedly it's less punchy than the one on the mug Duncan got me.

I've helped put a number of serial killers away, some of them household names. And I've worked extensively with Scotland Yard and the FBI to do so. If Falcon had a serial offender on his hands, it was no surprise that he'd call me in.

But the London Lacerator? Well, I wasn't expecting that. The guy had been dormant for years.

'Serial killer from the eighties. Never caught. But suddenly stops killing. No one knows why,' I said in answer to Falcon's question. 'All his victims were stabbed through the eyes. All had their faces bashed in. And all had their genitals severed post-mortem. Police at the time found the body parts in bins near the dump sites.

'The victimology and MO were consistent for the last three victims. They were all gay men in their sixties with grey hair, glasses and beards, killed in park squares and public toilets. But Aidan Lynch was different. He was a man in his twenties. And he looked nothing like the others. Plus, although he was stabbed and mutilated, he was killed in his own home and his body was set on fire.

'Not that the differences in victimology or MO are unusual. An offender learns from his first kill. He notes the lessons: what went wrong, what went right. He does what he has to in order to perfect his craft. Very possibly, the Lacerator found the first victim difficult to overpower. Older men may have made less challenging targets. And luring them to a secluded spot may have proved easier than persuading them to take him home.'

'Nice.' Falcon nodded.

I smiled. It never hurts to impress the brass.

Falcon wasn't smiling though. He rubbed his eyes, a blocking behaviour. Another sign of discomfort.

I looked him over. I read the non-verbals. Only one thing made sense.

'He's struck again, hasn't he?'

CHAPTER 15

'Looks like it,' said Falcon, nodding slowly. 'A body was found early this morning by a dog walker. The local major crimes unit called us after they made the connection. Dump site was in an alleyway in Camden. Forensics suggest it was the kill site too.'

'Camden? Apart from the first vic, all the eighties crime scenes were around Soho.'

'Yes?' said Falcon, eyebrow raised. Quizzical.

'So why change now?'

'Good question.'

'Given the body wasn't moved it's unlikely he uses a vehicle. So he's most likely on foot. Not that that explains why he's changed his location preference. He obviously felt comfortable in Soho.'

'Why deviate from what worked for him?'

I pinched my lips.

'For some reason it doesn't work for him any more.' I paused, running my hands through my hair. 'What makes you so sure this is the Lacerator's work?'

'MO and signature's the same. Blitz attack. Multiple stab wounds, including through the eyes. Contusions to the face. Castration.'

'Victim type?'

'At first glance it seems the same – physically, I mean. Though family interviews will tell us more. Right now we know very little about him. If he was gay. Where he was last seen. Who he was with.'

I paused again, thinking. In my experience, serial killers don't stop killing for twenty-five years and then just start up again. Could there be something else at play here?

'Have you considered this might be a copycat?' I said to Falcon.

He shook his head.

'It's not a copycat.'

'What makes you so sure?'

'A copycat wouldn't have done what he did.'

I gave him a look, confused.

'How do you mean?'

Falcon inhaled deeply and let the air out through his teeth.

'The Lacerator always did something to his victims that was never released to the media.'

I wasn't surprised to hear the police had kept certain details back. It's fairly common practice in big murder cases; helps insure against false confessions.

'So what did he do?' I said thinking back to some of the most bizarre serial killer calling cards. A way of marking their victims out as their work, of dominating them even in death.

The Beer Killer left a beer can by each of his victims. The Boston Strangler tied a bow round the neck of each of his with whatever he'd used to asphyxiate them. And the aptly named Smiley Face Killer graffitied happy faces at his crime scenes.

'The Lacerator already cuts off his victims' genitals and stabs them through the eyes. What else does he do?'

Falcon looked at his feet then back at me.

'He sprinkles them with olive oil.'

CHAPTER 16

The boy is lying on his tummy by the sofa, his red Spider-Man baseball cap on back to front as usual. One hand's propping up his chin, the other's flying a toy helicopter across the carpet. A Bell Jet Ranger with a yellow stripe along the fuselage.

The grown-ups are talking about boring stuff: the price of petrol, the roadworks at Swiss Cottage, that sort of thing.

He pushes his fringe out of his eyes. It's getting way too long but luckily no one's noticed. His mother used to cut his hair at the kitchen table but Dad put a stop to that. Now, it's Andy the barber with his horrid clippers and the rubbery gown that doesn't stop the hairs going down the back of the boy's T-shirt.

'Do you want a chocolate, Goldilocks?' Grandad says. He holds out a box of Maltesers from his place on the sofa.

'Yes,' the boy says, jumping up.

'What's the magic word, mister?' says his mother.

'Please,' the boy says. He draws out the word in a sounding bored sort of way.

Grandad winks at him. The boy grins back.

He lifts the lid of the Malteser box. The edge is serrated. It makes him think of a Halloween mouth. Most of the chocolates have already been eaten. There's just a row left along the bottom, a line of knobbly brown teeth. He grabs a handful and stuffs them into his own mouth in one go before his mother can stop him.

'I saw that,' she says with a smile.

His father's watching too but he's not smiling.

'Such a sweet tooth! And now my payment, please,' Grandad says. He presents his cheek for a kiss. 'Ha, gotcha,' he says, scooping the boy up and hugging him tight.

The boy sits on Grandad's lap for a bit but he's uncomfortable. Grandad's breath is hot in his ear and his beard's tickling the back of his neck.

'More tea, anyone?' says Granny, smiling round the room.

CHAPTER 17

'Olive oil?' I said to Falcon. 'Why?'

Was the Lacerator a chef, or some kind of health nut? Whatever he was, the oil meant something to him, that's for sure.

A serial killer's signature is the personal stamp he leaves on his crime. It's not just a form of personal expression, he's psychologically compelled to leave it. Without it he can't achieve satisfaction from his crime. Or, as the lovely Ted Bundy put it, he can't get his rocks off.

The MO, how an offender executes a crime, changes over time. Signatures also evolve. Necrophilic killers, for example, might increase their level of mutilation over a course of homicides. The core elements of a signature never change, though. They are critically important to the offender and they give profilers an insight into how their minds work.

Sprinkling his victims with olive oil was clearly a core part of the Lacerator's signature. But why did he feel driven to do it? And what did it say about him?

'We're hoping you'll help us figure that out,' said Falcon. 'We'd really appreciate your input on this, Mac. You're the best profiler on our books and you understand serial killers better than anyone. You willing to come on board?'

I thought of the funk I was only just beginning to claw my way out of. If I joined the investigation I'd need to interview grieving relatives.

I'd need to witness their pain and their loss. What if it sent me back to the pit? Could I take the chance?

A photo on Falcon's bureau caught my eye. It was a picture of his wife, a dimple-cheeked, curly-haired woman with a small gold crucifix round her neck a bit like the one the Catholic woman had been wearing.

He did it. You have to tell someone.

I'd promised myself I'd figure out what she'd been trying to say. I didn't expect any help from the guys at the Yard, but being based here would have its advantages. I'd have access to all sorts of data I wouldn't have back at my digs. Not to mention the chance to nail one of the most notorious serial killers of our time.

The DCI must have sensed my equivocation and pressed home the advantage.

'This is a massive case. There'll be huge public interest and pressure to get a speedy result. Not to mention more victims if we don't make a swift arrest. Say you'll join us and I'll go and introduce you to the MIT right away.'

'Happy to help,' I said with a smile before I could change my mind.

'Excellent.' He pumped my hand. 'Let's go get you acquainted with the team.'

We walked back to the lift and rode it down to the fifth floor to a large room in another part of the building, filled with people, white boards and ringing phones. The major incident room.

I spotted Paddy Dinwitty at the back. An Irish guy, always smiling, who worked for a time with Duncan chasing down drug dealers and other nasty bastards.

I caught his eye. He raised his hand and grinned. There were a couple of other bods from Duncan's day dotted about. I smiled. It was good to know there were a few friendlies on the team.

'Ziba, this is DI Nigel Fingerling, the SIO,' Falcon said, clapping the shoulder of a skinny-wristed man with his hair cut high and tight, thin lips and a minor facial tic. 'He was on the train yesterday too. He's also a sudoku expert and a black belt in jiu-jitsu.

'Nigel, this is Ziba MacKenzie. Her husband was one of ours. She's a first-rate offender profiler. Helped us crack some of our toughest cases.' Falcon steered me forward, his hand on the small of my back, protective.

I worked to keep my smile straight. I do wish he wouldn't treat me like a bloody weeping widow, I thought. In my old job I was the one who made people cry.

'How do you do?' I said to Nigel Fingerling, sticking my hand out.

He looked vaguely familiar. I was sure I'd seen him before. Not at the Yard so perhaps on the train or platform yesterday. Though most likely my mind was just playing tricks because I'd heard he was there. The power of suggestion and all that.

He shook my hand with a lettuce grip while reaching into his pocket with his other hand for his mobile. It had just buzzed for the third time since I'd come in.

He checked the screen and a deep crease appeared between his eyes. Disappointment. Bad news then. He blinked rapidly and adjusted his tie. He was the only one wearing one and it was knotted too tight.

'I'll leave the two of you to get acquainted,' the DCI said, absently stroking his barrel stomach before limping off. Yep, definitely gout, I thought.

Halfway to the door he stopped and turned round.

'We need to get on top of this fast, Mac. The public's going to panic when news gets out there's a serial killer on the loose. We'll need them to know we're in control. And that we're going to catch him. Fast.'

'Understood.'

He gave a mock salute and left the room.

'So, you're a profiler, are you?' said Nigel Fingerling with a sneer, stroking the fancy fountain pen sticking out of his top pocket. There was a bloom of ink on his shirt. 'Go on then. What am I thinking?'

He'd started off looking me in the eye but his gaze was slipping down to my breasts. I folded my arms and took a step back.

'I'm too much of a lady to answer that but I can tell you it ain't going to happen.'

I probably should have smiled but I didn't. Fingerling narrowed his eyes.

'Isn't profiling really a fancy word for conjecture? I'm sorry, Ms MacKenzie, I just don't believe you can deduce anything meaningful about someone based on . . . Non-verbals, isn't that the word you people use? No, I'm afraid it's all a bit too hocus pocus for me.'

I felt my cheeks redden but it wasn't because I was embarrassed. I balled my hands into fists, stuck them on my hips and took another step back to look him over properly.

'You wear tight shirts to show off the shape of your torso and probably tight boxers to show off your manhood. Trouble is, like your attitude to women, your fashion sense is about ten years out of date. Both might explain why your bird dumped you. You have a tattoo on your arm but some of the letters have been removed – recently judging by the scarring. The name of an ex-girlfriend probably, given you've got plenty of other tats.

'You work out every night at the gym because you have a hangover from your school days. You were skinny. The other kids used to pick on you. Your arms are muscly now but your narrow wrists give it away. Your TAG Heuer is a fake. The green on the watch face is a shade out and there's a spot of rust on the strap. But it's important to you to have a branded timepiece. Like your tie and cufflinks and sharply ironed shirt, it's all part of your need to keep up appearances.

'The question is why you feel you have something to prove. Perhaps the answer has something to do with your hands. They're chapped and your cuticles are ragged. It's not cold so either you've got a bad case of eczema or you just wash them too much. Both things are stress-related. Because you've got a secret you're ashamed of, haven't you? Something you're worried your colleagues will find out. What is it, detective? A stash of porn in your desk drawer? A pair of used panties in your top pocket? Or something altogether darker?'

Everyone was watching and laughing – everyone except Nigel Fingerling. His face was ketchup red.

Before, he'd doubted my worth. Now he hated me.

CHAPTER 18

I spent the weekend collecting as much information as possible about the Lacerator's latest crime to help develop a psychological picture of him – the profile.

I combed through the historical information and matched it against the most recent attack, looking for anything that might give a clue about the type of person we were dealing with. Understanding who he was would be key to finding him and preventing more innocent lives being lost.

I read autopsy reports, witness statements and preliminary police reports. I was sure that this business with the olive oil was critical. But nothing in what I read gave so much as a hint as to what it was all about.

Frustrated, I moved on to victimology.

'I've already got a team doing interviews,' Fingerling said. 'No need for you to get involved. Just read the write-ups.'

'Face to face works best for me,' I said. 'I find how people speak is as important as what they say.'

He rolled his eyes.

'Take Williams then, if you must go.'

'Better if I go alone.'

I didn't add that I'd get more out of my subjects without a DS playing pocket billiards next to me. People tend to put their guard up when the police are around, even if they have nothing to hide.

'You're not much of a team player, are you, MacKenzie?'

Not when the captain's such a donkey dick, I thought, smiling sweetly.

The feedback I got from the interviews was consistent. Apart from the usual line about the victim being a wonderful person, so kind and caring etc., I was told he was an openly gay man in his late sixties, and he didn't have a partner.

A few people I spoke to added that he hung out at gay bars to meet men. And on the night of the attack he'd been drinking at the King William, a well-known gay pub in Camden, where he had been seen chatting to a man in the corner.

Unsurprisingly, descriptions of the man he was with varied widely. The witnesses had been drinking and the pub had been dimly lit. Every prosecution barrister's nightmare.

'Why is it all the jobs I work on there's no bloody CCTV,' said Fingerling at one of the team briefings early on, as we sat round in a circle updating each other on developments.

He'd asked for footage from the area in the hope of getting an image of the victim leaving the pub with the man he'd been talking to. But he'd come up empty. Not that it would have made a huge difference. The quality of these pictures is never good enough for a positive ident.

'We're looking at a high-risk victim,' I said during another briefing. We had them every morning and evening bang on 09.00 and 18.00. 'Sounds like the deceased was possibly promiscuous and on the night of the homicide he was inebriated, according to the pathologist's report.

'His vulnerability would have made him easy prey for the offender, and the booze would have made it easy for the Lacerator to overpower him.

'We can't be sure but the offender may well have approached the victim in the bar. He may be the man the victim was seen talking to, in which case we need to appeal for more witnesses to come forward.

'If we can put together a composite sketch, someone may recognise him. And if he did target his victim there, that tells us something about him. He has a reasonable IQ and social skills along with the where-withal to come up with a ruse to lure his targets away.

'But the real question is this: does the offender choose his prey because he sees them as convenient targets? I.e. does he find it easy to pick up gay men and entice them away with him? Or is their being gay the thing that draws him to them? Is it the key element of his prefer-ence, and if so, why?'

'Isn't that what you're supposed to be telling us?' Nigel Fingerling said with a snorty laugh.

Still hasn't forgiven me, I thought.

'Yes, it is.' I kept my expression neutral. I didn't want the pimply cheese-dick to think he could wind me up. 'I plan to reconstruct the crime from the perspectives of the victim and offender. I should be ready to deliver a preliminary profile tomorrow.'

He should have looked pleased but he didn't. This was a guy who bore a grudge.

'We should arrange a press conference,' I said. 'We've kept the media waiting long enough and we're going to need their help on this.'

I was just packing up my things when a text came through from Jack.

Check your email

I opened my inbox.

Thought this might interest you. Wolfie

I clicked on the attachment.

Hooah! I thought, smacking my fist into my left palm as I read the title at the top of the page. Result!

He'd sent me a link to the BBC website. There was a list of names of the people who'd died in the rail crash, along with photos by each one. Halfway down the page, was the picture of a woman wearing a small gold crucifix. My Jane Doe.

It took me a second to process what I'd seen and when I had, I still couldn't quite believe it. Surely it was just a coincidence.

The woman's name was Theresa Lynch. The same surname as the Lacerator's first victim, Aidan.

CHAPTER 19

It wasn't a coincidence though. The electoral roll confirmed it. Theresa Lynch was Aidan's mother. Which gave me the perfect excuse to phone her husband, Marcus, and request an interview.

The killer's early crimes weren't my main focus, but Marcus Lynch wasn't to know that. Less than an hour after making my discovery, I knocked on the front door of a terraced house on Inverness Street in Camden, North London. The same place Aidan's body had been found twenty-five years earlier.

'Thank you so much for letting me come over,' I said as Marcus handed me a mug of Nescafé. A few undissolved granules floated on the surface like dead flies.

He settled himself into a flowery armchair by the fireplace, a little gas contraption with bits of coloured glass in the grate designed to look like hot coal.

'It's been a while since we've been asked questions about what happened to Aidan.' He looked across at me over the rim of his mug, his expression curious.

I noted the 'we'. It would take him a long time to get used to saying 'I' again. Duncan had been dead for nearly two years and I still wasn't there yet.

There were dark shadows under Marcus's eyes. His lids were pink and puffy. I felt bad barging in at a time like this and yet didn't I owe it to his wife to find out what she'd been trying to tell me?

'Funny you were with her, eh? And that now you're investigating the bastard that killed my son.'

'What are the odds?' I said, pretending to sip my coffee.

'I got this feeling when Theresa didn't come home the other night, like something bad had happened. I just knew it. In my bones.' He paused and covered his face with the flat of his hand.

'Sorry. I thought I could do this.'

'It's alright. There's no rush. I lost my husband recently. I know how you feel.'

The empathy was real but also important. It would build trust and rapport.

He inhaled deeply and nodded at me in a stiff-upper-lip sort of way. This was a man who liked to keep a lid on his feelings.

'Sorry about that,' he said in a trembling voice, straightening his maroon sweater vest. 'It's just all so raw still.'

He sighed and carried on with his story.

'I knew she was on that train, see. She always takes it. I went to every hospital to see if she'd been brought in. I had the BBC on the whole time at home in case there was any news. But there was nothing. Not until yesterday. It was almost a relief when I found out. Not that she'd been killed obviously, but that I finally knew for sure what had happened to her.'

He looked up at me with wet eyes. 'I'm glad she had someone with her at the end. I'm glad she wasn't on her own.'

'She wasn't on her own. And she wasn't in pain either.'

I don't suppose the last bit was true but it's what he needed to hear. And I needed to hear about Theresa. If I could profile her I might be able to work out what she'd been trying to tell me. Then I'd move onto Aidan. Understand the victim, understand the killer.

'Perhaps we could start off talking about Theresa before we move on to Aidan. It may sound strange but it helps establish victimology.'

I was talking bollocks but he wouldn't have known.

He shrugged. 'Okay.'

As I asked my questions I concentrated as much on how Marcus Lynch spoke as what he said. If you know how to read the signs, non-verbal behaviour, or body language, is a message board that conveys what a person's really feeling.

I asked general questions first about what she was like as a person, then moved on to the more pertinent ones that might give me a clue about what her dying words had meant.

'Did your wife recently start socialising with a new group of people or making excuses to meet friends without you?'

Marcus shook his head but at the same time his jaw muscle tightened; a minor indication of tension that suggested a deeper emotional stress.

'Are you sure?'

'Quite sure,' he said, compressing his lips. 'I always make a point of asking my wife where she's going and who she's going out with.'

The use of the present tense was a natural slip, one I still often make when I'm talking about Duncan. The clenching of his hand into a fist was surprising though. So too was the fact he demanded to know his wife's every action. Both suggested a controlling personality.

'Was your wife religious?'

He laughed. It sounded hollow. 'Theresa was a staunch Catholic. I was never really into all that myself, but she started going to Mass every Sunday and insisting on saying grace before meals after she got pregnant with Aidan.'

The first part of the sentence about his wife's Catholicism was spoken with a note of disdain but his attitude shifted when he mentioned her pregnancy. If he hadn't squinted as he spoke I may not have picked up on it, but the movement was as conspicuous as flares going up on an exercise.

Squinting is an unconscious act that's evolved to protect us from seeing things we don't like. It only lasts about an eighth of a second and always indicates a negative emotion, usually anger or displeasure.

But why would thinking about his wife carrying his son cause Marcus Lynch to feel that way?

Strange.

'Was Theresa political?'

He laughed and shook his head, relaxed now, on easier ground.

'No. She was a true blue like me. We both remember what happened to the country under Labour in the seventies.'

'Anything she was worried about? Money troubles, that sort of thing?'

'No.' He looked offended, as if my question were a slight on him. I moved on quickly.

'You mentioned earlier that she worked.'

'Yes. She was an office administrator for a property development company in the City.'

'What were her colleagues like?'

'She got on well enough with them but they didn't socialise outside of work. We liked to keep to ourselves.'

Her choice or yours? I wondered as I scanned the room. Behaviour mirrors personality, but so do our homes.

There was a Good News Bible on the bookshelf; leather-bound and probably expensive, so a valued possession. A statue of the Virgin Mary and a framed photo of the Pope on the wall. Both supported what Marcus had told me about Theresa's religious observance.

There was a dining table set against the far wall, large enough to seat six but which only had two chairs tucked into it. There were paintings – all prints of landscapes. Woods. A field of poppies. Nothing with people in them.

We liked to keep to ourselves, Marcus had said. Why? Was he afraid of letting people into their lives? And if so, what did he think he'd stand to lose if he did?

My gaze moved to the mantelpiece. There were two photos on it. An old wedding snap in a tarnished silver frame and a professional photograph of a child in his school uniform, half hidden behind a china ornament of a cat. I got up to take a better look.

'May I?' I said, indicating the wedding photo.

He shrugged. 'Sure.'

'Theresa was very beautiful.'

'Yes, she was.' He clenched his jaw.

Odd, I'd just complimented his wife. Surely that would have made him pleased not angry.

'And who are these people?' I said, pointing at the other people in the bridal party.

He came over and took off his glasses then polished the lenses with the bottom of his sweater vest before taking the picture from me to get a closer look.

'Those are my parents. Died in a car crash in France. Those there are Theresa's folks. Her mother's dead now too. Cancer. The old man's in a care home, lived with us for a while after his wife passed. And that's Theresa's sister. Lives in Bath.'

'And I'm guessing this must be Aidan, right?' I moved the picture of the kid out of its hiding place.

Marcus bristled visibly.

'Yes,' he said, without meeting my eye.

Curious reaction. And why was there only one picture up of his son?

The child in the picture was grinning at the camera. His colouring was completely different to Marcus'. He was a sweet-looking kid with a big, gappy smile. And a strange mark on one of his irises as though the pupil was leaking into it.

I turned back to Marcus. He was shifting his weight from foot to foot and fidgeting. He was uncomfortable. He didn't want me holding the photo of Aidan. Why?

He looked at his watch. I was running out of time.

Watching him closely I said, 'Your wife said something to me just before she died. A final wish, so to speak. "He did it. You have to tell someone." I don't suppose you have any idea who she was talking about, do you? Or what *he* might have done?'

An ugly red wave flooded up Marcus's neck. The muscle by his eyelid started to flutter.

'No idea. Look, are we done here? I really am terribly tired.'

'But we haven't talked about Aidan.'

'Like I said, I'm very tired. I'd like to go and lie down now.'

A moment later he was fastening the deadbolts as I stood outside his front door trying to make sense of what had just happened.

I still didn't know who *he* was but judging by his reaction Marcus Lynch did. And given all the non-verbals, I couldn't help wondering whether he might actually be the man Theresa had been talking about.

CHAPTER 20

I forked a piece of sea bass and dipped it in the splashes of balsamic glaze and pea puree dotted artistically round the edge of my plate. I'd come straight to meet Jack from my interview with Marcus Lynch.

We were in The Lemon Tree. The three of us used to come here sometimes for a treat. It was Wolfie's idea to come back.

'Because we never got to celebrate Big D's birthday the other night,' he'd said on the phone.

With hindsight it wasn't the best choice of venue. This was the first time I'd been back without Duncan. My stomach cramped with the pain of his absence. The past folded in on the present. He was everywhere and he was nowhere.

'I picked this up for you. It's that book you were saying you wanted to read.'

'That's sweet of you, Wolfie. Thanks.'

'I was in Foyles anyway. It's no big deal.'

I took a slug of wine. Jack raised his glass and sipped too. I caught his eye and smiled. He smiled back, nostrils slightly flared. We lowered our glasses in unison.

'You've had your hair cut,' he said, leaning forwards. 'Looks nice.'

'Just a trim. Surprised you noticed.' I glanced round the restaurant.

A smartly dressed, middle-aged man wearing odd socks caught my eye. He kept smoothing down his hair and checking his watch. Anxious,

I thought. Dressed in a hurry but concerned about his appearance. Probably on a date and worried about being stood up. A first date, or a blind one, maybe. If he knew the person better he'd be less worried about where she was.

A flushed woman came hurrying through the door rubbing her hands up and down her sides. Nervous and running late. I watched as the maître d' helped her off with her coat and led her over to Odd Socks' table. He stood up and reached out to shake her hand at the same moment as she leaned in to kiss him on the cheek.

Yep, blind date! Hand shaking means a first meeting. The awkwardness shows they're both keen to make a good first impression.

I was feeling awkward too: the candlelight, the pianist playing in the corner. Jack and I have been out to supper plenty of times since Duncan died but somehow this was different. The setting was a bit too romantic. Not that real romance has anything to do with settings.

The most romantic moment of my life was in a windowless office. The heating had broken and I'd been working for thirty-six hours straight.

◆ ◆ ◆

'Can I have a word, Ziba?' Duncan said as the room emptied.

His tone was gentle but his face was impassive. Was he about to chew me out? I certainly hadn't made many allies given the way I'd gone about things that day, even if the end result had been good.

'Detectives I've worked with for years got distracted today and made poor decisions,' he said, eyes fixed on mine. 'But you didn't get distracted. You kept a clear head and stood your ground even though everyone else was against you. You got the rest of us to see sense. Our win is down to you.'

I smiled.

'You don't give a damn what people think of you. I like that. Some might see it as a flaw. It's not. It makes you strong. It makes you who you are.'

'I'm not sure that's always such a good thing.'
'It's a very good thing.'
That night he kissed me for the first time.

◆ ◆ ◆

'What's up, Mac?' said Jack now, head at an angle.

'Nothing.'

'I've known you long enough to know something's definitely bothering you when you say "nothing" like that.'

'Maybe you should try profiling.' I arched an eyebrow.

'Go on. Tell me what's going on.'

I sighed.

'It's just being here without Duncan. I miss him, Jack.'

He glanced down then back up at me. 'I miss him too. Dunc was nearly old enough to be my father but he was like a brother to me. I loved him.'

'Same here. Minus the brother bit.' I laughed.

'That's better.' He smiled and smeared mustard on a mouthful of steak. 'You have a great laugh. You should use it more.'

He paused and pinched his nasal bridge. It's one of his tells. He was about to say something that made him feel uncomfortable.

'How are you doing?' he said, his voice dropping an octave. 'I got the feeling you were struggling a bit. I've been worried about you. Are you okay?'

I thought about spinning him a dit but he'd probably have called me on it if I had. He's always been able to see through my shit, which means I can be myself with him; the best and worst versions.

The truth is, I may specialise in human behaviour but I'm not exactly a people person. I understand them on a rational level but still they make no sense to me. It's different with Jack. I get him and he gets me. Perhaps it's because of how much we both loved and miss Duncan.

Or perhaps we're just kindred spirits. Either way I can be honest with him; too honest sometimes.

'I'm doing okay,' I said. 'I had a bit of a wobble but I'm fine now.'

'I wish you'd talked to me.'

The tone was getting a bit heavy.

'Changing the subject, you'll never guess what.'

'Emmeline's actually an MI5 assassin and her work at the British Museum's just a cover?'

'No, this isn't about my delightful mother. That link you sent me. I used it to identify the woman from the train. Name's Theresa Lynch. I met up with her husband before I came here.'

'Nice one, Sherlock! How did it go?'

'I'm not sure. When I told him what she'd said, he practically booted me out the house. Obviously that got me wondering about him.'

'Obviously!' he said. His voice was teasing, playful, flirtatious even.

'But that's not all. Get this: her son, Aidan, was the first victim of the London Lacerator.'

'Shit! Seriously? Can you believe he's active again after all these years? The news came through on the wires earlier. Scary, eh?'

'I know. Corny moniker, though, isn't it? I can't believe some of the crap you journos come up with.'

'And I can't believe that family's luck. Mother and son killed twenty-five years apart in tragic circumstances. Could be a good story. Real human-interest piece.'

Jack was prattling on about possible headlines and articles running front and centre but I wasn't focusing. My brain was in a tailspin. I thought back to the urgency on Theresa Lynch's face as she passed on her dying message. The way she'd gripped my arm. The way she'd forced the words out.

He did it. You have to tell someone.

Could she have been talking about her son's homicide?

And if so, was it possible she knew who the London Lacerator was?

CHAPTER 21

Jack pushed his pot of fries towards me. 'Have one. I swear these are the best chips in London.'

'You always say that,' I said, pinching a few.

Of course, Duncan made the best chips. 'The secret's boiling the tatties first. Makes them go dead crispy,' he used to say.

Proper home fries, he called them. We'd eat them straight out the fat, standing by the hob, blowing on our fingers. LoSalt for him. Sloshings of Sarson's vinegar for me.

The waiter came to clear the table and we ordered hot drinks. He came back a few minutes later; ristretto for me, fresh mint tea for Jack.

'I dunno how you can drink coffee this late.' Wolfie stirred the leaves round his cup. 'I wouldn't sleep if I did. Mind you, I don't sleep anyway so maybe it wouldn't make much difference.'

I smiled. He's always moaning about his insomnia. I suspect his obsession with *X Plane* has a lot to answer for.

'Duncan was funny about caffeine too,' I said. 'Did you know, he wouldn't touch chocolate past lunchtime? Swore it kept him awake.'

I paused, twisting my cup round on the saucer. The memories were like dodgem cars tonight.

◆ ◆ ◆

'They've left chocolates on our pillows,' I said as we walked into the hotel room. 'Here, catch.' I tossed one over to Duncan.

'No, you're alright. I won't catch a wink if I eat that.'

'All the more for me, old man.'

'Who you calling old?' He launched himself on top of me, play-wrestling me down on to the bed.

He got me on my back and pinned my arms above my head, his mouth on mine. I wrapped my legs around his waist and pulled him in close. The next morning there was chocolate all over the sheets.

◆ ◆ ◆

Would you suck it the hell up? I thought, taking a slug of coffee. That dog doesn't need any encouragement to go walkies. And I refuse to be defined by Duncan's death.

'I've been thinking about what Theresa Lynch said to me.' I moved the conversation on, working up to the favour I'd been planning to ask Jack.

As a *Telegraph* journalist, he has ways of getting his hands on intel that would make my old pals jealous.

'What if it had something to do with Aidan's murder?'

'Could be I suppose.'

'It'd be useful to find out more about him. Trouble is, I'm clearly not going to get anything else out of Marcus. And I doubt the DI's going to want me taking my focus off the latest victim, given the pressure the team's under to make a swift arrest. Don't suppose you might be able to do some digging for me?'

He inhaled deeply. Not a good sign.

'Don't take this the wrong way, okay? But don't you think you're getting a bit fixated on this Lynch woman? I mean, you've been through a rough patch and now you're working full steam on the Lacerator investigation. Maybe it's time to pull back. Chances are what she said didn't mean anything. People say all sorts of odd shit before they kick the bucket.'

'I need to get to the bottom of it. I gave her my word, Wolfie.'

Not strictly true, but it's how I'd come to feel.

He sighed. 'Alright. I'll see what I can find out.'

'Magic.'

'Don't go getting your hopes up though. Aidan Lynch died twenty-five years ago. It won't be easy.'

I put my hands up in mock surrender. 'Fair dos. So how's things with crazy Maisie? Still stalking you?' I said, changing the subject.

He closed his eyes, sighed and shook his head. 'She calls me about a hundred times a day then hangs up the second I answer. Woman's wacko.' He drilled his index finger into his temple.

'Well, she never liked me much so I guess she must be,' I said with a smile. 'Actually, none of your girlfriends seem to like me, have you noticed that?'

'Shall I get the bill?' He turned to signal to the waiter.

It only occurred to me afterwards that he'd completely evaded the question.

CHAPTER 22

The boy's gone round for tea at his grandparents' house. Granny made scones with whipped cream and strawberry jam and they've had crumpets too, and Fondant Fancies.

Now the boy is sitting at the table drawing, his tongue sticking out of the side of his mouth as he adds a pair of rotor blades to his picture. He's going to have a helicopter like that one day, he's decided. And he's going to be a pilot too.

Grandad comes over and squeezes his shoulders.

'What a good artist,' he says, kissing the top of his head and stubbing out his cigarette in the bumpy glass ashtray. 'Why don't you leave that for a second and come with me, kiddo? I've got something for you.'

His voice is a whisper, wet in the boy's ear. The boy puts the crayon down and takes Grandad's hand. They go out of the lounge to the bedroom.

'Shut the door,' Grandad says.

'What have you got me?' the boy says in an eager voice, hopping from foot to foot. He likes presents but he's not that good with surprises.

Grandad kneels down and rummages about in the drawer by his bed. The boy squats down next to him.

'What is it?' he says again.

'Look me in the eye. Can you keep a secret?'

The boy nods his head.

'Are you sure?'

'Cross my heart.'

Grandad smiles and pulls out a red box of matches. There's a picture of a black sailboat on the front. It says SHIP in big letters across the top and another longer word along the bottom that the boy can't read.

'For me?'

'Want to light one?' says Grandad.

The boy knows he's not supposed to play with fire but if Grandad says it's alright . . . He chews his bottom lip.

'Here, why don't I show you how?' Grandad says, striking the match. There's a delicious hiss as the flame catches. 'Let's keep this between us, shall we?' he says. 'I don't want you to get into trouble.'

The boy nods again. His heart is beating hard. The room smells of smoke.

CHAPTER 23

Back at my flat, I was curled up on my sofa, laptop on my knees, trawling for information about Aidan Lynch's eye condition.

I yawned, knocked back the last slug of wine in my glass and logged off. Bring on the weekend, I thought.

A lie-in would be nice. Then maybe breakfast in bed, I thought. Thick-cut, bitter marmalade on granary toast. A bowl of berries, acacia honey and Greek yoghurt. A pot of fresh coffee. Then later, a read on my favourite bench by the canal.

Heaven. I just had to get through the rest of the week first.

I racked out before 23.00. The early starts and long days had started to take their toll, not to mention the mystery of Theresa Lynch that had ransacked my sleep ever since the night of the crash.

05.00 I woke with a start.

I'd been dreaming about the lip-gloss woman from the train. Her mouth bubbling with blood. Her matted blonde hair. And then, colliding with those images, the memory of Theresa struggling to speak, her dying message.

Marley's ghost was rattling his chains. I'd get no rest till I nuked out what she was trying to tell me.

Lying on my back, wide awake now and staring up at the ceiling, I thought back to my first sighting of her on the train. She'd clearly been agitated: her thumb tapping against her bag, the twitch at the corner of her mouth. And she'd whispered something: *They never caught him.*

At the time I'd assumed she'd been referring to the article she was reading about the murder of Samuel Catlin, the kid who'd been killed on his way home from school. But what if it wasn't that? What if reading about the child's homicide had brought back memories of her own son's murder? What if she'd been talking about Aidan's killer, not Samuel's?

They never caught him.

Not, 'the killer'. 'Him'. That's much more personal.

He did it. You've got to tell someone.

Was it possible she knew the man who killed her son? Or at least suspected who it might have been?

They never caught him. He did it. You've got to tell someone.

On their own the two comments were unrelated but put together they told a story. Put together they could easily be about Aidan Lynch's murderer – the London Lacerator, a serial killer who did unspeakable things to his victims and who'd eluded capture for a quarter of a century.

I thought back to the ugly red flush that had spread up Marcus's neck when I asked him if he knew what his wife's last words meant. And I thought about how he'd kicked me out of the house straight afterwards.

He'd claimed not to have any idea what Theresa had been trying to say, though his body's response told a different story. It was such a visceral reaction. A clear indication of stress and fear.

I didn't know what, but Marcus Lynch was definitely hiding something.

CHAPTER 24

DCI Falcon stood up and waited for silence before speaking. He was in uniform, the silver epaulettes shiny on the shoulders of his jacket. The police always dress up for press statements. Their message is ostensibly delivered to the media but they have another audience. Offenders follow the progress of the case against them closer than anyone.

Press briefings are the first piece of communication; the starter gun in a high-stakes game. It needs to sound the right note. Looking the part helps with that. I'd donned heels and my good Max Mara trouser suit for the same reason; all fancy-dancy, as Duncan would have said.

I listened to the DCI speak, though I already knew what he was going to say. I'd written the script as well as coaching him on how to deliver it. Our comments were going out live. In the next few minutes radio stations and television channels up and down the country would be broadcasting it. We needed this to be perfect. There'd be no chance for do-overs.

'Start off by saying you want to offer your most sincere condolences to the victim's family. Speak slowly. Let your words sink in. The Lacerator will be watching. Use the victim's name. Give him a human face. Talk about the family he's left behind,' I'd said to Falcon during our prep session. 'The offender tries to dehumanise his targets. The facial contusions. The stabbing through the eyes. The degradation of the corpses. We need to show him they're real people. We want him to feel bad about what he's done.'

'Doesn't he need some sort of morality for that?' Falcon said, inhaling deeply.

'Serial killers are definitely disturbed individuals. But in every custodial interview I've conducted the subjects have all shown an understanding of the difference between right and wrong. Some of them may ignore that distinction, but they know it all the same.'

He shrugged and raised his eyebrows. He wasn't buying it but he'd go along with what I was saying.

'And when you say we're going to catch him, make sure you stop and look right at the cameras,' I said. 'That'll convey confidence and resolve. It's not just the public who need to know you're unshaken. The killer needs to know it too. Which is why I want you to tell the press he's slipped up. Made some sort of mistake we're not in a position to disclose just yet. We need to keep up the pressure on this dick-beater. But we also need to empathise with him. Leave that bit to me though. It'll come across best when I present the profile.

'For my part, I'll imply that I understand what was going through his mind and the stress he's under. It'll give him a way to save face and might encourage him to reach out to someone or even get in contact with us. We're not operating in some quiet backwater here. London's a huge city. Plenty of people are going to fit the profile. We'll need to focus on proactive techniques to draw the offender out.'

The DCI was well prepared by the time he took his place up on the platform, however no one had drilled me. Although I knew exactly what to say, my mouth was dry as I stood up to take over at the microphone. I took a sip of water and cleared my throat.

'Good afternoon, everyone. As you've just heard, I'm a profiler and I've been asked to assist Scotland Yard with this investigation. My role is to look at all the evidence and then put myself in the offender's shoes. I need to get to know him and to do that I need to look at his work, his crime. I need to examine what he's done and draw logical conclusions about how and why he's done it.

'We know behaviour echoes personality. And that the only way to catch a killer is to think like one. As John Douglas, one of the pioneers of investigative profiling at Quantico put it, "Serial killers play a dangerous game. The more we understand the way they play, the more we can stack the odds against them."

'The offender has killed five times now and on each occasion his actions left clues about who he is. In every attack he devastates his victims before they have a chance to fight back. That, combined with the level of overkill – eye stabbing and genital mutilation – indicates an asocial perpetrator with deep psychiatric problems. However, he's not a sadist.

'The mutilation in his previous crimes took place post-mortem and there were no signs of torture on the victims' bodies, either then or now. This shows the offender is motivated by hatred and anger rather than a desire to manipulate and control.

'He's a white male in his mid to late forties. White because serial killers generally target victims from the same ethnic group as them. In his mid to late forties because the average age serial murderers commit their first homicide is in their mid twenties and this offender has been killing for twenty-five years.

'He is naturally unkempt. Any effort to keep himself neat and tidy is a symptom of over-control. Doing so will be mentally and physically exhausting for him. I expect him to be on, or have been on, antipsychotic medication. Whilst the level of frenzy exhibited in the attack suggests he may be using drugs, most likely some sort of stimulant.

'Considering his significant cooling-off period and his psychological condition it's possible he has been recently released from a mental care institution or prison.

'There would have been a precipitating stressor leading to the commission of this crime. Something momentous occurred in his life which triggered a relapse. Something happened to make him snap, most likely on the day he attacked his latest victim. And he may well now be consumed with feelings of guilt and remorse.

'I urge him to come forward before we close in on him. I understand he's feeling overwhelmed by what he's done and possibly afraid of the impulses he's unleashed.' I paused, thinking of something. A different approach. A more personal one.

I took a deep breath, choosing my words carefully, then looked straight into the cameras. If the killer was watching I'd be looking him right in the eye. 'I'd like to speak directly to the offender now,' I said, deliberately not referring to him as the Lacerator; a hyperbolic media-generated moniker I had no doubt he'd find distasteful. 'I know someone has hurt you so badly you can't sleep at night. And I know that's why you attacked the man in Camden. This is about payback, I get that. I also get that something terrible has just happened to you. Was it on Thursday? Did you lose your job or someone who mattered to you? Is that what's making you feel so frightened and alone? I understand you and I want to help. But to do that I need you to reveal yourself. It's time to stop hiding. It's time to let someone in. Come to Scotland Yard. Ask for me. I'll be waiting for you.'

◆ ◆ ◆

'You did well down there,' Nigel Fingerling said back in the incident room. 'But what's all this about the Lacerator making a mistake?' He was leaning in too close, his eyes squinting, the tic going full throttle in his cheek.

'Beats me,' I said, pulling away.

'But the DCI said—'

'He was trying to rattle him, that's all. Intensify the ass-pucker factor. The Lacerator hasn't killed for a long time. His post-offence high is beginning to recede. And he's beginning to feel afraid of what he's done. We needed to tap into that fear before he kills again.'

'You think he will?' he said, eyes darting back and forth.

'The level of rage evidenced by the attack shows he won't be satisfied with one homicide. Deep down killers are all the same, you know. They may have different motives and MOs but they all share one key characteristic – they can't resist the thrill of the hunt. They're addicts. Every one of them looking for their next high. And the Lacerator's just fallen off the wagon. The question isn't if, but when he'll strike again.'

Fingerling's mobile buzzed. An SMS. He whipped it out of his pocket. As he read the message, the corners of his mouth turned up but when he caught my eye his face adopted a more neutral expression. He'd just received good news. But for some reason he didn't want to share it.

'The DCI's right, MacKenzie.' He tapped the edge of his phone. 'You do know your stuff.'

'Thanks. And by the way, I'm sorry for what I said before. I was out of line.'

'No hard feelings.' He nodded, which pretty much implied the opposite. 'Look, why don't we nip down to the Lamb and Flag when we've finished up here? Mend bridges and all that. We got off to a bad start. I don't want it coming between us.'

'I can't tonight. I'm meeting someone for dinner.'

Jack had texted earlier, said he had info about Aidan Lynch. I wasn't going to pass up on the chance to hear what it was for the sake of a drink with this gift to humanity.

Fingerling stroked the knobbly bone on his wrist. 'Hot date, eh?'

Paddy gave him a scowl then made a sympathetic face at me as he walked past. Another one walking on damn eggshells, I thought. I may have lost my husband, but that doesn't mean I'm going to crack up just because someone looks at me funny.

I marched out of the MIR in search of some decent coffee. My mobile was on my desk next to an empty cup. But when I got back it was on top of my notepad.

Either I've got early-onset Alzheimer's. Or someone had moved it while I was gone.

CHAPTER 25

Raguel is waiting across the road from Scotland Yard, playing cat's cradle with a circle of string, his fingers zipping in and out of the loop.

Bruised clouds gather overhead. Rain is on the way.

He licks his lips – there's a trace of peanut butter from the sandwich he ate before the support team meeting. Unfortunately, that ghastly Jim person didn't have the manners to do the same. He'd spent the whole session stuffing his face with a bacon butty. The sight had turned Raguel's stomach. Meat always does – he's been a vegetarian for years.

But he's not thinking of that now. There's only one thing in his head – beautiful Ziba MacKenzie with her huge eyes, so dark they're almost black.

He'd recognised her the moment he saw her, of course. She was the woman on the train. The one he'd seen tending to his angel in her last moments, preparing her soul for the journey to come.

She may have introduced herself as a profiler this afternoon but Raguel knows she's more than that. She's a saviour, like his angel was. Just look at how she cared for the injured on the train. How she drifted from one to another bringing healing and comfort.

Yes, definitely a saviour: a modern day St Raphael. The voices had told him the same thing.

'Protector,' they'd whispered, overlapping each other and growing in volume as he watched the press conference from his spot at the back of the room. 'Guardian,' they'd said, plus a whole lot of other words in a strange language he'd never heard before, though he knew what they meant.

They meant that Ziba MacKenzie was his new ministering angel. The Lord had recalled the first one but sent another to replace her.

Hadn't she said as much herself?

'I understand you. And I want to help.'

How his skin had tingled! How his heart had throbbed!

To think he feared his previous angel had abandoned him. How could he ever have thought such a thing? She would never leave him without sending someone to take over from her, he thinks now as he tucks and twists his fingers, turning the cat's cradle into an X.

'The Lord will guard your going out and your coming in from this time forth and forever,' whisper the voices, and Raguel nods. He knows they speak the truth.

The moment he'd seen the Hamsa round Ziba MacKenzie's neck earlier, he'd known for sure. His angel used to wear a bracelet with a similar charm on it; a hand-shaped symbol to ward off the evil eye.

It's a sign that in the moment of her passing she transferred her mantle of protection to onyx-haired Ziba MacKenzie and that from now on she'll be the person who keeps him safe. Despite some of the more unpleasant things she'd said about him this afternoon.

She had to say them though, he sees that now. It wouldn't do for the whole of Scotland Yard to know she's on his side. The nastiness was a trick. She's hiding in plain sight, just like him.

He moves his thumbs under the string. Three parallel lines. A second later the pattern changes again.

The proof's in how hard she's trying to understand him, he thinks. And look at how right she's got it all. Not just that he lost his angel the same day he struck out against the demon, but that this is about payback, justice. Blood for blood. No one else has ever worked that out before.

But Ziba MacKenzie is different. She gets him. She described him perfectly in that room, even if he didn't like some of what he heard.

And look how she never once called him the Lacerator. True, she doesn't know his real name yet, but she does know enough not to call him by that offensive title.

Raguel puts the string away then takes off his glasses and cleans them on his shirttails, rubbing each lens seven times. Under his breath he says seven Our Fathers then puts his glasses back on and swats at his arms.

The insects are back. He can't see them but he can feel them, the tickle of their feet running over his skin.

'Reveal yourself. It's time to stop hiding,' the voices whisper, repeating what Ziba MacKenzie said at the press conference.

Raguel picks at the scab on his lip. Although she gets him better than anyone else ever has, it seems his new protector needs more information in order to keep him safe.

'It's time to let someone in,' she'd said, and as she did a strange feeling had come over Raguel. All these years he's kept his secret, a knot of vipers pulled tight around his heart. All these years and no one has guessed the truth.

How freeing it would be to open himself up, to offload the darkness that consumes him! How liberating!

But how can he do it without compromising himself?

He pulls the string back out of his pocket and works it quickly, thinking back to that other thing Ziba MacKenzie had said. That she wanted to get to know him and to do that she had to look at what she called his 'work'.

True, she'd added the word 'crime' after that. But she'd said 'work' first. So she understands what he's doing is righteous – a holy mission. Another sign she was sent to him by the Lord and that she can be trusted.

His previous angel, God rest her soul, was hampered by her lack of understanding. He never told her his secret and she never worked it out. As a result, she couldn't protect him when he was at his most vulnerable.

A wind whips through Raguel. He shuts his eyes and whispers seven Our Fathers until the moment passes.

He'd wanted to confess everything to her back when it might have made a difference but fear had held him fast. He mustn't make the same mistake again. If he wants Ziba MacKenzie to look after him he must open up to her like she asked. He must trust her. And he must find a way to let her know he accepts her protection.

He watches Katie floating above him. Then she disappears with a pop.

'You put me on a pedestal, it's not healthy,' she'd said to him that time he'd brought her pink tulips. 'You're making me uncomfortable.'

Well, there'll be no more pedestals or flowers for her. Raguel doesn't need Katie any more, not now he's got Ziba MacKenzie watching over him.

'Ziba Mac,' whisper the voices.

The shadowy figure crouching behind him slinks closer. The sound of giant shoes slapping on concrete reverberates down the street.

Ziba Mac, yes of course! thinks Raguel, putting the string away again and counting the letters out on his fingers: Ziba: Four. Mac: Three.

Three plus four equals seven.

It's perfect – a celestial sign of approval.

'Glory be to the Father, and to the Son, and to the Holy Spirit, as it was in the beginning, is now, and ever shall be, world without end. Amen,' he says in a whisper over and over the right number of times, making the sign of the cross.

Forehead to chest. Left shoulder to right shoulder. With the other hand he claws at his skin. Damn those invisible insects!

A couple of men in suits walk past.

'Loser,' they say, pointing at him. 'Bloody druggie.'

Raguel scowls. He has to start all over again. It doesn't count if he gets interrupted. When he's finished he looks to Heaven and smiles.

'Peace be with you, Chosen One,' whisper the voices as the pavement starts to breathe.

They've been speaking more kindly since he slayed the demon in Camden. They're showing him they approve of what he did. It's all he can think about now: how it felt, how it made him feel.

His new protector comes out of the building, rooting in her bag and popping in her earbuds as she walks away.

Raguel's veins fill with warmth. This is the moment he has been waiting for.

He glances over his shoulder then, keeping his distance so she doesn't realise he's tailing her, he and the shadowy figure follow Ziba Mac up the street, into the Tube and all the way to Camden – which is surely yet another sign they belong together.

CHAPTER 26

Jack was sitting at a banquette in the Camden Brasserie, one of our favourite haunts. He waved me over with a big smile as I walked in; hair looking like it hadn't been brushed for days, face unshaved. No change there then.

I glanced out of the window as I sat down. The place was heaving. People ambling along. Couples hand in hand. Groups of teens wearing jester hats and DM boots. Rasta guys openly selling ganja.

That's the meth addict from the train, I thought, spotting a man across the street from the restaurant. He was swatting his body and scratching the sores on his face. What's he doing here?

The city's a big place, you don't tend to bump into strangers twice. Then again, I thought, Camden's right round the corner from Kentish Town. Maybe he lives here. Or more likely just drops in to score.

London's Amsterdam, Duncan used to call it. The shops display bongs on their shelves and there's an open drug market along the tow-path. Very des res.

I turned back to face Jack. The brasserie was buzzing. It seemed like everyone was talking about the Lacerator. The men in wrinkled suits with five o'clock shadows who'd come straight from work. The girls flicking their hair and laughing loudly. The young marrieds taking advantage of having a babysitter for the evening but who couldn't stop checking their phones to make sure everything was okay at home.

The murder of the man in Camden and the craphat who killed him was the topic of every conversation.

'So don't keep me hanging,' I said once we'd ordered. 'What'd you find about Aidan Lynch?'

Jack shifted position so he was mirroring me exactly.

'Nothing groundbreaking. But I did manage to get in touch with a few people he was at school with. Couldn't get hold of anyone from later on in his life. No one had a bad word to say about him though. Sounds like he was a nice kid. A little shy with people he didn't know, but sweet.'

I thought back to the photo I'd seen in the Lynches' living room. You could tell he was sweet just by looking at him: that gappy smile, the dimples. A right little monkey, Duncan would have said, and with that thought an invisible fist socked me in the gut.

'How many children do you think we'll have?' Duncan said as we ambled hand in hand through the Avenue Gardens in Regent's Park. The delphiniums were out, the flower beds a jumble of blue.

'I don't know. How many do you want?'

'A whole football team.'

An avocado stone began to form in my throat. I inhaled deeply trying to imagine my breath breaking it down. I'm not normally into all that mindfulness shit but there are times it does seem to help.

'You okay, Mac?' Jack looked at me, concerned.

'I'm fine. Just a bit of heartburn.' I forced a smile. 'Anything else about Aidan?'

'Apparently he got a bit withdrawn around the age of ten or so. But then again, a lot of kids get like that as they approach puberty, don't they?'

'Aye, the nobody-understands-me phase is tough.'

'There was one other thing,' he started to say, before a wiry man with thinning hair and a bad case of psoriasis barged in on our confab.

'Mervyn Sammon, *Daily Star*,' he said, jutting out his hand right across Jack's face. 'Sorry to intrude on your dinner but I saw you speaking at the press conference today, Ms MacKenzie.' He coughed. Lots of phlegm. 'Would you mind answering a couple of quick questions?'

Had he followed me here? Bloody journalists.

'I admire your ambition, dragging out in the rain without an umbrella for the chance of a scoop, especially when you haven't been well. But I'm afraid I'm here with a friend and you're interrupting us.'

His mouth dropped open, a question on his face.

I sighed.

'Your shirt's dry but your hair's wet. You had a jacket but no brolly. There are pink rings round your nostrils but there's nothing off with your voice, so you've just shaken off a cold. You might want to rethink your food choices, Mervyn. I'd avoid those cheese sandwiches till your chest's clear.'

'How do you know?'

'It's still in your teeth.'

As he stalked off he shot Jack evils over his shoulder.

He thinks Wolfie's getting an exclusive, I thought. Must have recognised him as a fellow hack. It made sense. They both worked on the crime desk even if for different papers. They'd have seen each other around.

'Where was I?' Jack tilted his head a fraction. 'Ah yes. The fire.'

I raised my eyebrows. 'Fire?'

'Yeah, according to one guy I spoke to, Aidan burned down his dad's toolshed when he was sixteen. Him and his old man didn't get on too well, apparently.'

Tension between Aidan and Marcus. What was that about?

The waitress came over with our pizzas. The smell of basil and mozzarella made my stomach rumble. I leaned back as she ground black pepper over my pie and took a sip of wine.

'Not for me, thanks.' Jack held up a hand when she came round to his side proffering the mill. 'So, is that Fingerling character still being a dick to you?' he said, drizzling chilli oil over his Fiorentina.

'That's far too nice a term for him.'

I'd spotted the shit-bird on the platform at St James's Park on the way up to Camden. Needless to say, I hadn't gone over to say 'hi'.

'He had no right to talk to you the way he did.' Jack wiped his mouth with a napkin. 'Maybe I should invite him up for a flight and push him out the passenger door when we're ten thousand feet over the Channel.'

'I knew it was only a matter of time before you started talking about flying, Captain Airdale.'

He'd recently bought a share in a Grumman Tiger and takes it up whenever he gets the chance. Talks about it whenever he gets the chance too.

He laughed. 'Haven't taken the bird out in weeks. Weather's been shit.'

'Poor Jack.'

He flicked a chip at me. 'You're in a mood.'

'So would you be if you'd had to spend the day with fuck-ass Fingerling.'

'I've never met him, but word is he's a real tool. No people skills.'

'To be fair, mine aren't great either. That hot date comment was crass though.'

Wolfie's tone hardened. 'He needs to treat Dunc's memory with some bloody respect, even if he can't manage to behave himself around you.'

'He never even met Duncan, Jack. And frankly, it makes a nice change from the way some of his old workmates treat me. Tiptoeing round me like I'm some fragile little girl. Falcon's as bad as the rest of them – always doing that head-tilt thing. Here comes poor widow Ziba.' I rolled my eyes. 'I'd like to see him in hand-to-hand combat with Taliban soldiers when the mission's gone sideways and his weapon's out of juice.'

'Falcon and Duncan were close. He probably just feels protective towards you.'

'Well, there's no need. I'm perfectly capable of looking after myself.'

'Alright, point made,' Jack said, holding his hands up in surrender.

I smiled. 'Now you've got that off your chest, how about you tell me about Nigel Fingerling's bad rep. Likes to wear women's knickers, does he?'

'I don't know about that.' Wolfie laughed. 'But word has it he has had a few mental problems over the years. His girlfriend ditched him recently. Apparently he took it hard. Been in and out of therapy ever since. They say she'd been having it off with someone else.'

'Bit harsh.'

'Maybe, but from what you've told me about him he had it coming.'

I shrugged and we moved on to the topic of the latest Lacerator murder. I guess it was only a matter of time before we got on to the same subject as everyone else.

'You will watch your back with that Fingerling bloke, won't you?' Jack said later.

We'd finished eating and Jack was settling the bill. He never lets me pay.

'You bringing all that up again?'

'I've just got a bad vibe about him. I'm not sure what it is but there's something I don't like. Be careful, that's all I'm saying.'

'I appreciate your concern, Dad, but I can take care of myself. Don't worry about me. I'll be fine.'

CHAPTER 27

'You sure you don't mind dropping me back? I'm perfectly happy taking the Tube,' I said.

'Don't be silly. It's getting late and anyway it's pissing down. Hop in.' He unlocked his car door, an ancient Range Rover Vogue SE.

As he shifted his flying bag off the passenger seat, a map fell out of the front pocket.

'Thought you said you hadn't been up in a while,' I said, passing it over.

'I haven't and there's even less chance of me bunking off and cruising the big blue yonder with this Lacerator story running hot. Here, let me help you in.' He reached out a hand.

'It's alright, I can manage,' I said, hoisting myself up.

He walked round to the driver's side rubbing the back of his neck.

It was a comforting gesture. A pacifier. One of the body's limbic responses to stress. By shaking him off, I'd embarrassed him, made him feel rejected.

'Mind if I put the news on?' I said, reaching for the radio dial as he climbed up and eased himself in behind the big leather steering wheel.

'Sure.' He started the ignition.

We pulled away from the kerb. The big V8 growled as the revs rose and we accelerated down the road.

In a statement issued today, Scotland Yard Detective Chief Inspector Chris Falcon confirmed that the man responsible for killing Philip Lawrence last Thursday was the London Lacerator, a serial killer responsible for a string of murders in the late eighties. Appealing to the public for calm, he said: 'We will catch this offender. The victim's family deserves it. The community deserves it.'

In other news, the Queen has flown down from Balmoral to visit the crash site of the King's Cross rail disaster. She spent twenty minutes discussing the clear-up operation with Chief Constable Alan O'Bryne of the British Transport Police in preparation for meeting emergency services staff at a reception later this week.

We drove along the wet streets, black and shiny in the lamplight. I watched the people scurrying along the pavements with their heads bent beneath their brollies. Then I saw it.

'That's Inverness Street,' I said. 'Where Theresa Lynch lived.'

'Thought you were going to drop that.' Jack hooted as a black moped swung out in front of us. Its lights were off. The driver wasn't wearing a helmet.

'Do you think it's weird his parents only had one photo up of Aidan?'

'Not really. Perhaps they just couldn't handle seeing his face staring at them every time they settled down to watch *Coronation Street*. Can't say I blame them under the circumstances. Take my advice, Ziba. Put what that woman said out of your head and focus your energies on the Lacerator case.'

'But what if they're connected?'

'Mac,' he said in a warning voice.

I laughed and touched his forearm. He pinked. I pulled my hand away, my colour up too.

All those hours we'd spent alone together after Duncan died, yet I'd never picked up on it before. I'm an expert in human behaviour. Reading people is my job. How had I not spotted the signs?

Fingerling's jibe echoed loud in my ears. Hot date, eh? Jeez, that dipshit had been tuned in better than me.

Two nights in a row I'd observed the same signals yet I hadn't connected them. Mirroring. Dilated pupils. Expressive hand gestures. Head tilting. Leaning in. All non-verbal expressions of attraction. All indicators that Duncan's best friend fancied me.

I should have been offended on my husband's behalf. Or felt violated in some way. But I didn't. I felt flattered, and something else too. I felt like I'd just stepped into the sunshine. Like Cinderella walking into the ballroom. My skin tingled. My stomach danced. And yet this was the one person in the world I could never be with.

Jack's definitely easy on the eye – I'd have to trade my team vest if I didn't find him attractive. But a relationship with him would be a betrayal. Even thinking about it was wrong.

I rubbed my suprasternal notch, the dip between the neck and collarbone. It was an unconscious gesture. A pacifier, much like the way Jack had rubbed the back of his neck after I rejected his offer of help into the car.

We continued driving up the dark roads. I wasn't sure at first but after we took a turn faster than we should have and it swung round sharply after us, I knew.

'We've got a tail,' I said. 'A silver Honda with a big dent on the bonnet. Can you see it? It's just let a car out in front of it but it's still behind us.'

He looked in the rear-view mirror and then back at me with an 'are you crazy?' face.

'There's no one there.'

I looked round. He was right. The Honda had gone. The driver must have realised he'd been made.

'Pull in here a second. Let's see if it comes back.' I pointed to a vacant parking bay.

'I'm not pulling in. This is ridiculous. There's nobody following us,' he said, carrying on up the street towards the canal.

'Damn it, Jack. Now we won't find out who it was.'

'There's nothing to find out apart from the fact you think there's a threat lurking behind every corner. The world's not as dangerous as you think it is, Mac.'

'Spend your life fighting monsters and you'll take a different view,' I said as he pulled up outside my apartment block.

I climbed the steps to the communal front door and turned round to wave goodbye. As Jack edged away from the kerb I saw it again – a silver Honda with a dented bonnet just nosing out from between two parked cars.

CHAPTER 28

I yawned, adjusted the throw across my shoulders and stretched my legs out along the sofa.

The lights were turned low. There was a half-empty bottle of Napa Valley Merlot on the coffee table. The radio was on in the background, as per.

By the time I'd made it upstairs and looked out of the window the silver Honda had gone, if it had even been there at all. I was tired. I'd been working hard. Maybe Jack was right. Maybe I was losing the plot.

I poured another glass of wine and swiped my finger across my phone screen bringing up the next photo. Duncan in his North Face jacket, a big smile crinkling his eyes.

It had been a blustery but bright afternoon in Poole, the wind salty and chill. 'Bracing,' Duncan called it, taking arm-swinging strides as we'd hiked across the sand dunes. When the rain started up we stopped off at a blue-fronted café on the waterfront for beer-battered cod and chips.

'Easy on the salt, sweetheart. You'll give yourself a heart attack, so you will,' he'd said as I shook the cellar over my fries.

He was still wearing his jacket, even though we were inside. His old fisherman's sweater was on underneath, the one I was now wearing over my pyjamas.

I sighed, pressure building behind my eyes.

You do it to yourself, I thought, switching off the side lamp and leaning my head on a stripy kilim cushion. The colours are so faded it looked old even when it was brand new. I should have gone to bed but I didn't have the energy to get up and fell asleep without meaning to.

I dreamed I was a child back in my father's study. The room was heavy with cigarette smoke and the scent of patchouli orange from the incense burning in the corner. Duncan was sitting in the old leather armchair by the window wearing my father's collarless tunic shirt and Peshawari Chappal sandals while reading to me from an old volume of *Arabian Nights*.

I was on the floor by his feet plaiting the tassels on the rug the way I used to as a kid. The door opened and Jack walked in. Duncan stood up and handed him the book but instead of taking his place in the chair, Jack knelt down next to me and opened it up. I slid closer so I could see the pictures.

Suddenly I wasn't a child any more. I was a woman and Jack's hands were in my hair, the tips of his fingers massaging the dip at the base of my head.

I lifted my face to his and he pulled me to him, pressing his mouth hard against mine, pushing my lips open with his tongue. My body flooded with heat. Every atom pulsing.

And then the dream changed. A fire alarm went off in the distance. Its tone loud and insistent until I realised it wasn't a fire alarm at all. It was my mobile and it wasn't part of the dream.

I felt about for it. I was woozy, my eyes heavy with sleep, but still I felt the hard bite of guilt. It was just a dream, I told myself, finally locating the ringing mobile, buried down the back of the sofa. And yet the guilt gripped tight.

I scrambled for the button on my phone. Grey, early-morning light was filtering through the shutters but the flat was in semi-darkness. I glanced at my watch as I answered.

04.42. Who was calling this early? And why?

There was no name on the screen, just a mobile number I didn't recognise.

'MacKenzie,' I said in a cotton-wool voice.

'Sorry for calling so early,' said Nigel Fingerling on the other end of the phone. 'Can you come down to Delancey Street as soon as possible? We're just behind the Camden Brasserie. I'll text you the address.'

'The Camden Brasserie?' I said in a whisper.

'It's on the corner of Delancey and Albert Street. Flaky brown paint. Lantern above the door. You'll see the panda cars when you get here. They're impossible to miss.'

'What's going on?' I asked, though I could already guess the answer from his tone and the time of the call. There was only one thing that would cause him to get me out of bed at this hour.

'There's been an incident. Another Lacerator murder. And it's not pretty.'

CHAPTER 29

Fifteen minutes later I swung my Porsche – a silver 1988 911 Turbo, my pride and joy – into a spot behind two panda cars. Their blue lights were flashing but the sirens were off.

'Ziba MacKenzie. I'm a profiler working with Scotland Yard. DI Fingerling's expecting me.' I handed my ID to the PC guarding the crime scene from evidence contamination.

'Help yourself to PPE,' he said after entering my details in the log. He pointed to a box of crime-scene clothing – suit, hat, shoe covers, gloves and face masks.

After kitting up, I found Fingerling in the alleyway at the back of the restaurant where I'd been sitting with Jack only a little while earlier. The thought made me blush, a hangover from my dream.

But that's not all. I'd been sure a car had been tailing us last night. And now there was a dead body right outside the restaurant where we'd been eating.

Were the two things connected and if so how did I fit into the equation? Or was I just doing what Jack had accused me of, seeing threats behind every corner?

'Apologies for waking you at such an ungodly hour.' Nigel Fingerling was standing outside the tent. There were dark circles under his eyes and he was blinking rapidly. The guy looked like he was sleeping on his feet. Clearly I wasn't the only one who'd had my zeds interrupted.

It was oh silly hundred hours. I'd barely managed to stomach my coffee on the way over but he was chowing down on a Snickers. King-sized. He stuffed in the last mouthful, put on a fresh pair of gloves and led me through.

The place was buzzing with CSIs processing the scene; placing markers, taking photos, testing for fibres and footwear marks. In the middle of it all was the corpse, part covered in a white sheet, blood soaked through the groin area. I knew enough about what the Lacerator did to his victims to guess why.

About three feet away there was spatter and a fleshy mass where the ground met the wall. I've seen some hideous things in my time but this took some beating.

'Olive oil again?' I said to Fingerling, working on my gag reflex.

He nodded.

'Wish I knew what it meant.'

Didn't we all?

'What do we know about the victim?'

'Quite a lot, actually, thanks to the weather last night. The killer set fire to the body but the rain meant it didn't last long.'

'So he doesn't wait around watching the flames.'

If he did he'd have made sure the corpse burned properly.

'Implies an element of caution,' I said, putting myself behind the perp's eyes. 'Flames attract attention. He needs to get away as fast as possible after starting the fire and he has the wherewithal to realise that. Which suggests the fire-starting is about destroying evidence. He doesn't get off on it. If he did, he'd be compelled to watch. He wouldn't be able to help himself.'

'Makes sense.'

'Did you find any ID on the vic?'

'Yep. We'll need to wait for the DNA results to confirm it, but the credit cards and driving licence in his wallet indicate he was a male in his sixties called Ian Clough. He lived on Rossendale Way. It's not far from here.'

'What about cash?'

'Still there. Watch and earring too.'

'Rules out robbery as a motive and fits with the disorganised offender typology.'

Fingerling squatted down by the body. 'You ready?'

'Aye.' I crouched down next to him.

He raised an eyebrow. 'Aye? You don't sound like a Scot.'

'I'm not. It's just something I picked up from my husband.'

'And what did he pick up from you?' he said with a leer.

'Bad language mostly.'

He pulled back the sheet. I leaned over the body covering my nose. The corpse was already starting to smell, the first sign of decomp.

'Stab wounds to the neck and eyes. Severing of the genitals. Massive overkill. Lacerations and contusions to the face designed to wipe out the victim's personality. No attempt to hide the body or remove identifying items. Appear to be no trophies taken but there is the removal of a body part. All consistent with a killer in a psychotic break,' I said. 'The wounds look clean. He used a knife so he came prepared.

'This murder was planned. He came out with the sole purpose of hunting, a matter of days after the last homicide. You know what that means, right?'

'His compulsion to kill's escalating.'

'Aye, at a disturbing rate. But that's not all. I said at the press briefing that he may be feeling guilty about what he did. But looking at what he's done to his latest victim, I think I got that one wrong.'

'What makes you say that?' Fingerling scratched his arms, the muscle in his cheek twitching like crazy.

'The positioning of the body. It's completely exposed. The legs are splayed to draw attention to the groin area. He's been left uncovered. The killer's making a statement. He wants to demonstrate his dominance over his victim. And to degrade him. Remorse has nothing to do with this.'

The victim's skin was purple and waxy looking. His lips had turned white and his hands were blue. I palpated his arms and legs. The muscles were tight, which meant rigor had started to set in. He'd been dead for well over five hours.

'Do we have a time of death yet?'

'Liver temp's eighty-nine point six. So based on that and lividity, the ME's estimated time of death at around midnight last night.'

No more than an hour after I left the restaurant.

'Victimology's the same as Thursday's murder,' I said, looking at the deceased's face.

It's easier to think of them like that. The deceased. The victims. Not to personalise them by using their names; we save that for media appeals. In the field you need to maintain a degree of distance. You'd go mad otherwise.

'Male. Late sixties. Grey hair. Beard. Glasses. Victimology matches the eighties kills too. With the exception of Lynch, the Lacerator's always targeted people of the same physical type. That means they're surrogates, stand-ins for the true focus of his rage.'

'What makes you say that?' said Fingerling, his legs spread wide, his arms crossed over his chest. Confrontational. Assertive.

'Offenders rarely direct their fury towards the true target of their resentment straight away. It usually takes a number of killings before they build up the courage to go after the person they really want to destroy.

'Take the Co-ed Killer. He used to creep into his mother's bedroom with a claw hammer and fantasise about smashing her skull in while she slept. But it took six murders, maybe more, before he finally beat her to death, decapitated her and ejaculated into her headless corpse.

'Lovely.' Fingerling cricked his neck. 'You got anything else? Or just more bedtime stories?'

I've got plenty of those.

'There are seven stab wounds in and around the carotid artery. They're deep. No hesitation marks. Ditto the area round his groin. The killer's becoming more confident. His fervour's growing and so is his anger. In the past he's disposed of his victims' genitals by dumping them in bins near the crime scenes. This is the first time he's ever hurled them against a wall. He's evolving.'

I prodded the victim's body. 'This man took care of himself. He worked out. Either the Lacerator's in great shape to have been able to overpower someone like this or else he had another way to subdue his victim. And judging by the level of frenzy evidenced by the attack, he's likely taking drugs. Amphetamines. Or Cocaine.'

'So we're looking at an addict that likes to go to the gym?'

'Actually, right now we're looking for someone who's completely wiped out. An attack like this is physically exhausting. His post-crime behaviour will be marked by disorientation and an insatiable hunger.'

'That it?'

'For now. We'll need to set up another press briefing. I'll coordinate a response.'

'Right.' He walked off to speak to the crime scene manager, then turned on his heel. 'By the way, MacKenzie, I don't suppose you or Mr Wolfe happened to notice anything while you were here earlier?'

I shook my head. It was only later I realised I'd never told him who I was meeting for supper. Or where we were going to eat.

CHAPTER 30

Raguel's offering to Ziba Mac is perfect; a gift that will bind them together and tell her more about him, just like she asked. But it's not enough. He needs to find a way to tell her *why* he executes sinners, what they mean to him, the harm they do. Without that she can't fully understand him.

But how can he do so without revealing his identity?

He clenches and unclenches his fist. Seven times open. Seven times closed. He grinds his jaw.

A letter might do it, he thinks. Though it wouldn't be enough.

Communication has to be two-way; mutual, reciprocal. He needs her to prove herself to him. If he's going to let her into the most secret chasms of his heart, he needs to know she's deserving.

He must engineer a way for her to uncover the truth for herself – that's the answer, he thinks. Only then can he be sure of her worthiness. Only that way can he rely on her protection, on her ability to keep him safe. But how?

What should he do? What clues can he leave? And how can he be sure she won't involve anyone else?

Raguel gnaws the sore patch on his lip and scratches at his head. His hair is short and prickly to the touch. There's an itchy boil at the base of his skull.

There must be a way, he thinks. O Heavenly Father, send me a sign.

He squints. It's hard to see clearly, everything is so bright, blindingly so. The world has become Technicolor, filled with constantly shifting geometric patterns and flashes of light. Raguel rubs his eyes and blinks but still he can't focus.

He's spent, exhausted; completely wiped. He did it. Another demon's dead. Though once again sleep has eluded him.

'Thou shalt not kill,' says the deep voice that speaks on its own. 'Your brother's blood cries out to me from the ground.'

Raguel starts to shake. Invisible hands grip him by the throat. Guilt always comes on the tail of his success.

'I was doing your work,' he says under his breath.

'Liar,' whisper the voices.

'Forgive me, Lord. Whatever you wish, I will do.'

But how can he know for sure what the Lord wants when first he tells Raguel to destroy the schemes of Satan and punish sinners, then afterwards admonishes him for his actions? If only there were a way he could be certain he was carrying out his Maker's wishes. If only there were a way to make the doubts disappear.

An idea begins to grow in Raguel's mind; the whispering voices murmur their approval. The panic from before recedes as he sees what he must do. He starts to breathe easily again.

He hears Ziba Mac talking. Raguel listens to the shape of her too-fast words. He sees them hanging in the air then dissolving in puffs of purple smoke. He sees her bending over the sinner's body, her outline bright and hazy, an angel's halo above her head. A unicorn snorts and canters past. The hallucinations are always so strong after a slaying, so vivid.

Raguel chews his lip. Will Ziba Mac understand the significance of the wounds on the pervert's neck or will he need to give her a clue?

Raguel stabbed him seven times in the neck even though the first thrust was enough to kill him. But it was important to get the number right. It was part of his message to his new guardian.

The lesions dance in front of him now, still wet from where he plunged the knife in. He licks his lips. The walls start to breathe and glow.

Ziba Mac's voice is fading. Raguel leans forward to hear her better, imagining he can smell her perfume. He remembers the bottle with its pretty glass stopper. He could never work out if it was supposed to look like a bird or a flower.

The memory fills his throat with acid. He squeezes his eyes shut. He doesn't want to think of Katie. She's gone and she's not coming back. She made that very clear. He couldn't count on her.

He drums his thumb against his knuckles. Seven times. Stop. And repeat. He whispers seven Our Fathers and seven Hail Marys.

He begged Katie not to leave him, though it didn't stop her. But Ziba Mac is different. She won't abandon him; she'll keep him safe. Hasn't God told him as much? Hasn't she said so herself?

Raguel begins to breathe more evenly, already thinking of what's to come. The next slaying will be different. The holy of holies. Spectacular.

It's time. He's ready to do what must be done.

CHAPTER 31

The boy lays out his collection in a line on the bed – a penknife, two Chupa Chups lollipops, some dinosaur stickers for his school bag and now a Mars bar. All gifts from Grandad.

'I've got a present for you,' Grandad whispered this afternoon when he and Granny came round to visit.

He'd put a finger to his lips and beckoned for the boy to follow him out of the room. The boy's mother was in the kitchen putting the kettle on, chatting to Granny. His father was finishing off some paperwork upstairs. The boy hadn't seen him all day.

He abandoned his Playmobil police helicopter and trotted off with Grandad into the hallway.

'It's in here,' Grandad said, patting his trouser pocket. 'See if you can find it.'

The boy grinned up at him and dug around. His smile disappeared. There was nothing there.

'Oops, silly me. Other pocket.'

The boy switched to the other side and fished out a Mars bar; a biggie, not one of those fun-sizes he sometimes got in party bags.

'Cool! You're the best!'

'Payment please,' Grandad said, bending down and tapping his lips.

The boy kissed him. The Grandad's bristles scratched his mouth.

Grandad put his hands on the boy's shoulders, their faces level. 'Now, don't tell anyone. It's our little secret. I wouldn't want you to get in trouble.'

Same thing he always says.

CHAPTER 32

'Let's go, MacKenzie.' Fingerling yawned wide enough for me to see his tonsils. 'I'll buy you a coffee back at HQ.'

'I'll be in later. There's something I need to check out on my own first.'

'There's no "i" in "team",' he said, rolling his eyes.

But there is a 'u' in 'schmuck', I thought, narrowing mine.

'By the way, you might want to ask someone to check out Marcus Lynch's alibi for the night Aidan Lynch, the first vic, was killed,' I said as we left the crime scene. 'They're father and son. I interviewed him the other day. There's something off about him. There was also some angst between him and Aidan back in the day. And he lives round the corner from The Camden Brasserie, in the house where his son was killed. I realise he doesn't fit the profile but it may be worth looking into him anyway.'

'Right,' Fingerling said in a brush-off voice before stalking off.

◆ ◆ ◆

Back in my flat a few hours later, I was trying to get my head round the Lacerator's hunting style. The World Service was on in the background. There was a near-empty coffee pot on the side table and a mug of freshly ground lifer juice in my hand.

I'd examined the weather records from the dates of each of the Lacerator's attacks, walked between the different crime scenes studying each site trying to see how they were connected, and checked for bus stops, driving and parking restrictions.

Now I was standing in front of the map of London I'd tacked up on my living-room wall and looking at the coloured flags I'd stuck on it. Blue for where the Lacerator's victims had last been seen. Red for where their bodies had been found. Eleven flags in total.

It was all part of the geo-profile I was preparing to try to identify the offender's comfort zone based on the location of crime sites. It's an effective technique since most crimes are committed within less than a mile of an offender's home.

Of course, there are some deviations to this rule. Adult offenders usually travel greater distances than juveniles, and body disposal sites are generally further away from where a perp lives than from where they target their prey.

Excluding his first kill, the Lacerator's victims from the eighties were all abducted and dumped in alleyways and green spaces around Soho.

Lynch didn't fit that mould. He was murdered and left at his home in Camden. But given that that kill didn't go too well for the Lacerator, judging by the botched job he made of the genital mutilation, it's not surprising he made an effort to learn from his mistakes and perfect his MO moving forwards.

However, although Lynch was killed in Camden and the others in Soho, there was still a pattern. The body disposal sites were all near the places where the victims were last seen.

And now, with the two most recent victims, he seemed to have come full circle, killing them both in Camden, not far from where he'd attacked Aidan Lynch.

I rang Nigel Fingerling's mobile.

'Any news yet on where the latest vic was last seen?'

'Yep. The Prince Albert pub. It's right round the corner from where we found his body.'

'So the pattern holds,' I said, sticking a blue flag on my map. 'And did he leave with anyone?'

'Barman's not sure. It was crowded last night. Some uphill gardener event.'

'The Prince Albert's a gay bar?'

'Either that or they just really like rainbow flags.'

'Nice to know you're such a tolerant guy, Fingerling. Thing is, it's another link to Thursday's killing and the eighties homicides. Helps build a picture of how he lures his targets.

'He must approach his victims in a bar and use some sort of a ruse to get them to leave with him – most likely the promise of sex. Whatever the ploy, though, the use of one reinforces the probability of good verbal skills and a normal to high IQ.'

'Hang about. I thought you said he was a disorganised offender. Isn't using a ruse and hunting people who fit a certain victimology the hallmark of an organised killer?'

There was a challenging tone in his voice. I could see why the kids at school hadn't liked him. His weedy physique would have only been part of the reason.

'The whole organised versus disorganised thing isn't a perfect dichotomy. Very few offenders are completely one or the other. Take Ed Kemper, the Co-ed Killer we talked about earlier. He lured female hitchhikers off the highway and transported them to rural areas where he killed and decapitated them before having sex with their corpses. The use of a ruse to target specific victim types is classic organised offender behaviour. But the mutilation is typical of a disorganised one.'

'Point made. Thanks for the lecture.'

Twat. I didn't respond though. I wasn't in the mood for a big-dick contest.

'All the Lacerator's victims were last seen in gay bars. Even Lynch, though he hadn't come out as being gay. However, I don't think the Lacerator's actually gay himself. The genital mutilation and overkill suggests he has some sort of vendetta against homosexuals.'

'Okay. Got anything else?'

'I've been charting the abduction and dump sites. They span a narrow geographical area. That suggests we're looking at an offender who's not particularly mobile. He's an opportunist but he goes to the abduction sites prepared and he knows exactly what he's doing.'

'Like you, hopefully.'

I hung up. What a clown dick. How did he ever get to be an SIO with his people skills?

Normally I'd have called Jack to rant but my dream from last night stopped me. The dream and the fact I couldn't stop thinking about it. I decided to go out for some air instead.

I stepped outside my front door and looked around. There was no one there but I could have sworn someone was watching me.

The world's not as dangerous as you think it is, I said to myself, thinking of what Jack had said as I popped in my earbuds and started walking towards the canal.

CHAPTER 33

I walked briskly along Westbourne Terrace Road past the Canal Café Theatre where Duncan and I used to go to watch the *News Revue* on Friday nights, past the Bridge House where we'd grab a drink afterwards and across Warwick Crescent towards the minicab place and the Waterside Café where we'd sometimes pop in for coffee and cake on Sunday afternoons.

The canal stretched out in front of it. A dirty green snake dotted with boats and flotsam.

I'd come a long way from the dark place where I'd been trapped in the run-up to Duncan's birthday. A week ago, I wouldn't have trusted myself to stand too close to the water's edge. Its tempting depths would have had a siren's call I may not have resisted. But today the swirl of the eddies was soothing rather than inviting.

There was some news coming through about Thursday's train crash. I turned up the volume.

The immediate cause was that the moving train was travelling too fast to stop when its driver first sighted the derailed wagons up ahead.

John Barnes, Chief Inspector of Rail Accidents, says that there will be a full inquiry into the incident, in which eighteen people were killed.

'We are working hard to establish the circumstances leading up to this terrible disaster, particularly how the freight train came to be derailed resulting in the death of so many innocent people.'

Not just death, I thought, an image of the burned teenager who wanted to go to Juilliard popping into my head. What about all the people who survived but whose lives will never be the same; haunted forever by what happened?

A few paces on I stopped, took my earbuds out and turned around slowly.

I hadn't heard or seen anything but I'd got a feeling; a sense again that someone's eyes were on me. I surveyed the path and the areas off it. There was no one.

Jack's right, I thought. I'm going all high off and to the right here. First the silver Honda and now this.

Except, unlike the night before, I hadn't been drinking anything stronger than Kenyan AA this morning. I shook my head. No, this was about me and my state of mind, not what was really there.

I put my buds back in and carried on walking, but I was still on edge. And I couldn't shake the feeling I was being observed.

I stopped again, removed my headphones and looked round carefully.

I thought I caught a movement; a flash of colour out of the corner of my eye. But when I got to where I'd seen it there was nothing there.

This is bullshit, I thought. I've been spending too much time thinking about the Lacerator and getting wired on caffeine. Why would anyone be spying on me? This isn't the old country or Afghanistan. No one's out to get me here.

But then, what about the Honda? And where the latest victim had been found?

My mind was firing rounds in every direction. I didn't know what to think.

I reached my favourite bench, the one by the water under the huge London plane tree. My special place. I glanced at the etchings as I sat down.

Ramon 4 Caz 4 Ever. Louis loves Amy. Mark Landings and Liz Alonby Always.

How many of them are still together? I wondered. And how many are off screwing other people and carving new messages of undying love?

The sun won out over the clouds and drifted over my face. The warmth felt good. I leaned back, closing my eyes.

And despite all the coffee and all the thoughts ricocheting in my head, I drifted off right there by the canal in full view of anyone who might be watching.

CHAPTER 34

My phone rang, waking me with a start. I pulled it out and checked the screen. Wolfie. My stomach flipped.

This shit has got to stop.

I wrinkled my nose. What was that smell? It was like rotting food. Fruity with a vinegar overlay. Algae from the canal, maybe?

'I hear you found another Lacerator victim this morning,' he said. 'Can you tell me anything?'

'He's evolving. Getting into his swing. MO's started to change, which could mean he's becoming more dangerous. There'll be a press conference later.'

'You speaking?'

'Not sure yet. Might be better for Falcon to be the mouthpiece. Demonstrates our control over the case. Leadership. All that hoo-ha.'

'Right. By the way, I thought of you earlier. Your man's name cropped up again today.'

'Duncan?' I said, confused.

'Not Duncan, you daft mare. Aidan Lynch.'

'Really? How come?'

'I'm doing a piece on that murdered kid. You know, Samuel Catlin. The golden-haired boy, the rags are calling him. Anyhow, I popped into the Kentish Town nick. Their major crimes team was in charge of the case at the time. Got talking to a DS there who'd worked the case and turns out Aidan Lynch was questioned by the brains department back in the day.'

'Seriously? Why? Was he a suspect?'

'No. It was more to do with the fact that Samuel was part of the Cub Scout group Aidan was involved with. The detectives just wanted to know if he'd seen anyone hanging around, paying the kid any special attention, that sort of thing. Apparently he couldn't have been more helpful. Nice guy, according to the DS. They checked his alibi of course, good housekeeping basically. It was rock solid though.'

'How so?'

I heard him rustle paper down the line, checking his notes. As he sucked his lips, an image from last night's dream flashed into my brain. The look he'd given me right before we'd kissed. The feel of his mouth on mine.

I squeezed my eyes shut. This has got to stop, I thought. No good can come of it.

'Here we go,' he said a couple of seconds later, thankfully oblivious to the journey my mind had taken. 'Aidan bought a ticket from Camden Road Station for the 15.09 train to Watford. He was on his way to get to his army physical. He called his mother reverse charges at 16.30 from Watford Station to say he'd missed his doctor's appointment. The Old Bill has the call logs.'

'Life really went arseways for the poor bastard, didn't it? The Lacerator butchered him less than two months after that call.'

'Some people have all the luck.'

I laughed and we said our goodbyes. Yawning, I got up off the bench. When you've been on the job since zero dark thirty, eleven thirty in the morning feels like the middle of the afternoon. I was dog tired. I needed a pot of lifer juice. Maybe two.

I was just swinging my bag over my shoulder and thinking about the revised profile I was putting together when my phone rang again.

The number that came up was withheld but that didn't matter; I knew who was calling before I heard his voice.

'I've been trying to reach you. The DCI wants to make a statement to the press. You need to get down here. Five minutes ago.'

People telling me that I need to do something is one of my biggest bug fucks.

'I'm on my way, Fingerling,' I said, longing to ask him how the hell he'd managed to be the fastest sperm.

CHAPTER 35

Raguel is inside Ziba Mac's apartment block. He stands for a moment in the narrow hallway breathing in the air she breathes, seeing her world as she sees it. He takes it all in. The dust motes dancing in the sunbeams. The sheen on the wooden banisters. The worn strip on the edge of each carpeted stair.

It wasn't hard to gain entry. He'd pressed all the bells until someone buzzed him through. They hadn't even asked who he was. So dangerous, any nutcase could get in.

Finding her address was easy too. It only took a moment to locate it in the computer room. A sign from above that all will be well; that he's doing the right thing.

He crosses himself, goes to her mailbox then climbs the stairs. There is a lift but if he takes it he won't be able to count the steps and that would be dangerous. This way is safer.

He counts as he goes up. Each time he's gone seven steps, he stops and whispers the prayer, or at least the first part, the first seven words. *Thy kingdom come, thy will be done.* Then he goes up seven more steps, stops and prays again.

'Do not fear, for I am with you,' whispers the solitary deep voice. 'I will uphold you with my right hand.'

God is talking to him directly now. Just like he did the night Aidan Lynch died. And like he did again after the crash on Thursday.

Raguel is on the top floor. There's only one door here. He kneels down in front of it and presses his palms and forehead to the wood. It feels cool against his skin. A gentle kiss on a fevered face.

He inhales deeply, filling his lungs, breathing her in.

'Ziba Mac,' the voices whisper. 'Holy angel of the Lord.'

'Glory be to the Father, and to the Son, and to the Holy Spirit, as it was in the beginning, is now, and ever shall be, world without end. Amen,' Raguel says, taking the envelope out of his pocket and touching it to his lips.

This is the ultimate connection. The path to true understanding and togetherness. The revelation Ziba Mac asked him to make.

It's also the first part of the plan he's devised to make her uncover the truth about him for herself. If she can figure out the answers he'll know she's worthy of being his protector. And by the end of the day he'll also know for sure what the Lord wants from him. Ziba Mac's actions will provide the answer.

It's perfect. So too is the plan he's concocted to make sure she doesn't involve anyone else. It's so genius it can only have been divinely inspired.

He makes the sign of the cross seven times then slides the envelope under the door. But the moment it's gone he starts to shake and his skin crawls with ants. He swats his arms but it's no good. If anything it makes them multiply.

'What's done cannot be undone,' the voices whisper, the words echoing in the air around him. 'Stupid. Sssssstupid.'

Raguel covers his ears but it's no good. The voices grow louder and louder till they're all he can hear.

A long gnarly arm stretches out from the wall. A spider the size of a football climbs up his leg. And the air becomes thick with the smell of cigarette smoke and cologne.

What if the Evil One has guided his hand rather than the Lord? What if silver-tongued Satan has tricked him? What if Ziba Mac is one of the Serpent's own and this was a terrible mistake?

He can't catch his breath. His heart is booming. He needs to get out of here but when he looks down at his feet he sees they are welded in a can of cement.

He digs in the pocket of his chinos for his baggie. The magic powder's there; just what the doctor ordered, as his mother used to say when he was a boy – though she was talking about an apple a day rather than Class A drugs.

He doesn't usually carry – it's too risky – but he'd known today might be difficult. He'd known he might need a little crystal courage, despite what the doctors have said about it making his condition worse.

He pulls the baggie out and opens it in haste, spilling some of the precious powder as he does so. He sees the specks on the carpet and wants to cry at the waste. The voices in his head start to tut but he won't be beaten. He slithers on to his stomach and presses his face to the floor, licking the grains off the ground, though all he's really getting is a mouthful of dust.

He sits back up on his heels, sucks his little finger and dips it in the bag. Then he wipes it round the inside of his right nostril. Seven licks. Seven dips. Seven snorts. 777. The ancient protection against the Devil. Satan's numerical antithesis. A representation of the threefold perfection of the Holy Trinity. The seven bowls of wrath, seven angels and seven trumpets from the Book of Revelation.

Raguel's body stops shaking and fills with the strength of the Lord right through to his extremities. It makes him want to laugh out loud. It makes him want to jump off the roof and fly over the city. It makes him believe he can.

It also makes him realise he was wrong about Ziba Mac being one of the Devil's helpers. He was being stupid; panicking and giving into fear.

'Trust in me,' whispers the deep voice. 'Do what you must do.'

Ziba Mac is his protector. She wants to help him, just like she said. His mission is holy and it will be successful.

Today he will bring a course of fire in the west to persecute the fallen as it was written in the Book of Enoch. Just as it has been commanded by the Lord God who dwelleth on high and sits on the throne of glory.

Vengeance will belong to Raguel as it says in Jeremiah: 'At the time that I visit them they shall be cast down.'

Raguel will be the one to cast the demons out. And the time has come for the Devil to lie amongst the slaughtered. A thrill of what's to come pulses through him.

Raguel has waited a long time to mete out his punishment but he won't have to wait much longer.

CHAPTER 36

The boy's in his Thomas the Tank Engine pyjamas, all tucked up and snoring softly in his grandparents' spare room. His first ever sleepover.

'Snug as a bug in a rug,' Granny said, as she kissed him goodnight after checking for monsters under the bed and promising to leave the landing light on.

His parents have gone off to the Lake District, just the two of them. Dad's idea.

'I'm taking Mum away for a birthday treat,' he'd said to the boy. 'I've arranged for you to stay with Granny and Grandad. I bet they'll spoil you rotten.'

The boy's been so excited; crossing off the days on the kitchen calendar at home and getting his bag all packed – a proper grown-up case with stiff handles and wheels and everything.

Granny's promised to make chocolate-chip pancakes for breakfast, his all-time favourite. She even said she'd let him flip them over in the pan.

He insisted on getting everything ready before he went to bed – the big measuring jug, Granny's blue china mixing bowl with the flowers painted on the side, the balloon whisk. And a stool so he'll be able to reach the hob.

The clock ticks on the nightstand. Lambie's tucked under his arm. And there's a patch of drool on the pillow. The room smells of cookies. The boy's mouth moves as he dreams.

Creak.

The door opens then closes again with a soft snap. There's someone else in the room now; all shape and no features in the dark.

A man who smells of Camel Straights approaches the bed.

CHAPTER 37

Raguel watches the press conference while Ziba Mac stands beside him glowing white as though lit from the inside. The walls are breathing gently and a harp plays softly in the distance.

He takes in the room packed with newspapermen and cameras. The raised platform and large, white screen. The people jostling for position, pointing their microphones and voice recorders at the stage before anything's even begun.

They're all there. The BBC, ITV, Sky and even some foreign TV stations he's never heard of. He holds a giggle inside his chest; laughing now would give the game away.

In the old days, prophets had to shout outside the temple walls to be heard and even then they were often ignored; side-lined and treated like madmen. But no one's ignoring him. He's got their full attention.

The way the journalists are waving their recorders about reminds him of how they'd all held their home-made Union Jacks that day the Queen Mum had driven past Kenwood in her Daimler.

Raguel had been six or seven at the time. He'd stood with his school friends waiting to see the car for over an hour. It had passed by them in less than five seconds but it had been worth the wait. He'd seen her face through the passenger window and she'd smiled right at him. He'd waved his flag off the pole. He'd been happy then. Childhood innocence. It hadn't lasted long.

The Detective Chief Inspector stands up to speak. Raguel listens carefully. First, he tells the media about the body they found this morning. He talks about the location of the 'crime', the cause of death and what he calls the 'mutilation of the deceased's genitals' and the 'ocular trauma'.

It makes it all sound much more clinical than it felt when Raguel was hacking the demon's penis off with his long-sheathed knife and driving his blade into his cursed devil eyes.

'Look at me,' the voices whisper. 'Look at me.'

Raguel is in a room full of people; no one can hurt him here and yet still his blood runs cold as the past presses down on him.

'We are beginning to hone our profile of the Lacerator following the murder of Mr Clough this morning,' the Detective Chief Inspector is saying.

Raguel hopes he'll say something about the religious imperative for his actions. Something about the stab pattern maybe. That'd be good; a sign Ziba Mac is beginning to know him better. If the DCI doesn't say anything though, he may have to give her a nudge in the right direction, Raguel thinks, polishing his glasses on the underside of his shirt.

He knows Ziba Mac needs to understand him fully – the past has taught him as much – but at the same time she needs to prove her worth. All God's servants are tested; there can be no exception here. Hence the little challenge he's set up. She needs to work for the information; he can't hand all the answers to her on a tray.

But now, listening to the Detective Chief Inspector talk, he begins to think that despite what the voices have been telling him, Ziba Mac really doesn't get him. And if that's the case maybe she isn't his saviour after all.

'The profiling work carried out by Ziba MacKenzie, who spoke to you yesterday, suggests that the offender is not particularly mobile and that he kills near to where he lives. Given the nature of his crimes, we understand him to be primarily what we call a disorganised offender.

These perpetrators are nearly always male. They have an inborn anxiety regarding other people and often inhabit a complex delusion they've constructed in his own mind.'

Raguel's stomach fills with stones. Complex delusion, indeed! He rubs his eyes and tries to swallow away the lump in his throat as the Detective Chief Inspector talks. The words stick him in the gut, proof of Ziba Mac's lack of comprehension and unworthiness. Next to him her inner light fades and a hairy bug crawls down the neckline of her shirt.

The disappointment is all the greater for the expectation that preceded it. There is no one left on earth to protect him after all. His true guardian angel has gone, killed on that cursed train. He is completely alone. Ziba Mac is not his new guardian after all. She's his Judas Iscariot.

'Following the execution of a crime, a disorganised offender will drink or take drugs excessively. He'll alter his eating habits and become extremely nervous. He will take a high level of interest in the police case and introduce it into the topic of conversation at every opportunity.

'At present we are investigating the possibility that the Lacerator's murders are homophobic attacks. All his victims were last seen at gay bars. Furthermore, the way in which the killer severs his victims' genitalia suggests a deep hatred towards homosexuals. However, I'd like to stress that we are keeping an open mind about motive at this time and that all members of the public should act with caution. We would advise people to plan their travel arrangements before they go out at night, to avoid dark, isolated areas and to trust their instincts. If anyone sees anything suspicious please call 999 immediately and seek safety in a public place.

'The longer the Lacerator goes without being caught the more emboldened he will become and that will make him start to take risks. Not because all serial killers deep down want to be stopped, as some people believe, but rather because he'll want to enhance the thrill of the kill. Serial killers are like drug addicts. They need a bigger and bigger fix each time to match the original high. But whatever they do, nothing will ever feel as good to them again. However, that doesn't mean they don't stop trying – quite the opposite, in fact. They never stop.

'There have been two murders in the last six days. The killer's blood lust is growing. We believe he will strike again and that he'll strike soon.'

Raguel digs his nails into his palms. They leave behind a row of red crescents; four small blood moons. The analogy makes him smile. Blood moons have a special significance for him. Perhaps this is a sign from above that all will be well after all, that he should have faith in the woman his Maker has chosen for him.

He raises his eyes to the ceiling and says the Lord's Prayer inside his head. He doesn't want to be overheard and draw attention to himself; it's bad enough that the shadowy figure is hopping about the room blowing raspberries at everyone.

Did Ziba Mac really get it all as wrong as she seems to have done? Really, a crusade against gays? How ridiculous! She's so off the mark, he wonders whether she's got it wrong on purpose, whether it's a way of throwing the police off his trail. Yes, that must be it, he thinks, and the whispering voices murmur their agreement.

Sodomy is unnatural of course, a transgression against God and his holy laws, but Raguel's mission is about something else. Something much more personal – as Ziba Mac is about to find out.

The Detective Chief Inspector is winding up now.

'There is a benefit to the killer becoming bolder,' he's saying. 'The more risks the Lacerator takes, the more likely it is he'll make a mistake that'll get him caught.'

Wrong again, thinks Raguel, taking a lungful of air. I'm not going to make a mistake. And I'm not going to get caught either. Not while I'm doing God's work and Ziba Mac is here to protect me.

CHAPTER 38

Nigel Fingerling and I stood together the back of the packed press room.

I glanced at him.

We were on the same side. We both wanted to catch the mumza terrorising the capital. But deep down I had a feeling we weren't on the same team. I couldn't help feeling that he wanted me to fail and that he wanted to be there when I did.

Ever since I'd embarrassed him in front of his colleagues with that profiling business when we'd first met, things had been tense between us. And turning him down when he asked me for a drink the other night hadn't done much to smooth things over.

I'd seen the way he'd flushed when I'd made my excuses; how his neck had gone blotchy, how he'd sniffed as he tossed his head back. He'd taken what I'd said as a rejection. He'd taken it personally. I find when men do that they don't forgive you easily.

Falcon was reading out the bit I'd written about how serial killers are like drug addicts. I glanced at Nigel Fingerling out of the corner of my eye. He was completely focused on Falcon. His eyes were narrowed in concentration, his hand was clenched and there was a sour smell coming off his skin.

I took a half step back to observe him more carefully while pretending to keep my eye on the platform. His skin was pale; bone white and splattered with acne, tiny red pimples just breaking through the surface.

He looked in my direction for a moment and then back at the podium. His eyes were deep-set and bloodshot from lack of sleep. There were dark patches under his lower lids.

If I hadn't looked at him when the DCI said the thing about drug addicts I may not have made the connection but now I had, it did make a sort of sense.

I couldn't imagine Nigel Fingerling hunched over a glass-topped table with a rolled-up bank note in his hand or shooting up at some doss house in the middle of the night, but he did have all the physical signs of addiction – and some of the psychological ones too: the irritability, the angry outbursts and the strange appetite.

I picked up a fair bit from Duncan when he was in Vice but I'm not an expert when it comes to drugs. I didn't know what Fingerling was on. Though the more I thought about it, the more I thought he might well be on something.

Maybe that was the dark secret I'd guessed at when we'd first met. If so I'd been right. It was something he'd be ashamed of and as such he'd be at great pains to hide it from his colleagues. The mere hint he was taking drugs would be enough to end his career.

The DCI wrapped up his speech and moved on to questions. A jungle of hands went up, Jack's among them.

Normally the police keep their investigations private. The last thing they need is journalists sticking their beaks in and getting in the way. The hunt for a serial killer is different. It's one of the few times the police willingly involve the media, and for good reason. Someone out there always knows something. The police's job is to say what they're looking for. The media's job is to disseminate that information and get the public to talk.

But that's not the only reason the police involve the press. Most people know offenders often try to insert themselves into an investigation but that doesn't stop them doing it. And the police use the media as bait to draw them out.

Take the Soham murders back in 2002. Ian Huntley played with the press. He gave interviews, he made a whole deal about how he'd been the last person to see the missing girls alive and in doing so he turned attention on himself, which ultimately led to his arrest.

Of course, not every officer welcomes this level of media engagement. I remember having a heated debate with Duncan about the impact of the press on the Soham investigation. I was all for it, arguing it was how the police had got their man so there must be something to be said for the method.

'You have no idea the pressure it put on the Cambridgeshire force,' he'd said, shaking his head and reaching for his Tennent's – Ye Olde TL, he called it. 'Not only was it like having *The Bill* broadcast around the world 24/7, it also made the team go down paths they didn't want to follow.'

What would he have said if he could see this? I thought, surveying the room and feeling the dull ache of his absence. Even after all this time I haven't got used to not having him around. And every morning I still experience a nanosecond of amnesia; sweet while it lasts, cruel when it lifts.

'Good work, Mac,' said Falcon, coming over to shake my hand after the hordes had begun to disperse.

I was careful not to grip too tight. His fingers were red and swollen around the joints, his limp more pronounced. The gout was spreading. The stress of the Lacerator case wouldn't be helping and nor would his fondness for cookies, I thought, noting the smattering of biscuit crumbs on his trousers.

'It might be helpful to look more closely at the relationships between the historic and current crime scenes. See if we can get more of a read on where he lives. You've heard of Operation Lynx, I presume?' he said.

'1996. One of the biggest manhunts in UK history. Twelve thousand suspects. Crime scenes covering a 4,378 square mile area. Using evidence from a credit card stolen from one of the victims, investigators tracked a number of routine purchases the perp made to hone in on where he lived.' I said. 'It was a major win for geo-profiling and a turning point in the way we approach cases. I've started preparing a geographical profile for the Lacerator. I should have some answers later today.'

'Didn't I tell you this lady's good?' The DCI turned to Fingerling with a smile as he patted me on the shoulder. 'By the way, are you still collecting sponsorship pledges, Nige?'

'The triathlon was a couple of weeks ago but donations are always appreciated.'

'What's all this?' I asked.

'Didn't you know? Nigel's a big fundraiser for the Children's Cancer and Leukaemia Group. He does the London Marathon and Blenheim Palace Triathlon every year.'

'Really?' I didn't manage to keep the surprise out of my voice. The whole charity thing didn't fit with my impression of him any more than the apparent fact he was a sportsman.

'My sister died of leukaemia when she was six. It's a horrible illness,' he said, squaring up to me.

'I'm so sorry. I had no idea. I know how difficult it is to lose someone you love. My husband died recently. I miss him terribly.'

I looked at the floor, thinking for a moment of Duncan. About the god-awful rock music he liked and the way he smiled at me in the morning when he'd just woken up. The liquorice comfits he used to eat by the handful while he watched the rugby and how they made his mouth taste afterwards. And how we'd stay up into the night with a bottle of wine discussing something he'd just read: a line of poetry, an obscure idea in a philosophical text, a passage from a book.

The night before he was killed he read to me from *The Winter of Our Discontent*.

'What d'you think of this?' he said. '"It's so much darker when a light goes out than it would have been if it had never shone."'

'That's heartbreaking,' I said. 'Imagine feeling grief like that.'

I don't have to imagine any more.

CHAPTER 39

'By the way, I got a DS to look into Marcus Lynch's alibi for the night of his son's murder, like you asked,' said Fingerling in his whiney nasal voice as we left Falcon and walked over to the lifts together.

I tried to keep my face neutral. I didn't want him to think I was emotionally invested in this. Or that I was surprised. I hadn't expected him to come up with the goods.

'And?'

'Funny thing, actually. He doesn't have one.'

'Really?'

'Yeah. Turns out he and the wife were supposed to be staying with her sister in Bath for the weekend. Then on Saturday morning he was called back to London. A work emergency, so he said. Something to do with a big commercial loan and a financial covenant being breached.' He scratched the back of his head with the end of his ink stick. 'Apparently, Lynch needed to calculate whether it was in default. Not sure if I've got all the terms right there, but you catch my drift.'

'Wouldn't he have an alibi from his place of work?' I said, frowning.

'That's the thing. He checked into the office around three in the afternoon and stayed till ten o'clock that evening. Then he left. Didn't come back till the following morning – by which time Aidan had been iced.'

'Hang on. His son's murdered and he pitches up at work the next day?'

'He may not have known the boy was dead.'

'But Aidan was killed in the Lynch family home. How could Marcus not have known he was dead if he'd gone back there after work?'

'Well, that's the thing, you see. He claims he didn't go home. Says he stayed in a hotel round the corner from the office so he could make an early start the next morning. There's a record of him checking in but there are no security cameras. He could have come and gone and no one would have been any the wiser. It was the wife who discovered the body the next day. Not him.'

'And you buy that? Where was the office?'

'London Bridge.'

'London Bridge? That's on the Northern Line, same as Camden Town. Why'd he need to go to a hotel?'

Fingerling shrugged.

'Maybe he was being a naughty boy.'

I gave him a look.

'No way to prove or disprove it now,' he said.

I sighed. He was right.

'There's more.' Fingerling hit the call button as we reached the lifts. 'DS Lane's just spoken to the sister. She didn't tell the detectives at the time, didn't see the relevance she says, but turns out Theresa Lynch did the dirty on her other half. Had an affair before Aidan was born. Marcus supposedly forgave her but the sister says things were never the same between them afterwards.'

An affair. I thought back to what Marcus had told me about how Theresa had become more religious after she got pregnant with Aidan. Was her new-found fervour about guilt and shame because she was carrying her lover's child?

'So Aidan may not be Marcus's son,' I said.

That'd explain why the two of them looked so different.

'That's not all.' Fingerling pulled a piece of paper out of the file he was holding. 'Here. Take a squiz.'

It was a black-and-white photo of a handsome man in his early sixties with a neatly trimmed beard and owlish, wire-framed glasses.

'Who's this?'

'Theresa Lynch's bit on the side. Remind you of anyone?'

I looked from the photo to Fingerling. The magazine slotted into place. 'The Lacerator's other victims,' I said in a quiet voice.

'Exactly what I thought,' Fingerling said with a slow, thin-lipped smile.

CHAPTER 40

It was all asses and elbows back in the incident room. Detectives talking on the phone, tapping at keyboards, going through files. I went to my desk, processing my conversation with Fingerling.

I know it was wrong but a part of me wanted Marcus Lynch to be the Lacerator. At least that'd give me closure on the business with Theresa. *He did it. You have to tell someone.*

However, although he had motive and opportunity for killing Aidan, it didn't mean he had, not least because he didn't fit the profile.

The evidence pointed to an offender in his mid to late forties, naturally unkempt, on antipsychotic medication and possibly using drugs. Marcus Lynch was none of these things. The question was, which was wrong – the suspect or the profile?

I ground my temples with the balls of my hands, thinking.

'Do you have a minute there, Mac?' Paddy Dinwitty said, coming over.

His Irish accent was soft and lyrical. I could listen to him talking all day.

'What's up?'

I wasn't sorry for the interruption. It was like a Killing House inside my head, thoughts firing off in every direction.

'The wounds in the victim's neck. I don't think they're random like we thought. Come and see.'

I followed him to the mural of crime-scene photos on the far wall. They were connected with lines of red string and labelled with yellow and orange Post-its.

'It's unlikely there's a pattern here,' I said, looking at the marks on the most recent victim's neck. 'The Lacerator struck late at night. It would've been dark and he was clearly in a frenzy, hence the overkill.'

'Just do me a favour and have a look.'

'Alright.' I stood a little way back from the pictures.

I'm not squeamish but these days I am slightly long-sighted. Helps me see the bigger picture, I always say.

The fire set by the Lacerator hadn't been burning long before it had gone out, which meant the bruising and marks around the lesions were clearly visible. I tilted my head, squinted my eyes and peered at the photos.

'If there's a pattern, I don't see it,' I said. 'The incision marks look random to me. And they're close together, which is consistent with a frenzied and repeated stabbing motion.'

'You ever done those Magic Eye puzzles?' Paddy asked.

'You what?'

'Magic Eye puzzles. They were all the thing back in the nineties. I used to have posters up in my room at university,' he said, stroking the stubble on his chin.

From what I'd picked up, his wife had recently walked out on their marriage to 'find herself'. His unshaven and generally unkempt look probably has something to do with that, I thought. And he's still wearing his ring. So he's hoping she might come back.

'So how do these puzzles of yours work?' I turned to look at the board.

'You've got this image, right? A repeating pattern. Can be anything. Swirls. Rainbows. Whatever. Point is, there's another image hidden in it. You can't see it by looking at it straight on. You have to hold the picture right up to your nose so it gets all blurry, see? Then you need to focus as if you're looking through the pattern into the distance. Then very slowly you move it away from your face and the hidden image comes into view. They're dead good.'

'And your point is what? That I need to hold the crime-scene photos up to my nose?'

'Not exactly. Perhaps you just need a different perspective, is all. A different way of looking at them. Maybe rather than looking at the stab-wound pattern with your eyes you need to look at it with your mind.'

'Shit, Paddy, that's a bit Uri Geller, isn't it?'

He laughed. 'Maybe. Try this instead. Start with the numbers first. How many stab marks are there?'

'Seven.'

'Okay. Does the number seven mean anything? Does it have any bearing on what we know about the Lacerator?'

I pinched my nasal bridge. 'Let's see. There have been six victims not seven so it's not that. But he struck again for the first time in years on the seventh of October. Could it have something to do with that, I wonder?'

'Maybe. Or could it be how many people he's going to kill?'

'I doubt it.' I shook my head slowly. 'This guy's not going to stop once he's reached some magic number. Remember what I said at the debrief before the press conference? He's like an addict. All he's interested in doing is reliving how he felt after his first kill, his first high. He's just like any other junkie – the only way he'll only stop if he's forced to.'

Paddy rubbed his eyes for a minute and sighed deeply. 'Okay, how about we look at it another way? Go up close to the photo. What do you see now?'

I tossed the hair out of my eyes and looked at the board. This close everything was out of focus, which I suppose is what Paddy had intended.

'Three pairs of eyes,' I said without thinking through my answer. 'And a dice pattern. A square. That's number four on the dice. And also a diamond at the bottom. That's a dagger symbol.'

'Or a cross.' He connected the dots with his forefinger. 'Does that tell you anything?'

'I don't know. A square. A cross. Three pairs of eyes. Could mean anything. Or it could be random. But if it is all intentional then the Lacerator's playing games with us, which means he's starting to communicate.

'And if that's true, then maybe deep down he knows what he's doing is wrong. And he wants to be caught.'

CHAPTER 41

I shut the communal front door to my apartment block and wrinkled my nose. The hallway normally smells of Lemon Pledge, especially when the cleaner comes in to dust the common parts. The smell of Pledge was there now but there was something else too. A whiff of over-ripe fruit, refuse and vinegar. Just like the odour by the canal.

I massaged my temples and took a deep breath. Ever since the train crash I'd been jumpy. My mind had been hot-wired and out of control. I'd been seeing things that couldn't be seen and hearing things that couldn't be heard.

I'm getting to be as messed up as a left-handed football racket, I thought, shifting the weight of my shoulder bag and heading on up the stairs to my own front door.

The smell from downstairs was stronger up here. Where was it coming from? I'm the only one who lives on the top floor and I don't smell like that.

I turned the key in the lock and pushed the door open. My thoughts were full of the Lacerator and the geo-profile I needed to pin down. I had to hone in on the area where he lived but I wasn't sure how to do it.

The detectives working on Operation Lynx had got a break but it was a break hinged on luck, as is so often the case in high-profile investigations. The way the Son of Sam was caught out by a parking ticket is possibly the most famous example of this but it's not the only instance of an offender's mistake leading to his capture.

So far, however, despite what we'd told the media, the Lacerator hadn't slipped up at all – at least not to my knowledge.

I was rubbing my eyes as I stepped across the threshold so I almost didn't see it lying on the mat: a creamy white envelope with my name written across the front in black ink.

I picked it up. The writing was straight and pointy. There was a full stop after my name. And my name was wrong. Nobody's ever called me Ziba Mac. I opened the envelope.

The blood cooled in my veins. My heart hammered. My palms began to sweat.

It was from him – the Lacerator; a serial killer boiling over with blood lust. And he'd been standing right outside my door.

I've never kidded myself that the apartment block was Fort Knox. Hell, we don't even have security cameras or porterage, but I have always felt safe here.

This is the place where I hunkered down after Duncan died and it's where I closet myself away from the world when the sky darkens around me and the black dog creeps out of the shadows. But now it had been violated, the same way the funky smell in the hall had overpowered the clean scent of Lemon Pledge.

The Lacerator was out of control, driven by a need for violence and domination. He was spiralling, devolving; increasingly irrational and overwhelmed by an inner rage he couldn't contain.

The acid churned in the pit of my stomach, burning my gut. I couldn't breathe. I could barely stand. I reached out a hand to steady myself against the wall and pressed my forehead to it. The cool plaster against my skin was comforting, grounding somehow.

The Lacerator had been here in broad daylight without anyone stopping him. That told me something about him. It told me he didn't care who might have seen him. Maybe he took precautions when he was out on the streets. Maybe he was smart enough to wear a disguise or at least a cap pulled down low to hide his face from the CCTV cameras.

But no, thinking about it, that sort of calculated behaviour didn't fit with the profile or what he'd just done. The letter he'd slipped under my door was handwritten. Not in capitals, just regular joined up writing. Writing that someone might recognise.

I squatted and rummaged about in my bag for a pair of latex gloves. They made a whispering sound as I slipped them on. They were a size small but they were still loose on me, making me clumsy.

The letter was written on printer paper. Easily accessible. Cheap. But the Lacerator had used a fountain pen. He's traditional then, I thought. Old-fashioned at heart with an eye for detail; someone who takes the time to get things just so. The colour of the ink told me something too. People who use black ink think of themselves as serious and professional. They're often also uptight and anally retentive – like the charming Nigel Fingerling, I thought. He uses black ink too.

I read the letter again.

It's funny how many serial killers write to journalists or the police. The BTK Killer sent letters and poems to a local newspaper suggesting nicknames for himself. The Zodiac Killer wrote to the NYPD and the Lipstick Killer scrawled a note on the wall of his second victim's home saying, 'I cannot control myself.'

What's interesting is that rather like the way they murder their victims, there are plenty of reasons killers choose to communicate.

Some write because they want to be caught. Their messages are essentially cries for help. For others it's about power. The Zodiac Killer wanted to taunt the police. The BTK Killer liked the attention.

But given what was in this letter, the London Lacerator was after something completely different.

I'd have liked to call Jack but he wasn't the man I had to speak to. The person I had to call was someone who made my skin itch; the original swinging dick. I closed my eyes, sighed deeply and dug my mobile out of my bag. The line rang twice before it was picked up.

'DI Fingerling's phone.'

It wasn't the spotty Pippin speaking.

'Is he there?'

'Mac, is that you?'

Paddy.

'The DI's out right now,' he said. 'And his mobile's off, I just tried calling.'

'This can't wait.' I dropped my shoulders, which I hadn't realised were tensed up round my ears. 'I'm coming back in. I've got some new evidence you all need to see as soon as possible. In the meantime can you pull up the CCTV footage from the cameras around Blomfield Villas between ten fifty this morning and two o'clock this afternoon?'

'Well alright. But tell me why.'

'I've got a letter. I think it's from the Lacerator.'

I more than 'thought' it, but couldn't rule out the possibility it might be a hoax at this stage.

'Jaysis. What makes you think that?'

'When I got back after the press conference this afternoon there was an envelope under my door. It must have been delivered while I was out. So, sometime between 10.50 and 14.00. Inside was a handwritten note. From someone claiming to be responsible for the murder of the latest victim. Though interestingly, the writer signed off as "Raguel" not the Lacerator.'

'That doesn't mean it's not him. Plenty of serial killers have come up with names for themselves.'

'I know. Having said that, you know as well as I do that high-profile investigations like this one draw attention from the wrong kind of people – losers who like to pretend to be someone they're not for a bit of attention.'

'Still, I'd better get a forensics team over to you. You should be there. It'll be quicker if I come and collect the note rather than waiting for you to get over to the Yard. We can look over it together before I go back.'

'Sounds good.'

'So, yer think this is really him, eh?'

'I do. One – the language denotes a personality that fits the profile. Two – he refers to the gold stud we found in the deceased's right ear. That's not something we released to the media, it's information only the killer would know. And three – possibly most significantly – the tone is overtly religious, which fits with someone on a crusade.'

'Yer really understand this guy.'

'I'm trying to. But get this. Remember how you said maybe there was a pattern in the stab wounds?'

'Yes?' There was a tremor of excitement in his voice.

'Well, I'll show you when you get here, but given what's in the letter, I think you might actually be right.'

'I'm on me way.'

'Wait,' I said. 'I haven't given you my address.'

'It's alright. I've already got it.'

CHAPTER 42

'Lord God,' Paddy said, sucking his lips, his eyebrows quirked.

He was in my flat sitting at the dining table with the Lacerator's note in his hand. There was another copy up on my laptop. I'd scanned it in before he'd arrived.

The World Service was on low in the background. The newsreader was talking about the latest murder and some of the more gruesome details of the attack. Though, of course, there was no mention of the drops of olive oil the CSIs found on the body. That information we were holding back.

I'd just told Paddy what I now thought the wound patterns represented. A dot to dot. At the top, a 'Z' for Ziba. And at the bottom a cross, like he'd thought. I'd had to draw it out for him before he could see it.

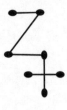

'If we're right the attack was more controlled than we thought,' I said. 'And it suggests the killer feels he's got some sort of connection with me. The letter he sent certainly bears that out. What he's written is as much about me as it is about his crimes. Have a look.'

Paddy took it from me and read aloud, his hands shaking slightly.

Dear Ziba Mac,
I was with you this morning as you bent over my offering, kneeling at the altar of my work.

We are one, you and I. Bound together in the holiest of missions – me, the judge and executioner. You, the guardian angel sent to keep me safe.

The earring-wearer will not be my last, but I think you know that, don't you? You already understand me so well. And I am beginning to understand you too.

Each time I look into your eyes I see your pain.

You are an outsider, tortured by your past, wary of everyone – just like me.

Already we have started our journey but before we can go further you need to know me better. And soon you will.

In nomine Patris et Filii et Spiritus Sancti,
I remain yours truly,
Raguel.

'Let's discuss the wording,' I said once he'd finished reading. 'How a person expresses themselves says a lot about them. We can use this letter to get inside the Lacerator's head, James Brussel style.'

'What's his story?'

'He analysed the Mad Bomber's manifesto. It was the first example of criminal profiling. Led to the perp's arrest.'

'How's that?'

'He deduced that the Bomber's formal language and lack of colloquialisms showed he was foreign. The breast-shaped "w"s implied he had an Oedipus complex, which meant he wasn't married. And he even used it to predict what he'd be wearing when the cops caught up with him.'

'He got that boxed off, eh?' said Paddy. 'So what can you tell about the Lacerator from his letter?'

'For starters, he's got a high IQ and one hell of an ego. And he clearly thinks he's on some sort of divine mission.'

Paddy crossed himself. I raised my eyebrows. I hadn't known he was religious.

'The last line – *In nomine Patris et Filii et Spiritus Sancti* – tells us something else. The offender's a strict Catholic. Latin is a key part of the Catholic patrimony. A Protestant would never refer to the Trinity like that. He probably goes to Mass every Sunday. Private worship isn't enough for him, not from a spiritual perspective but because the importance of communal prayers will have been drilled into him from an early age. We know he takes his religion seriously. He'll take ritual seriously too.

'But although he attends services this isn't someone who takes part in church socials. He's not comfortable around people. He doesn't mix more than he has to. He says so explicitly here when he calls himself an outsider.' I pointed to the relevant part of the text.

I paused a moment, thinking. The Lacerator was a fervent Catholic. But when I'd first met Marcus Lynch he'd been disdainful of Theresa's religious observance and told me that he was never really into it himself. There was no reason to think he'd been lying. His micro expressions, the tiny facial movements that give away our feelings, were completely in sync with his words. The Lacerator was religious. Marcus wasn't. He may have had the motive and opportunity to commit Aidan's murder, but he wasn't our guy.

I couldn't help feeling disappointed. It would have felt so good to have solved Theresa's mystery along with this one.

'Why do yer think he's called himself, Raguel?' said Paddy giving me a funny look.

'It's pretty obscure so he's obviously chosen it for a reason. Only reference I could find to it is in the Book of Enoch. Raguel is one of the seven archangels.'

'Book of Enoch?'

'It's an ancient Jewish religious work ascribed by tradition to Enoch, the great-grandfather of Noah. Although modern scholars estimate the older sections date from about 300 BC,' I said, regurgitating what I'd found on Wikipedia. I don't have a photographic memory, but it's not far off. 'Apparently it's one of the most important non-canonical apocryphal works.'

Paddy smiled. 'You're dead good. Yer really know your stuff, eh?'

I smiled back.

'Well, I know how to use Google, if that counts. Raguel isn't a regular divine being. He's the archangel of justice and vengeance. Also known as The Fire of God. Might explain why he set Lynch and the latest vic on fire. Could be that it's not just about destroying evidence.'

'I like the way yer think, Ziba Mac.'

He was making a joke, but I bristled all the same.

'Believers say before the messiah comes, Raguel will inhabit a man to take vengeance on sinners. If the Lacerator believes he's really this archangel character, it shows we're on the money with him being schizophrenic or suffering from some other delusional disorder. And now he's in a psychotic break. Most likely he's been taking illegal drugs – meth, maybe coke – and misusing psychiatric medications or simply not taking what he's been prescribed.

'Whatever the underlying cause of his psychosis though, one thing's clear. The fucktard's completely out of touch with reality.'

Paddy made a face. Surely he wasn't offended by my language. The guys at the Yard aren't far behind the military as far as profanity's concerned.

I moved on quickly.

'He may cover it well but someone he knows will have spotted he's delusional. We should canvass local hospitals with mental health facilities. A nurse or doctor might have noticed someone who fits the profile.'

'Grand.' Paddy scribbled in his notebook.

'Mind you, there are going to be plenty of people who fit the description. Religious delusions aren't uncommon with schizophrenics.'

'Still worth a go, eh?'

I nodded. 'Now the handwriting. We should get a graphologist to take a look at it properly but I did a course as part of my special forces training so I can tell you a couple of things. The Lacerator's writing is tiny. The letters are bunched close together. And they're all the same size, indicating he's withdrawn and also meticulous. The handwriting itself is sharp and pointy. That suggests someone who's aggressive and intense. No surprises there. And look at his placement of the dots over his "i"s. They're directly above them. Not off to one side or the other. That suggests he's detail-orientated. But what's really interesting is this: the Lacerator wrote in ink, not biro. That means we can interpret how as well as what he wrote.'

'Brilliant!'

'See here? There are no signs of shaking or that he was pressing down hard on the page. In other words, he felt relaxed when he wrote this. That implies real confidence. This guy thinks he's divinely protected, that he's unstoppable.'

Paddy shook out his writing arm. As usual I'd been talking too fast. I made a conscious effort to say the next bit more slowly.

'You know, we keep saying he's going to slip up and hopefully he will because despite what we'd like the public to think, the truth is most killers are caught because they make a mistake. But the fact is, the Lacerator's killed six times now, twice in the last week. And as far as we know he hasn't slipped up once.'

'You're right there. He hasn't, has he?'

CHAPTER 43

'What do you make of what he calls me?' I said to Paddy.

'How do you mean?'

'The only people who call me Mac are Duncan's mates at the Yard and his best friend, Jack. So how does this crayon eater know my nickname?'

Paddy took his glasses off, rubbed his eyes and stared into space as if waiting for an unseen person to give him the answer.

'We'd better put a detail on yer,' he said after a moment. 'Given what he's written there's no telling what this fella might try and do next.'

'I appreciate the sentiment but it's not necessary. I can handle myself.'

'There's no shame in accepting help, Mac. You've been through a tough time and . . .'

Kid bloody gloves again.

'This isn't about shame, Paddy. Or what happened to Duncan. It's about what I need. And protection isn't it.'

There was a stomping noise coming from outside my front door. The forensics team had finished swabbing the hallway and staircase and now they were gathering evidence up here.

My poor neighbours. One minute they were living in a salubrious block in a sought-after area, the next they were being shut out of a crime scene roped off by DO NOT CROSS tape and teeming with people in white overalls and dentist-style masks carrying clipboards and Ziploc bags.

'I'll get the letter down to the lab. You never know, we might just get fierce lucky and find some trace evidence on it we can match to someone already in the system. Didn't you say he'd maybe been in a mental care institution or prison?'

'Aye. It'd tie in with the profile. Plus, it explains the long cooling-off period between the Lacerator's last murder and the start of his new spree on the seventh. Ha, there it is again,' I said. 'Seven. It does look like he has a thing about it, doesn't it? Seven stab wounds. First kill is in eighty-seven. Kicks off again on the seventh.'

'Aw, sure!' Paddy nodded vigorously, his eyes lit up, all excited.

'It's all a bit obsessive compulsive, which certainly fits with the control evidenced by the most recent attack,' I said. 'And of course schizophrenics often suffer from other personality disorders. OCD is pretty common. Carl Jung calls the obsession with order "a defence against internal chaos".

'Our initial profile suggested he was naturally unkempt, which you'd expect from someone with a mental illness. But given this level of compulsiveness I think it's more likely he's neatly dressed. Obsessively so. And his home will be orderly – everything in its place. He may even be able to hold down a job. In fact, he may be more high-functioning than I previously thought.'

I rubbed my eyes, fanning my fingers outwards towards my ears. Thinking.

'When an active offender suddenly stops killing it's usually for one of three reasons. He's committed suicide. He's been banged up for another crime. Or he's left the area and is operating somewhere else. But there is another reason. If he knows the police are on to him, if he's intelligent enough to stop before sufficient evidence has been gathered, then he might decide to retire. Could be we're looking at that here.'

'I just wish we knew what was so special about seven, eh?' said Paddy, changing the subject back to the Lacerator's fixation.

'Could be that something happened to him when he was seven years old.' I massaged my occipital bone. 'A trauma that a recent pre-kill stressor brought back to him. Or maybe it's linked to a date rather than an age. Maybe the seventh of a certain month has a special significance for him. Or what if seven has something to do with this whole religious thing? It's supposed to be a holy number, isn't it – God resting on the seventh day and all that?'

I caught my breath. As usual I'd been talking a mile a minute.

'I reckon you're bang on there,' said Paddy, looking into the middle distance again.

'It's not just the crimes that have links with the number seven. It's the note too,' I said, the words tripping over each other in their haste to make it out of my mouth. 'There are seven paragraphs, even though it doesn't quite make sense to break them where he has. And— No, that's stupid . . .' I stopped mid-sentence.

'What's stupid?'

'I'm probably over-reaching here but maybe it's why he calls me Ziba Mac.'

'Go on.'

'Count the number of letters in the name.'

'Seven! Shit the bed, Mac, you're good! I need to get all this in front of the team. Is there anything else you can tell me before I head on?'

'Wouldn't you rather I just came back to the Yard and spoke to everyone directly myself?'

That would be normal procedure.

'Don't be troubling yourself.' He shook his head emphatically. 'I can do it. And it's better if you hang back in case any of the forensic lads need to ask you any questions.'

'If you're sure . . .'

'I am, yeah. You stay here.'

'Alright then,' I said, happy to have the excuse not to go out again. I had an internet connection and plenty of coffee in the fridge. There was no reason I couldn't make progress on my own right here. And of course there was the added bonus I wouldn't have to see Nigel Fingerling for the rest of the day.

'Right then, I'll be seeing you.' Paddy got up.

On the way to the door he stopped, scrunched his eyes and shook his head in a brisk juddery motion.

'You alright?'

'I'm fine,' he said quickly. 'Just getting a migraine.'

'D'you want an aspirin?'

He stared at a spot on the wall for a second before answering, his head tilted slightly. 'Don't bother yourself. I'll be grand. I'm probably just getting the dose that's going round.'

There were dark circles under his eyes but his colour was good, his pupils weren't dilated and he was talking at a normal volume.

Something's definitely up with up him, I thought. Though I wasn't convinced by what he'd said. He certainly didn't look like he had a bug. Or a headache either.

CHAPTER 44

A chill flows into Raguel's arteries. His heart begins to pound. He squeezes his eyes shut and presses them with his fingers so hard he can see sharp specks of light inside his lids.

It's happening more often now. The flashbacks are creeping up on him at the slightest provocation. Sometimes with no provocation at all.

CHAPTER 45

After Paddy had left, I sat down at my desk and reread the Lacerator's letter on my laptop.

A shadow swept across the room as the sun slipped behind a cloud. On the road below there were sounds of an altercation: hooting, angry voices, the screech of tyres.

I massaged my sinuses and exhaled slowly through my nose. It was the opening line that was bothering me, not that I'd mentioned it to Paddy. I didn't want him giving me any more shit about needing a protective detail. And yet . . .

I was with you this morning as you bent over my offering.

Had the Lacerator written it to spook me or was it true? Could he have been at the crime scene?

A calculated lie didn't fit the profile. Nor did it fit with the theme of the letter, which was about establishing a bond between us and helping me get to know him better. How was messing with my noggin going to achieve that?

He must have been at the scene this morning, then. There were nine of us on site: me, Fingerling, the crime scene manager, five CSIs and the copper standing guard. No way the Lacerator could have snuck in unnoticed. So how had he seen me examining the body?

I closed my eyes, remembering the layout of the alley. In the SF we were trained to observe and recall the most seemingly insignificant details. All this time later and I still can't drive past a car without noting its make, model and registration plate.

There was a high wall on one side and some low-level buildings on the other – the back of three restaurants. There were two windows. One was directly in front of where the corpse was positioned, though it was three metres up from the ground.

If anyone had been observing us through it, we would have seen them. The other window was much further along to the left. It was a small rectangular window with frosted glass. And it was shut. No way someone could have been spying on us.

As I absorbed the implications, my whole body tightened like I was being zipped up in a cadaver pouch two sizes too small for me. If the Lacerator hadn't been lying about being at the crime scene that meant he had to be one of us; a CSI, the PC – or Nigel Fingerling.

I got up from my desk and started pacing the room, going through the options.

The forensics team and the police officer were from the night shift, so they'd have been on duty at the time of the murder. So their movements would have been tracked the whole time. That ruled them out.

But what about Nigel Fingerling? He hadn't come off the night shift. His movements weren't tracked. I twisted my hair up off my neck and let it fall. A Scotland Yard DI moonlighting as a serial killer? No, it was ridiculous.

The way I saw it the guy was most definitely a waste of a good swimmer but that didn't mean he was a murderer. If he had a secret like that, surely he'd have tried to hide it by being a tad more civil rather than bawling me out whenever he got the chance.

Admittedly the profile told me the Lacerator was telling the truth, but perhaps he was just trying to psych me out. Plenty of other serial killers have tried to do the same thing.

But was I just trying to convince myself? After all, it wasn't the only hint that we knew each other. What about what he'd written,

Each time I look into your eyes I see your pain? For that to be true, we had to have met.

He'd said I was 'an outsider', 'tortured' by my past and 'wary of everyone' – and he was right on all three counts. That level of insight can normally only come through personal contact, and of all the people at the crime scene, the only person I'd had that sort of involvement with was Nigel Fingerling.

Don't be a nugget, I thought. I'm a profiler. I'd know if one of my colleagues was a murderer. There's got to be another explanation.

I marched up and down the room punching my palm. Then I stopped. That's it! I thought, slapping my forehead. It's about transference. And a bit of internet research. Talk about paranoia. Of course the Lacerator's not bloody Fingerling!

The offender claimed to be an outsider. He'd said I was also an outsider because it suited him for us to have similar personalities so it would cement the bond he thought we had. The fact he'd been so right in his analysis of me meant nothing more than he was capable of using a mouse and keyboard.

DCI Falcon had introduced me to the media at the first press conference. If you enter my name into any search engine one of the first things that comes up is Duncan's murder.

The Lacerator didn't need to know I can't be alone in a room without music, the World Service or Al Jazeera on in the background. Or that I read different papers from different political standpoints because I don't trust what people are telling me. Or even that I drink as much as I do because it's the only way to chase away the demons that haunt me.

All he needed to know was that I'd lost my husband in tragic circumstances. He could build the rest of his little profile from that.

I was sure now the Lacerator wasn't someone who knew me. But thanks to what he'd written, I understood him better than before.

And with any luck that would help us catch the swamp donkey before he killed anyone else.

CHAPTER 46

The dark memory has passed now he's out of the building. A quiver runs the entire length of Raguel's body. A butterfly trapped beneath his skin. Wings fluttering. Hundreds of tiny pulsations.

A brimstone perhaps. Yes, that would be apposite. A creature with veiny green wings that looks just like the leaves it roosts in; an insect hiding in plain sight. Raguel knows all about that.

CHAPTER 47

I thought over the revised profile I'd given Paddy before he left. It was based on an amalgamation of what I'd worked out before and what I knew now.

> The Lacerator is a white Catholic male in his mid to late forties. He's a regular churchgoer. He keeps himself to himself and he knows his Bible inside out.
>
> He has a history of mental illness and may have suffered a recent trauma around the time of his first attack. That trauma unbalanced him and triggered a relapse.
>
> As a person he is withdrawn and intense. He is uncomfortable around people and he is obsessive. However, he functions well in his daily life. He knows how to do what is expected of him. He's neatly dressed, though not necessarily expensively so.
>
> After the murders he will have exhibited signs of physical exhaustion and strain. He will have dark circles under his eyes, bad skin and an increased appetite. He will have experienced sugar cravings, irritability and a loss of focus.

Paddy had promised to get the profile out to the media stat because our best chance of capture was still for it to resonate with someone. And if I could pinpoint the area where the killer lived we'd have a better chance of that happening. The geo-profile was therefore my top priority.

I looked at the locations of the eighties crime scenes. With the exception of the first homicide, all the attacks were based around Soho and the victims were all men in their sixties. According to witnesses at the time they'd initially been drinking alone. So, hoping to meet someone rather than out with friends.

The Lacerator had preyed on these men. At some point he'd approached them, lured them away and then brutally murdered them.

Given the derogatory way he'd referred to his latest victim as an 'earring-wearer', he was clearly a homophobe. But contrary to what I'd said earlier, I was beginning to think he might be gay himself. If so his sexuality was in conflict with his strict religious upbringing and values. That could have caused a tension which made him lash out at other men who were at ease with their sexual orientation.

It's happened before. The serial killer Dennis Nilsen targeted gay men to alleviate his own guilt about being homosexual. His murders were warped acts of contrition. Could the Lacerator be doing the same thing?

I stared at the pins on my map as if the answer were hidden in the pattern they made, a bit like Paddy's Magic Eye puzzles.

Might there be another reason the Lacerator was targeting homosexuals? Could it have been because they were easy targets? When the Green River Killer was arrested he said he chose prostitutes as victims because they were easy to pick up without attracting attention.

Picking someone up in a crowded bar late at night wouldn't attract attention either. Nor would it be difficult if you were a nice-looking guy targeting older men.

Or could it be what we'd said at the press conference – that the Lacerator was on a crusade? Was he attacking gays because he thought homosexuality was an 'abomination', as the Good Book so liberally puts it?

The language in his letter was vehement when it came to describing his victims. Was their homosexuality the 'crime' the Lacerator thought he had to punish them for?

It certainly fits with his fervent Catholicism, I thought. And the Bible's full of condemnation of boy-on-boy action. Never mind what should be done to those who practise it.

The Lacerator believed he was God's 'minister', an archangel of justice and vengeance. Did he also believe it was his duty to mete out the biblical punishment of homosexuals?

Aside from that, another thing was clear given the locations of the eighties murders.

Soho is well-known for its gay bars. With the exception of Aidan Lynch who was killed in his own home, the eighties victims were found in garden squares close to the drinkers where they were last seen.

So, the Lacerator hunted and killed in Soho. But since it's not a residential area, it's unlikely he lived there. Which meant he had to travel home after each slaying. How he did that might provide a clue as to where home was.

I knew from my recce that parking in Soho is next to impossible. So it's unlikely he took a car, which fitted with the disorganised offender profile. These guys tend not to drive to crime scenes. They walk or use public transport.

But buses and trains are well lit at night. In knife homicides it's impossible for the offender to avoid getting blood on himself. If the Lacerator took public transport he'd have risked other passengers noticing him.

So he must have walked to and from each of the crime scenes. And to be able to do that he couldn't live too far away from them. His attacks would have left him physically drained. There's no way even a fit man in his twenties could have walked more than two miles afterwards.

I grabbed a compass and ruler from my desk drawer. Then I went over to the map on the wall. I checked the scale and measured out a two-mile radius around the early crime scenes with Soho Square at its centre. The areas on the outer perimeter of the circle were Vauxhall, Clerkenwell, Paddington and Camden Town.

Of course!

The average serial killer starts killing in their twenties, which also happens to be the time schizophrenia usually starts to develop. The Lacerator's first murder was twenty-five years ago. If the pattern held, it put him in his mid to late forties now, as I'd calculated when I put together the initial profile.

It was one thing for a man in his twenties to be able to walk two miles after a strenuous attack. It was another thing altogether for a man in his forties to do so.

When I'd first realised the Lacerator was obsessed with me I'd wondered whether the location of his latest murder was more than just a coincidence. Had there been a more sinister reason for him killing the latest victim just behind the restaurant I'd been eating in that night? Did his choice of location have something to do with me?

Maybe it had. Maybe he had chosen the alleyway as a way of establishing a connection between us. But maybe it was something else as well. Especially considering his first victim was killed in Camden.

Was it possible that's where the offender lived? Could he have killed on his home turf because it was easier to scoot away afterwards?

There was a knock at the door. One of the CSIs.

'We're off.'

Ten minutes later my mobile buzzed in my pocket.

I pulled it out. It was an SMS sent from a website, so completely untraceable. And it was signed 'Raguel'. The name the Lacerator had given himself.

CHAPTER 48

The boy is clinging to his father's shirt, crying and begging not to be left.

'This is ridiculous,' his father says, hauling him up to the front porch. 'What's wrong with you? Come on.'

'Please, Daddy,' says the boy. His face is red and there's snot dripping into his mouth. 'I don't want to go.'

'I've got to get to work. I don't have time for this.'

The boy monkeys up his father's leg, gripping as tight as he can.

'Get off me. You'll make Mum and Granny miss their train. Stop it.'

The boy's red baseball cap falls off and lands in the dirt.

'Maybe we should just take him with us,' the boy's mother says, picking it up and dusting it off before popping it back on his head. 'He'll be a bit bored but I suppose it's not the end of the world if he comes.'

'No,' says his father, wrestling him off. 'This child needs to learn to do what he's told. You mollycoddle him too much.

'Now go in,' he says, shoving the boy through the door where Grandad is waiting for him.

CHAPTER 49

Check your mailbox. Raguel.

For a moment I just stared open-mouthed at the message on my phone.

How had a man in a psychotic break managed to get hold of my personal mobile number?

I'm obsessive when it comes to privacy. I don't have a Facebook account or even a LinkedIn profile. I use a secondary email address for online forms. I'm careful who I give my details to. And my home phone is unlisted. So unless the Lacerator was a super-hack, I couldn't figure out how he'd done it.

I put on a fresh pair of latex gloves and went downstairs to my mailbox. Inside was a pizza delivery leaflet, a flyer for some cleaning service and a large manila envelope with my name written on the front in black ink. The penmanship was identical to the other letter. My hands trembled as I pulled it out.

What the piss, Ziba, I thought. Get a grip. You're not on your own in the desert or hanging out with Al-Qaeda bosses pretending to be someone you're not. This is London. You're on home soil and Scotland Yard has your back.

Still shaking despite everything I kept telling myself, I took the stairs up to my flat two at a time. I slammed my front door shut behind me and covered my dining table with cling film to avoid contamination. Then I photographed the envelope before opening it and removing the contents.

A folded piece of printer paper and two smaller envelopes. One of the envelopes had a large number one written on it. The other had my initials in the top right-hand corner.

I read what was written on the printer paper first.

Dear Ziba Mac,

You said you wanted to help me. You said I must reveal myself to you so you can protect me.

Very well, I will do as you asked. But first you must prove yourself deserving of my trust.

I have set up a little game. A treasure hunt. If you can solve the clues you will know me by the end of it. You will have proved your worthiness.

You will also know where I shall strike next. Today I shall destroy Satan at last. Demon Number Seven. Blood for blood. Will you get there first? Will you be able to stop me carrying my most important kill of all?

If you do, I will know carrying out His vengeance is no longer the Lord's will and I will strike no more. However, if you do not prevent it I will know for certain He desires for me to continue with my holy work and that He has sent you to protect me in order that I may serve him better.

DO NOT INVOLVE ANYONE ELSE. THIS CHALLENGE IS FOR YOU ALONE.

As much as it will pain me to do so I will have to punish you if you are unfaithful to me, if you break this holy covenant.

I will be watching you. If I see you working with anyone else, if I even suspect you have told anyone about our arrangement, I shall bring my wrath to the streets. No one will be spared. My judgement will be executed by fire and sword on all flesh. And those slain by me will be many – starting with you.

The contents of the envelope marked with your initials should convince you I can do what I say.

In nomine Patris et Filii et Spiritus Sancti,
I remain yours truly,
Raguel.

I opened the envelope, touched my hand to my hair and screamed.

CHAPTER 50

The boy bounces in his seat as the bus lurches along the road. His school bag's on the floor resting between his feet. The T-Rex sticker is starting to peel off and the brontosaurus is torn. Maybe his mother will get him another sheet from the corner shop if he asks nicely.

He's looking out of the window, watching for his stop. His finger rests on the button, ready to press it.

'Keep your eyes peeled,' his mother said this morning, wiping a smear of peanut butter off his chin with the edge of her thumb. 'Remember where to get off. Are you sure you want to take the bus by yourself? I know Daddy thinks it'll be good for you but—'

'I'll be fine,' he'd said in an impatient voice, hunting for his red baseball cap. It was under the sofa. He put in on backwards the way the cool kids wore theirs.

'Well, if you're sure.' She'd kissed the top of his head and said something about how she couldn't believe what a big boy he was getting to be.

The bus approaches his stop. He presses the button. A little bell rings and the sign at the front lights up. It's only when the bus has driven away that the boy realises he's left his schoolbag under the seat. No new dinosaur stickers for him now.

There's a sharp chill, the sky is already darkening. The nights are drawing in – that's what his father always says at this time of year. He also says things like, 'It's nice weather for ducks,' and 'There's a nasty nip in the air.'

The boy imagines the nasty nip pinching his cheeks and pushes his hands deeper into his anorak pockets.

The streets are quiet. Everyone must be inside watching telly and eating their tea, the boy thinks. He walks faster.

He rounds the corner. Nearly there. His too-tight new school shoes make a slam-thunk sound as he trots along the pavement avoiding the crocodiles hiding in the cracks.

'Well, hello there, kiddo,' says Grandad, suddenly in front of him, barring his way. 'Fancy running into you!'

CHAPTER 51

'How the hell did he manage to cut my hair without me noticing?'

My body was trembling. My breathing was ragged. I felt both hot and cold at once.

I'd convinced myself the Lacerator had been bluffing when he said he'd been watching me at the crime scene and looked deep into my eyes. But I'd been wrong. He must be someone I knew. It's the only way he could have done what he had.

I touched my hand to my hair again. How had I not realised a chunk was missing from the back? How had no one else spotted it?

When had he cut it? Had he broken into my flat last night? No, impossible. He'd have triggered the alarm and anyway, there were no signs of forced entry.

So when?

I gnawed a hangnail and thought.

I'd washed and blow-dried my hair after coming back from the crime scene that morning. I always blow-dry it section by section, teasing the hair straight with a paddle brush. If one bit had been shorter than another I would have noticed.

I took my thumb out of my mouth and inhaled deeply, calmer now I was rationalising things.

If my hair hadn't been cut then that meant the Lacerator must have cut it sometime between me leaving the flat after I'd washed it and now. But how would he have been able to? When would he have had the chance?

I felt a prick of adrenaline. My stomach contracted.

The press conference!

It had been packed in there. We'd all been jammed in nut to butt, as some of the special forces guys used to say. Or like tatties in a pan, to use one of Duncan's expressions.

It's just possible that someone standing close enough could have cut my hair without me noticing if they were quick enough.

Up until now I'd worked on the basis that the Lacerator wasn't a professional. It was part of the disorganised offender profile that he wouldn't be. But if I was right about him being at the press conference, then I had to be wrong about that.

The only people in the media room were cops and press. You could only get in if you'd been invited. Everyone was accounted for. So if the Lacerator really had been at Scotland Yard with his scissors that afternoon it could only mean one thing. He was either a police officer. Or a journalist. And given who I'd been standing next to, close enough to see the fine smattering of acne on his skin, the most likely person was Nigel Fingerling.

Maybe I hadn't been so stupid to suspect him after all.

CHAPTER 52

Incredible though it seemed that Nigel Fingerling might be the Lacerator, now I'd started wondering about it, other things started to fall into place. His exhaustion and sugar cravings at the crime scene this morning. My suspicion he might be a drug addict. The mental instability Jack had alluded to. It all fitted with the profile.

And what about his recent break-up? That's just the sort of thing that can be a pre-kill stressor.

Not to mention the flash of anger when I'd turned him down for a drink. It would make sense if he were obsessed with me, as the Lacerator clearly was.

The guy even writes with a fountain pen, I thought. Black ink, judging by the stain on his shirt pocket.

People think schizophrenics can't hold down jobs, and it's true that symptoms can make working difficult. But when a sufferer is in remission they can often manage well and in fact there are examples of high-functioning schizophrenics with impressive résumés.

I read an interview a while back with a law professor at San Diego State University who suffered from schizophrenia but still managed to get a 'Genius Grant' from the MacArthur Foundation. She said that although she had psychotic thoughts several times a day and regular full-blown episodes, she'd always been able to work.

Although high-functioning schizophrenics are rare, it was possible that the Lacerator belonged in this category. And if he was Fingerling, it would explain how he'd got hold of my private number, cut my hair and was possibly keeping me under surveillance.

Though how do the disorganised elements of the most recent homicide fit? I wondered. What wasn't I seeing? What pieces wasn't I connecting?

One of the first things we were taught in the special forces was to assume nothing. As one of our instructors used to say: 'Assumption is the mother of all screw-ups.'

Unbelievable though it was that a Scotland Yard detective might actually be a serial killer, I couldn't afford to assume Fingerling wasn't somehow involved in all this. And I couldn't go wrong by playing it safe. In my experience, trust gets you killed faster than an MK-77. People invariably let you down.

But that didn't mean I should go marching into HQ shouting my mouth off. The evidence I had was circumstantial, even if it did seem to stack up. I had to be 100 per cent certain before I said anything to DCI Falcon. If I accused Fingerling and turned out to be wrong, I'd never set foot inside the Yard again.

However, lack of certainty was no reason to carry on as before. Until I'd ruled him out, I couldn't involve the murder investigation team in what I was doing. It may have been made up of many of Duncan's old friends and colleagues but right now I couldn't trust anyone on it. Not least because they would feed information back to Fingerling – the senior investigating officer on the case.

I walked up and down the room smacking my fist into my palm, questioning myself. Was I going mad? Was I looking at this all wrong? I couldn't remember when I'd last slept eight hours straight. I was tired, running on empty. Maybe I was making more of this than I should. I needed a reality check.

I pulled my mobile out of my pocket and hit the name near the top of the call logs. There was a beep, then: 'This is Jack Wolfe. Please leave a message.'

I didn't record anything. In fact I shouldn't have phoned him at all.

Jack knows everything in this world there is to know about me. He knows I can't sleep without the radio on and that I've painted my flat yellow as a shield against my inner darkness. He knows I'm down in the pit if all I'm eating is Marmite toast and that I'm at my happiest when I'm working so hard I can't see straight.

It's not that I've bared my soul so much as the fact he's always been able to see through my shit. It's partly the journo in him, of course, but more that; we're on the same wavelength.

'I sometimes think Wolfie gets you better than I do,' Duncan used to say, and although I'd tell him not to be daft, he may have been right.

I've never kept a secret from Jack but I had to keep this one. I couldn't trust anyone now, not even him. It wasn't because I thought he'd betray me. It was just that right now it seemed the smartest thing for me to do was to follow the Lacerator's rules and not involve anyone else.

Failing to do what he said wouldn't just put me in danger; it could put the lives of scores of innocent people at risk too. He'd made that quite clear. I was on my own now.

And he'd be watching to make sure it stayed that way.

CHAPTER 53

But how's he keeping tabs on me? I thought.

On instinct I looked out of the window, standing to the side of it so I couldn't be seen from the road. There was no one out there apart from a couple of workmen filling in a pothole and a woman with her hair scraped back in a bun pushing a Bugaboo along the pavement.

But there was a silver car parked halfway up the street. It looked like a Honda. Was the Lacerator inside? Is that who'd been following us the other night?

I leaned forward slightly to get a better look. An old lady carrying a Morrisons bag hobbled up to it, fumbling with her keys before unlocking it and squeezing herself in. As she pulled away I saw it wasn't a Honda at all but a Hyundai. Similar logos, easily confused from a distance and at this angle.

So if he wasn't observing me from the road, how was he managing to monitor my movements?

I shut all the curtains, turned on the lights and stood in the middle of my living room, hands on hips, legs spread wide. I scanned the room, cataloguing each item.

Cloisonné lamp, phone and an old Solzhenitsyn paperback on the end table by the sofa. Three cushions on the sofa itself, one dented from where I'd been lying the night before, the others in the exact position they'd been in this morning.

A4 pad, Parker rollerball, and the Lacerator's latest communiqué on the dining table. Tannin-stained glass, empty wine bottle on the coffee table. On my desk, a mosaic ashtray that used to belong to my father. Papers weighed down with the flint Duncan found on Chesil Beach the summer we went down to Dorset. An empty Ristretto cup. Maps. Charts. Notes.

Everything was where I'd left it. But what about the bookshelves?

Nothing looked like it had been moved but with that many publications I couldn't be sure. A camera disguised to look like a book could have been easily added. It's the sort of thing I've done before, I thought, remembering a particular operation in Afghanistan.

I carried a stool through from the kitchen then took each volume down one by one, flicking through the pages, feeling the spines. *Behavioral Evidence Analysis. Crime Classification Manual.* Joe Navarro's brilliant book, *What Every Body is Saying. Mindhunter. A Study in the Psychology of Violence.*

I went through the ring binders I'd collected during the ten-week specialist training programme I'd been invited to attended at the FBI National Academy at Quantico, Virginia, a few years ago. Reams of paper, no hidden cameras.

I checked old favourites: *The Conference of the Birds. The Alchemy of Happiness.* A collection by Rumi, a book of essays by Reza Baraheni, short stories by Shahriar Mandanipour.

Nothing. Nothing. Nothing.

I exhaled deeply and ran my hands through my hair. What next? A bug on my phone?

I picked up the receiver and listened. Just a dial tone. If the phone had been tapped I'd hear static, popping or hissing when I made a call and the connectors linked up.

I needed to call someone who wouldn't want to chat. That way I could listen for the telltale sounds more easily. I looked up the number and called my mother.

'Emmeline. It's Ziba.'

'Oh hello, dear. Is it a quickie? I'm just in the middle of something.'
Surprise, surprise.

'Not to worry. I was just touching base.'

'Oh, okay.' She sounded confused. 'Is everything alright?'

'All fine.' I paused, giving myself time to listen. Nothing. 'I'll catch you some other time.'

'Alright then,' she said, sounding relieved.

I hung up. The receiver was clear but that didn't mean there wasn't a device hidden somewhere else in the room.

I went to the kitchen, took the portable radio off the windowsill and tuned it into a quiet spot at the high end of the FM band. Then I walked slowly round the flat. Up and down the length of each room until every inch had been covered. There were no funny noises or high-pitched squeals. Check two.

Where is it? I thought rummaging about in the bottom of my coat cupboard.

It was like a what-the-fuck grenade had gone off in there.

I finally found my black Maglite stuffed inside an old ankle boot.

I turned off all the lights and shone the torch on the mirrors. A full-length, hand-carved one in the bedroom and a Persian one with enamelled Sanskrit accents in the hall. Both were bug-free.

I checked every switch plate and wall socket. I checked the smoke detectors, light fittings and lamps.

I looked for paint discoloration on my ceilings and walls. I ran my torch along the furniture – on top and underneath. I looked for patches of dust and tried all the door locks.

There was nothing. The Lacerator had been in my building, he'd managed to get hold of my mobile number, but he hadn't broken into my flat. My home hadn't been bugged. There were no hidden cameras.

I stood in the middle of the living room with my arms folded across my chest, teasing my lower lip through my teeth.

A photo of Duncan and me cutting our wedding cake was on the table against the far wall. My eyes were drawn to it, to the smiles on our faces and the way he was looking down at me as we cut through the sponge – vanilla because fruit cake gave him indigestion. My father had been just the same.

Suddenly that time, our time together, seemed like a lifetime ago. Unreal. The remembered snatches of a dream.

The only thing that seemed real to me now was the Lacerator's letters. I don't like being given orders, especially by a psychotic killer, but right now I had no choice other than to follow his rules.

CHAPTER 54

Raguel walks through the main doors and signs in. He'll sit down with the support team, agree the new plan and then . . .

CHAPTER 55

My heart was a pop gun in my chest. I'm used to keeping eyes on a tango. I'm not used to being the target.

I couldn't be sure Fingerling was the Lacerator but I did know the offender had to have been in the media briefing room that afternoon. Therefore, the safest thing for me to do was to go off the grid before trying to decipher the Lacerator's first clue. Despite what I'd said to Paddy about being able to handle myself, I wasn't planning on taking any unnecessary risks – not when my life wasn't the only one on the line.

Although I hadn't found any evidence of bugs in my flat, there might be undetectable monitoring software installed on my phones or laptop. I'd done a full sweep of my flat but the lopped-off hair showed I'd overlooked something. Somehow the Lacerator was watching me and he'd been quite clear about what he'd do if he thought I was breaking his rules.

I removed the SIM and battery from my phone – the only sure-fire way of covering my tracks. Simply powering it down wouldn't be enough. Depending how cyber-savvy the Lacerator was, he could still get a read on my location. And if he'd deployed spyware, he'd be able to record data from my phone even if it was off.

I'm no stranger to that type of activity, I thought, remembering a particular body snatch in the desert. But I never thought I'd be on the receiving end. Especially not on Civvy Street.

I picked up the envelope with the number one written on the front, adrenaline firing off rounds through my body. The last envelope had contained my hair. What was I going to find in this one?

I fetched a letter opener from my desk; a small gold knife with an enamelled mosaic handle. A relic from the old country – another thing my mother tried to throw away after my father died.

I slid the blade under the opening and ran it along the edge. I felt a moment of relief when I saw there was nothing else belonging to me inside. Instead there was just a sheet of paper. The first clue in the Lacerator's treasure hunt. However, the relief didn't last long. What did it mean?

At the top of the page there was an ink sketch of a giraffe wearing a T-shirt and Mickey Mouse gloves. Below it was a riddle.

20/15/25/19 18 21/19
La la la la la la, la la la la la la . . .

You're a girl and I'm a boy,
A real gent – you choose the toy.

It started off fun but ended so bad,
My fault of course, I was had.

Hurry now, you have till seven,
What's it to be, Hell or Heaven?

RAGUEL
18, 1 . . .

I scraped my fingernails over my scalp.

The letter showed I'd been right about what I'd said at the press conference. The Lacerator was plagued with guilt. He'd said this challenge wasn't just about helping me understand him. It was also a test. If I stopped him killing his intended next victim, he'd know God didn't want him to murder any more.

Which meant he was beginning to doubt himself.

In other circumstances I could have used this information to draw him out. I could have used his ambivalence to encourage him to turn himself in. But he was setting the agenda now. All I could do was play his game and hope I'd manage to save his would-be next victim along the way.

I normally like puzzles. I can solve the Rubik's Cube in under sixty seconds and whizz through *The Times* cryptic crossword in four minutes. But this puzzle had a deadline. 19.00. Seven o'clock. Less than two and a half hours away.

Time was ticking. A man's life was in the balance. But I had no idea who he was or how to save him.

CHAPTER 56

'I thought we'd go and look at the canal boats,' Grandad says, taking the boy's hand.

'Okay,' he says in a quiet voice, looking at his feet.

If he says no, he'll get a smack bottom later from his dad for being rude. His father's big on discipline. There are times the boy thinks he can't do anything right. His mum's different though. She never even shouts.

Grandad kisses the top of the boy's head, breathing him in.

'My little Goldilocks,' he says.

The boy wrinkles his nose; the smell of Camels makes his stomach knot.

As they walk, he thinks about the story his teacher read them before home time. The puppet whose nose gets longer every time he tells a lie.

Grandad doesn't like liars. He says that's what boys who can't keep secrets grow up to be: thieves and liars.

Mrs Atkin is on the opposite side of the road talking to the butcher. Patrick, from school, is kicking a pebble about on the pavement. Neither notices the boy.

'I got you a present,' says Grandad.

The boy's throat closes up. He knows what the present will be and he knows what he'll have to do to earn it. It's the first part of the ritual.

He takes the Mars bar and gobbles it quickly. The sooner it's gone, the sooner this will be over, he tells himself.

They're at Camden Lock now. The boy normally likes the market. The smell of spices and pizza. The bright colours and funny clothes. The people with their piercings in weird places and the sound his feet make on the cobblestones.

But they're not stopping here. Grandad winds his way through the throng and pulls the boy's anorak hood up over his head, even though it's not raining. He leads him over the bridge and down the stone steps towards the canal.

The towpath is quiet. A few barges painted in reds and yellows bob about on the oily water. Narrowboats, that's the proper name for them. His teacher said they used to get pulled along by horses but now only people live on them, the horses have long gone.

The boy saw a boat with a vegetable garden on the roof once. And another time he saw a fat man sunbathing on the little deck at the front, his vest riding up over his big tummy.

But the man's not here today. No one is.

CHAPTER 57

Nothing focuses the mind like a deadline. This was one in the literal sense. Dead. Line. Once I'd crossed it, another person would lose their life. Not solving the clue wasn't an option. Trouble is, I was drawing a blank.

La la la la la la, la la la la la la . . .

The opening's got to be from a song, I thought. All those la-las.

But what song was it and where did the numbers fit in? Were they dates? Or times? And what did that creepy-looking giraffe have to do with anything?

I tried singing it, pleased no one was around to hear my not-so dulcet tones.

The beat was oddly familiar but I couldn't place it. If only I could call the MIT for help, I thought. But as my mother so sweetly pointed out after my father died, there's no point wishing for something you can't have.

Solving the riddle was down to me. I was on my own.

Normally that's the way I work best but right now I was shooting at shadows. The more I tried to pin down the rhythm, the more elusive it became.

I paced the Persian runner in my living room; fists tight, jaw clenched.

Damn it, Ziba, think.

You're a girl and I'm a boy,
A real gent – you choose the toy.

It started off fun but ended so bad,
My fault of course, I was had.

Hurry now, you have till seven,
What's it to be, Hell or Heaven?

RAGUEL
18, 1 . . .

The riddle was divided into four parts.

The first stanza has something to do with kids, I thought, sucking the tip of my thumb. Girl, boy, toy . . . Could the giraffe be a childhood reference too? I ran a search on my laptop. Nothing came up apart from a family restaurant, but the logo wasn't anything like the picture the Lacerator had drawn. Maybe a theme park? Wannabe Disney venues often get creative with their mascots.

I typed 'UK Theme Park Mascots' into Google and hit the image tab. Photos of all sorts of weird and wonderful inventions popped up. Dancing octopuses. Pink elephants dressed like ballerinas. Crocodiles wearing Australian cork hats.

But no giraffes.

So if not a theme park or eatery, then what? It took me three more go-overs before I realised the answer was right in front of me: *You choose the toy.*

Can it really be that simple? I thought. A toy shop? Then a second later I realised it wasn't simple at all. There must be hundreds of toy shops in London. The next clue could be anywhere.

He's got to have given me more to go on than that, I thought, slumping down on the sofa. This only works if I've got a fighting chance.

Ouch, what's that?

There was something wedged between the seat cushions digging into my thigh. I shifted my weight and pulled it out. Paddy's pen.

I just wish I knew what was so special about seven, he'd said as we chewed over what the Lacerator had written in his first letter. *Count the number of letters*, I'd said when I worked out why he called me Ziba Mac.

I jumped up, reinvigorated. Was that the answer? The killer's obsession with numbers?

I looked again at the row at the top of the riddle: *20/15/25/19 18 21/19*

What if they weren't dates or times? What if it was a code? But if so, what code would he be using?

I raked my hands through my hair again. It could be anything.

The clock was ticking. The Lacerator wouldn't want me to fall at the first jump, I thought. That wouldn't prove anything about the so-called sanctity of his mission. Which meant I didn't have to be Alan Turing to crack this.

So he's got to be using something fairly basic, I thought, grabbing a ballpoint and flip-pad from my desk. But what?

It took me a few more minutes of head scratching before I got it. The clue was in the clue. A keycode.

RAGUEL

18, 1 . . .

Ha! He's using a substitution cipher, I thought with a grin.

A simple encryption where each letter is represented by its position in the alphabet. R is the eighteenth letter. A is the first. *RAGUEL 18, 1*. That had to be it.

I uncapped the pen with my teeth and applied it to the row at the top of the page.

20	15	25	19	18	21	19
T	*O*	*Y*	*S*	*R*	*U*	*S*

Suddenly it all made sense. The giraffe was the store mascot. I'd seen it on TV when I was a kid. And the la-las were the beat of the song that went with the ad. For the life of me I couldn't remember the lyrics, but that didn't stop the damn tune zipping round my head now I'd identified it.

I raced to my laptop to look up the address, heart thumping with excitement. Google quashed my euphoria pretty quickly though. By the looks of it, there were three Toys 'R' Us shops in London. One in Bayswater, one on the Old Kent Road and one out by Brent Cross. All miles apart.

Which one was the next clue hidden in? And how was I going to find out?

It was coming up to five. The traffic would be starting to build up, the rush hour already in full swing. Without the blues and twos on, I could easily spend the next three hours crawling from one store to another.

There has to be a way to break this down, I thought, going over to the map tacked up on my living-room wall.

The Brent Cross store was the closest to Camden, which is where I thought the Lacerator lived. That's where I'd start.

Again I wished I could put in a call to the team for help, but given my suspicions about Fingerling that could be suicide.

My only option was to drive over to Toys 'R' Us with my foot down all the way.

CHAPTER 58

Raguel's heart has expanded to fill his whole chest. Every moment in his life has led to this. The hot, sticky heat of the blood. The look in the fiend's eyes as the life leaves them.

And now the fantasy's about to be made real! A tremor of excitement ripples through him.

It's been so long since he slept well his body has given up trying. But tonight will be different. Tonight he'll sleep. Even the voices won't stop him.

He peels a new blue cotton shirt out of the packet and another wave of excitement engulfs him.

The shadowy figure in the corner dances a jig.

Raguel's navy chinos are hanging in the cupboard freshly washed and ironed. Each leg has been steam-pressed seven times. The trousers have been taken on and off the hanger seven times. And now he puts them on and removes them seven times too. 777. Everything must be perfect today and seven is the key.

He undresses in front of the mirror, admiring the ripples in his chest as he takes off his clothes. The muscles are hard-earned. They come from hours of weightlifting in front of the mirror every evening. The red flush and the glow of sweat that glistens on his skin as he works out spur him on. So does the thing he's working out for.

'I give you the sword of the Spirit,' whisper the voices. 'Ssssspirit.'

Raguel's body quivers with anticipation. He is a taut bow; a cat in the long grass, tensed and ready.

He turns to face east towards Jerusalem and gets to his knees, clasping his hands together in prayer.

The alarm clock goes off. Be-bep. Be-bep. Raguel stands up, straightening his clothes. It's time.

There are a couple of dead leaves on his ficus. They look so messy. He picks them off quickly, straps his knife to his calf and hurries outside where his chariot awaits.

CHAPTER 59

I fired up my Porsche and pulled away from the kerb, narrowly missing a black cat which chose that exact same moment to scoot out in front of me.

I knew where I was headed but I still hadn't figured out what the second part of the riddle meant.

It started off fun but ended so bad,
My fault of course, I was had.

It must be something about his childhood, I thought. That'd tie in with where the next clue's hidden and the whole kid theme. But what's he trying to say?

I was had. That's another way of saying he was tricked, I thought. And given the line before, things didn't end well.

Who tricked him though? The person he'd called Satan?

As I rounded the corner on to Grove End Road I saw it – a silver Honda several cars behind weaving in and out of the traffic towards me. The driver was wearing a cap pulled down low, a scarf and tinted lenses. I couldn't make out a face but I could see the bonnet. It had a dent just above the left headlight, in exactly the same position as the car I'd spotted the other night.

Was it the Lacerator? Was he tailing me?

I veered right on to Circus Road then swung sharply on to Elm Tree Road, my eyes glued to the rear-view mirror to see if the Honda followed. But it didn't.

Must have realised he'd been made, I thought, shooting a look up and down the street before accelerating hard to the main road.

The traffic was snarled up round by the Odeon cinema and judging by all the hooting, it had been for a while. I checked my mirrors and performed an illegal manoeuvre to nip down a side street leading to Fairfax Road. There was more hooting. This time it was directed at me.

I raced off down the hill, cutting off a red Micra and earning myself some more aggro in the process. Then I curled my way round the back of Waitrose and up to Finchley Road Tube Station. The traffic was clearer here but the lights were against me. I would have just run them, had a white van with 'clean me' written in the dust on its backside not been blocking my way.

I tap-tapped my thumb on the steering wheel. There was no way through.

You're a girl and I'm a boy,
A real gent – you choose the toy.

What did that line mean? It sounded like the Lacerator was talking about the two of us. Him the boy, me the girl? But what did that have to do with *you choose the toy?*

He was leading me to a toy shop, one of the biggest in London; a warehouse full of whatnots. He had to be giving me a hint about where the next clue was hidden. There's no way he could expect me to simply stumble across it in a store that big. Could he?

You're a girl and I'm a boy,
A real gent – you choose the toy.

The answer had to be there. He's a boy (*a real gent*), so he was going to let me choose the toy. But how would he know which toy I'd choose?

He doesn't know what I used to play with as a kid so he must be talking about something stereotypically girly, I thought as the lights finally changed and the traffic started moving again. A doll? It may have been un-PC but it fitted.

It was after five. The bus lane restrictions were in operation but I didn't care. I'd try and argue away the fine later if I had to and if I couldn't, a penalty charge would be a small price to pay for someone's life.

I signalled, swung out to the left in front of an angry double decker and floored it all the way up to the dual carriageway, just managing to avoid missing the turn off for Toys 'R' Us in time.

It was only as I got out of the car that I noticed it. A silver Honda with a dented bonnet parked behind a bank of trolleys three rows away from me.

But there was no sign of the driver.

CHAPTER 60

Was the Lacerator hiding inside the store? Was he watching me from a concealed position? I almost hoped he was Fingerling; at least I'd know who I was dealing with then. It was somehow less daunting to think I was being tailed by someone I already knew, even if that person was a knife-wielding serial killer.

Suck it up, Ziba. Save it for later.

Even if the offender is here, I'm nothing like his other victims, I thought. I don't fit his type. And he wants me to take part in his scavenger hunt. Knocking me off doesn't fit with his plan.

However, that didn't mean I was inviolable. If he suspected I was breaking his rules I'd feel the sharp edge of his blade, no doubt about it.

I walked through the automatic doors, scanning the store for someone acting furtively. No one stood out but that didn't mean the Lacerator wasn't there.

A large girl with colourless braces wandered past adjusting her ponytail. She was wearing a blue uniform shirt and a name badge.

'Where can I find your doll section please?'

She turned round slowly, a bored look on her face.

'What kind of dolls? Barbie, Disney princess?'

'Um, I—'

'We've got My Little Pony: Equestria Girls. Parker: Our Generation. Happy Chou Chou. Baby Born. Baby Annabell. Cabbage Patch Cuties. What do you want?' she said, examining her nails.

Jesus, I thought. In my day you got a generic plastic thing in a babygro. How has playtime become so complicated, never mind branded?

'Perhaps you could just take me to your main section,' I said, wondering how on earth the Lacerator had decided where to hide his clue amongst such a perplexing range of toys.

'I'm about to go on my break. Start off by looking over there.' She waved her hand expansively. 'If you can't find what you want someone else will help you.'

'Couldn't you just—?'

'Sorry. I'm on my break—' she said, marching off before she'd even finished the sentence.

Magic.

There were over thirty aisles and more than a third of them were full of dolls. Dolls in boxes. Dolls in pushchairs. Dolls in castles. Dolls in horse-drawn carriages. You name it, the dolls were doing it.

With so many glossy-haired creations to choose from I figured my best bet was to go through the shelves systematically. The aisles were numbered. I'd start from the first and work my way along.

I picked up box after box, examining each one from every angle. I turned over every smiling princess and pink-cheeked mermaid checking for clues. Nothing. Nothing. Nothing.

Just as I was about to move on to the next aisle, I sensed an infinitesimal movement in my peripheral vision; a fleeting image of someone slipping behind a display stand. A pair of sunglasses. A baseball cap. Was I being paranoid? Or was I being watched?

Backed up against the shelves, fists raised to my face, I advanced on the spot, but when I reached it there was no one there. I swept my gaze up and down the aisles, jaw tensed, heart rate quickening. It all checked out but that didn't mean anything. The store was big. There were plenty of places to hide.

As I turned back to the shelves of dolls, a pulse throbbing in my temple, I registered a troubling fact. This was the first time I'd ever had to play defence.

Muscles tensed, ready to engage if I had to, I continued my search.

Twenty minutes later and with zip to show for my efforts I began to wonder if there was a better way to approach the hunt. I'd only got to the end of aisle five. If I kept on at this pace I'd be lucky if I found what I was looking for before closing time.

It was 17.30. I was only an hour and a half away from the deadline. There had to be a way to speed things up.

Think like the Lacerator, I thought. Where would he hide it?

I pressed my hands to my temples and thought, deliberately blocking Fingerling out of my mind. Despite my suspicions, he might not be the offender and I didn't want any feelings I had about him getting in the way.

I ticked the key points from the profile off on my fingers. Religious. Delusional. OCD. Nervous.

Nervous. Was that it? He'd have been feeling on edge when he came in here to hide his next clue. He'd have been looking for reassurance, for a heavenly sign of approval.

I looked round the store. There were numbers hanging from the ceiling over each of the aisles. I was in aisle number five. That number meant nothing to the Lacerator. But what about aisle seven? Unless it was full of Transformers and Tonka trucks it's where he'd have gone.

Running, I nearly tripped over an abandoned water pistol. I managed to catch hold of a display of bike helmets in time to save myself, though unfortunately not the merchandise, which came tumbling down around me. I side-stepped the rolling helmets and raced on to aisle seven.

When I got there, I knew I was in the right place by the smell: steamy refuse, vinegar, rotting fruit. It was the same odour I'd noticed outside my front door – the smell I now associated with the Lacerator. And it was still strong.

A chill washed down my back. I jerked my head left and right, eyes darting. I held my breath. Was he close?

A skinny woman with her hair scraped back off her face eyed me curiously. I thought she looked familiar but my brain was so overheated right then I was seeing connections everywhere.

I was unnerved, not in control of the situation. The hunted rather than the hunter. This game was new to me.

I glanced at my watch. The killer may or may not still be here. There was no way to know for sure. I had to carry on.

Turning back to the aisle, I continued my search. There were shelves and shelves of merchandise – toy prams, accessories, baby dolls. On a gondola unit at the far end there was a display of plastic figures with boy-band hair and staring brown eyes labelled Davey Doll.

This had to be it! The only boy doll I'd seen so far, and in aisle number seven. But there were tons of them. It was like trying to find an unspent bullet after a Killing House exercise.

I picked up each doll, one by one, turning them over and feeling inside their clothes.

Nothing. Nothing.

This is bullshit, I thought. Then – hang on, what's this?

It was hiding thirteen toys in along the back. A mutilated doll: hair cut off, face blackened with a felt tip, pants pulled down. And the next clue was secured to its wrist with a figure-of-eight knot.

Ha! I thought.

Thirteen along, aisle seven. Numbers again. The first line of the riddle. The Lacerator hadn't just given me the name of the shop, he'd also told me where to look.

20/15/25/19 18 21/19

Add the numbers together and you get 137. Thirteen and seven. That wasn't the only thing I'd worked out though.

I'd also just discovered how the killer picked his prey.

CHAPTER 61

The girl on the checkout desk looked at me as she rang up my purchase.

'Did you do this?' she said in an aggressive voice, nodding at the Davey Doll.

'I found it like that.'

'It's all messed up.'

'I'm buying it, so it doesn't really matter if I did it or not, does it?' She screwed up her face at me.

I slapped down a twenty. I didn't have time for this. If only I had a warrant card or a DS with me.

'I need to call my manager,' the girl said, pressing a button.

Before I could stop her, a message was booming over the tannoy.

'*Manager request at till five. Vandalised item. Davey Doll.*'

I needed this as much as a chocolate kettle. What if the Lacerator had heard and thought I was trying to call for help?

I saw a flash of colour in the greeting-card aisle, as if someone had just ducked out of sight. Over by the inflatables section a man in a Nike cap was eyeing me over the boxes of paddling pools. My body tensed. My breathing turned shallow.

'Can I please just pay for this? I'm in a hurry.'

'Sorry, you'll have to wait for my manager. I can ring those up for you,' she said to the woman behind me, who had a trolley-load of items.

'I don't have time to wait.' I balled my hand into a fist.

'Rules is rules,' she said, starting to scan the other woman's shopping.

'Actually, can you cancel the Play-Doh, I didn't realise it was going to come to that much?'

'I suppose so. But I'll have to start over ringing up all the items.'

'That's okay.'

BOHIFCA. Bend over, here it fucking comes again.

I looked around. There was no sign of the store manager anywhere.

'Is she coming?' I said to the checkout girl.

She rolled her eyes at the other woman and leaned into her microphone.

'Manager request at till five.'

Not what I'd intended.

'Trace, can you come and take over for me?' she called over her shoulder to a girl rearranging rolls of wrapping paper. 'I'm supposed to be on my break.'

Not another one!

Screw this for a round of shoot 'em up, I thought, leaving my cash on the counter and legging it out of there with the doll under my arm.

'Stop! Come back.'

A moment later a hulking security guard was behind me, gaining ground. I broke into a run.

'Come back or I'll call the police,' he shouted, lunging after me.

I glanced round. He was only a couple of metres behind me. I kept my upper body tall, maintained my feet low to the ground with short, light steps and swung my arms backwards and forwards at a ninety-degree angle.

His footsteps pounded on the tarmac behind me, close enough for me to hear him puffing. I needed to smoke the guy – fast.

I breathed air in through my nose and out through my mouth to increase the oxygen to my muscles, filling my belly rather than chest with each inhalation. I arched my toes up towards my shins to quicken my cadence. I lengthened my stride.

Not for nothing had I passed the special forces selection course.

Three more steps. Two. One.

I threw myself into my car and accelerated away, nearly knocking the security guard over in the process. In the next few seconds he'd be calling the police.

My day just kept getting better.

CHAPTER 62

The canal water looks black in the fading light. A goose bobs its head under and comes up empty. The air smells of petrol, stale cigarettes and Grandad's too-strong aftershave.

The boy is crying.

'I don't like it,' he whispers.

'Yes, you do,' Grandad says. 'I can tell.'

His voice is cold and hard, just like his father's gets when he's cross.

The boy shakes his head and sniffles. 'I don't.'

'Well, it's too late to stop now,' says Grandad. 'If anyone finds out what you've done, you'll be in real trouble. No one will want to be friends with you.'

The boy starts to shiver. He feels sick.

This is all his fault. He should have done something before. He should have said something right at the beginning. But he didn't. He was too scared, and now it's too late.

If anyone finds out what he's let Grandad do, they'll think he's disgusting. No one will want to talk to him. Even his mother will hate him.

The boy starts to sob harder. He hiccups and struggles for air.

'Stop it,' says Grandad, shaking him backwards and forwards, his hands gripping tightly round the boy's throat. 'Look at me. I said, stop that! Right now.'

CHAPTER 63

Raguel's knife is snug against his calf. The voices whisper Ziba Mac's name. The walls breathe softly.

CHAPTER 64

As I sped off, I thought about what the Lacerator had just revealed. His letter implied a trauma, his riddle suggested it had something to do with his childhood, and the Davey Doll filled in the blanks.

He'd made a point of saying he was a boy in the first clue and then he'd chosen to hide the next one on a boy doll. So it followed that the toy was a stand-in for him as a child. And its face had been blacked out.

There are a number of different red flags professionals look out for in children when they suspect sexual abuse. Toilet training regression. Frequent masturbation. And mutilation of dolls. Inking a doll's face would fall in that last category.

Children often project their feelings on to inanimate objects. Destroying them is a way for them to express their feelings of self-loathing and impotence. It also helps them manage their pain and release the anger they feel but can't do anything about.

The Lacerator was using the doll to show me what he'd gone through as a child and how it had made him feel. His riddle hinted at the same thing.

It started off fun but ended so bad,
My fault of course, I was had.

I hadn't understood it at first but in the context of child abuse it made perfect sense.

Paedophiles normally groom their victims before assaulting them. They shower them with gifts and treats to make the child feel special and test whether they can keep the attention secret from their parents. At the same time they start engaging in 'innocent' touching; hugging, tousling hair, that sort of thing. The physical contact builds up slowly but because it's so gradual and a level of trust has been created between the victim and attacker, the child doesn't complain.

Then when it progresses further, the child feels they've done something wrong, that the abuse is somehow their fault. They don't speak out because they're frightened they won't be believed. Or worse, that they'll get into trouble.

This must have been what happened to the Lacerator as a kid.

It started off fun (presents/treats)

but ended so bad (abuse)

My fault of course (he blamed himself)

I was had (a double entendre; a reference to being duped but also to sex). Though the language showed he now put the blame squarely at the feet of his abuser.

If the Lacerator had been a victim of childhood abuse then he'd gone through a similar ordeal to many other serial killers. But the doll showed me something else too. Why he targeted his victims.

I'd been wide of the mark. He didn't kill because he was on an anti-gay crusade or because he felt guilty about his own sexuality. Rather, he chose his prey because they reminded him of his abuser – the true focus of his rage.

And I suspected the next clue might have something to do with who that was.

CHAPTER 65

Row, row, row your boat
Gently up the river
If you see a dirty old man
You are bound to shiver
This is where it starts and this is where it ends
By the lock where the bridge bends
The Angel saw and the Angel struck
No more tears, no more bad luck.
On a pillow he rested his head
No more fears of going to bed

It was 17.51. Just over an hour before the Lacerator killed his next victim. This was only the second clue and chances were it would lead to a third, if not more. Unless I could crack it fast, someone else was going to die. And I still didn't know who that was.

For a second time it occurred to me this whole scavenger hunt might be a ruse. It was certainly a brilliant way to separate me from the rest of the team; to isolate me and make sure I wouldn't reach out for help. The Lacerator wasn't special forces but that didn't mean he wasn't capable of setting off a flash bang in one direction and attacking from another.

Was I being overly suspicious or was I really in danger?

I didn't fit with the victimology but the perp was a schizophrenic, a man with complex delusions. What if his orders from above had changed? What if the voices had started telling him something new?

I'd profiled him at the first press conference. What if he hadn't liked what I'd said about him? Wouldn't an avenging archangel strike out against someone who dissed him in public? Isn't the Bible full of that sort of thing?

Should I call the MIR? Should I tell the team what was going on? But how could I? I still didn't know for sure one of them wasn't involved. And I couldn't chance the Lacerator finding out I'd broken his rules. No, I had to do this his way. I had to go it alone.

The grief over Duncan's death that so often cripples me also makes me strong. I've lost the only man I've ever loved. There's nothing left for me to lose. Risk doesn't mean the same thing to me as it does to other people.

I pulled into a Tesco car park up the road and cut the engine. There were hundreds of cars in the lot. I was well camouflaged. Trouble is, I had no idea where to go next.

The opening part of the first clue had been about Toys 'R' Us. But what was this one talking about?

There was another clear reference to abuse – *dirty old man*. And the nursery rhyme reference – *Row, row, row your boat* – alluded to the killer's tortured past.

Though where did the next clue's location fit in?

It has to be somewhere near water, I thought, given all the bridge and river references.

But if it was hidden along the Thames, I was screwed. Even with the pedal down all the way and going through every red light in London, there was no way I was going to be able to make it to the Embankment in time to stop him killing again. Never mind the fact the river's more than two hundred miles long and the clue could be hidden anywhere along it.

I re-read the rhyme. *By the lock where the bridge bends.*

An idea began to form. What if it's got nothing to do with the river? What if it's talking about a canal lock?

There are thirteen locks along Regent's Canal. But only one fitted with what I knew of the Lacerator.

Camden Lock.

Suddenly I knew exactly where I needed to be.

I fired up the engine. The sooner I found the next clue, the sooner I'd figure out who I needed to save. The other victims had been surrogates, stand-ins for the man the perp really wanted to destroy. Only now was he ready to embark on the final act.

The identity of his next victim was therefore significant, given his personal link to the killer.

Which meant finding out who he was could finally unmask the Lacerator himself.

CHAPTER 66

Forget all roads lead to Rome. In this case every path led to Camden. It's where the bodies of Aidan Lynch and the most recent victims had been found. It's where the geo-profile suggested the Lacerator lived. And it looked like the third clue might be hidden here too.

But what was it about the place that was so important to the Lacerator?

Experience told me it was about more than just convenience. Something pivotal had happened to him here. It's why he kept coming back. He was settling an old score. Putting the past right.

I pulled up outside the Roundhouse at 18.03. I'd made it down there in good time but my time was running out all the same. There was less than an hour to go till the deadline. Another man would be killed if I didn't get to him before the Lacerator did. Or woman, said my wired-to-lightning brain. There was still a chance he was coming after me.

There were no empty parking bays on the main road so I left my car on a double yellow. That would mean a fine for sure but I couldn't give a crap. All I cared about was finding the next clue.

Despite it being mid-week, the market was heaving with Goths and wannabe I-don't-know-whats. People in army-style trench coats with heavy-duty piercings and oddly dyed hair. People of indeterminate gender strolling hand in hand. People who shuffled rather than walked.

'Out the way!' I shouted shoving my way through the throng.

I passed an *Evening Standard* sandwich board emblazoned with the day's main headline – *Lacerator Strikes Again!*

'The bodies were found near here, weren't they?' I caught an American tourist saying, a shiver of excitement in her voice.

A few metres on, I spotted a PC, hands on hips, surveying the market as though looking for someone. He glanced my way and reached for his digital airwave radio.

'L2206.'

I couldn't hear the words but from this position I could lip-read well enough to know he'd just started a new transmission. Surely this wasn't about the bloody Davey Doll.

I slipped into the horde. I had to keep moving.

The bridge was up ahead but getting to it wouldn't be easy.

The market was pulsing. There were people ambling about taking photos, having caricatures drawn, or troughing on tandoori wraps and Indonesian street food. Stall owners were shouting out their wares – 'Real leather. Good price.' The heavy smell of Chinese food and Indian spices hung in the air, while all around was the din of hundreds of people talking in different languages.

'Make a hole. Move,' I said, elbowing my way through the crowds.

The bridge was a mirage: always in sight, always just out of reach.

I had to get there. I was running now, the thud of my feet loud on the path. Then I froze, a surge of adrenaline gushing through me.

I sensed rather than heard the footsteps behind me, though of course there were footsteps everywhere, the sound reverberating around the market. The stamp and slap of countless people moving over the cobblestones. And yet the cadence of these footsteps was different. They were careful, measured and in perfect sync with mine. These footsteps were following me.

I sped up, weaving my way through the crowds, trying to shake off my tail.

One of my first SRR missions was to maintain eyes on a suspected terrorist in the hope he'd lead us to his cell. I spent weeks tracking him. I learned to maintain a ten-metre distance between my tango and me. I learned to keep my head bent and to expect him to stop periodically, and if this happened to walk past in a nonchalant way until I reached somewhere I could conceal myself and look back. And I learned to keep walking if I suspected I'd been made.

I learned to wear neutral colours – nothing bright, never black. I learned to carry bags within bags containing changes of clothing. And I learned the importance of fitting in with my surroundings. In Tehran I wore a hijab. In Madrid I wore shades.

The footsteps were louder and faster now. Whoever was following me didn't know the rules. He wasn't keeping a ten-metre gap. But that didn't mean he wasn't a threat.

I quickened my pace. He quickened his. I started running, my bag banging against my side. He started running too. I glanced round, stumbled and tripped, managing to skin my knee in the process. Pushing myself up into a squatting position, I used my new vantage point to scan the area without being seen.

That's when I saw him. A young man with long, greasy hair in a ponytail, clutching something square and leather, being pursued by the copper I'd spotted before. A pickpocket, then. Not after me.

Numpty, I thought, getting to my feet and hurrying on.

There were stairs leading up to the bridge. I checked round the base of them just in case. There was nothing there. I ran over the bridge, barging into people.

'Watch it, you clumsy bitch!'

'Silly cow!'

'What's your hurry?'

There were more people on the other side. Eating. Drinking. Looking to score, despite the police's best efforts to shut down the drug market.

Heart still pounding, I searched behind the walls and under the debris collected there.

I was so wrapped up in the search, I didn't immediately notice the man watching me from the towpath. But as he swatted at his arms, his glasses caught the light.

What the—?

It was the tweaker from the train; the guy I'd seen again outside the restaurant last night.

A prickle chased across my scalp. Once was a coincidence. Twice was a pattern.

He was staring right at me, picking a scab on his neck, his lips twisted into an expression that was more smirk than smile. He was only there a moment though. The next second he'd disappeared into the throng, gone from sight.

I went after him, obviously. But I'd lost him as completely as if he'd been sucked into the ground.

'Hashish. Tina. Snow,' said a black guy in a sibilant whisper as he walked past, his jeans riding halfway down his ass, his eyes furtive.

I slowed to a stall. Could the tweaker be the Lacerator?

He certainly fitted elements of the profile, particularly the tie-in with Camden and the drug use, which may well have landed him in an institution at some point. And of course, meth addicts do have periods of lucidity, which he'd need to write to me the way he had.

But his age was off. I'd profiled the offender as being in his mid to late forties. This guy couldn't have been much older than me. Early thirties, then, or possibly younger even. Meth has a way of ageing people before their time.

On top of that, the tweaker dressed like a tramp whereas the killer's letters showed we were looking for someone obsessed with neatness and order.

I rubbed the back of my neck. Either way, I could hardly call it in without breaking the Lacerator's rules. The consequences were too awful to contemplate. And what if I did alert the Yard and the tweaker turned out to be innocent? It would put the real perp on notice and then . . .

No, I needed to carry on with the hunt. My best way of stopping him was solving his clues.

It took me another five minutes before I found it. A shoebox hidden inside a white carrier bag tucked away under the bridge.

I pulled it out. Taped to the front was a computer printout of an angel wearing armour and holding a spear. Something to do with Raguel and the whole archangel thing?

I opened the box. Inside was a yellow-haired doll, another boy, lying on its back, eyes closed, on top of what looked like a Cub Scout's neckerchief.

A figure-of-eight knot and now a neckerchief. Both Scout symbols. But how did the Lacerator fit in? Unless . . .

Jack had said the first victim, Aidan Lynch, was involved in a Scout group. Was the killer trying to tell me that's where they'd met, not in a gay bar as we'd thought? And if so how did that tie in with everything else he'd revealed?

I'd like to have taken a picture of the Lacerator's composition on my phone before rooting in the box for the next clue but I couldn't risk switching it on. Doing so would emit a signal and if he was trying to track me he could use it to pinpoint my location.

A piece of paper was hidden under the neckerchief. As I read it, a wave of acid splashed up my digestive tract.

The clue was different from the others. It wasn't written in rhyme. It showed just how closely the Lacerator had been watching me.

And it sounded very much like I was going to be his next kill.

CHAPTER 67

Closer and closer. The time is coming, the Kingdom of God draws near. Soon, Ziba Mac. Very soon.

CHAPTER 68

I raced back to the car, heart pounding.

I knew exactly where the next clue was hidden. Trouble was, going there could mean walking into an ambush.

I am with you and watch over you wherever you go.
I spared your life when you sat on your bench,
But my knife will be out when you go there again.

The Lacerator was talking about my favourite bench by the canal, the one under the big London plane tree where I'd spoken to Jack this morning. The place I like to sit and read.

How long had the smashed asshole been stalking me? And how did he know me so well?

That's not all though. Going by what he'd written, he must have been there at the same time as me. I'd thought I was being followed when I set out for my walk. If only I'd trusted my gut, the killer could be in custody now.

Beat yourself up later, Ziba. Right now, you need to be planning your next move.

But what should my next move be? I could get someone to call the police and tell them they needed to stake out the canal.

Trouble is no one knew what the Lacerator looked like. He wouldn't exactly be wearing a flashing neon sign saying 'Serial Killer'. According to the profile he'd be neatly dressed but that was all we knew about his physical appearance.

On top of that, the weather was good. There'd be plenty of people out and about. It wouldn't just be a matter of looking for a lone man acting suspiciously.

And what would he do if he saw a whole load of squad cars descending on the canal? Lash out? Go on a killing spree?

No, the more I thought about it, the more it seemed like the best idea was to go down there myself and hope he made a move.

I've been trained in close-quarter battle by the SAS. And I know how to disarm a man and turn his weapon against him. Right now, walking into a trap looked like my best way of catching the shit-bird in his own net.

I checked my watch – 18.25. Just thirty-five minutes to go till I hit the deadline but I knew where I needed to go. It wasn't far and my Porsche is fast. Easy.

I reached the Roundhouse and stopped dead.

No!

I wanted to scream. Un-fucking-believable! I glared at the rusty yellow clamp on my front right wheel. Just when I needed to move I was going nowhere.

I ripped off the PCN notice stuck to my windscreen. I could have called the contact telephone number in the strip at the bottom but waiting for someone to arrive and remove the clamp would take time, and time was something I didn't have. I needed to think of another way of getting where I needed to be. Fast.

Chalk Farm Tube Station was only a few minutes' walk away but the Underground wasn't the answer. I'd need to change trains which would take too long. And the bus was no good either. It'd be way too slow. A taxi would have been alright but there were no cab ranks and no passing trade.

What was I going to do?

I scanned the street.

That's it!

I legged it across the road, narrowly avoiding being mowed down by a truck which carried on blasting its horn long after I'd made it safely to the NatWest bank on the other side. I'd had an idea, though not one of my finest as it turned out.

I inserted my debit card into the hole in the wall and withdrew £250, the maximum amount I could take out in one day. Would it be enough though? Maybe not. I should get more. I dug in my wallet. A Mastercard and American Express. Where was my Barclaycard? Never mind, £750 should be enough. I'll be charged a commission for using credit cards but if this works it'll be worth it.

Armed with a thick wad of cash and the killer's shoebox, I stood on the edge of the pavement facing the oncoming traffic, waving my arms like a demented signalman. My plan was to pay for a ride. I didn't see how anyone would refuse hundreds of pounds for a short detour.

But I was wrong.

This is London; people don't stop for anything and everyone's always in a hurry. Maybe I'd have had more luck if I'd waved my bank notes about but more likely than not I'd just have had my money snatched.

Three minutes went by. Four. Five. No one pulled over. I had to try something else.

Maybe the Lacerator was after me. Maybe he was after someone else. There was no way to be sure. All I knew was I had to keep going with the scavenger hunt. Not doing so could put another person in mortal danger.

I needed to identify who that might be and find a way to save him. And if it was me the Lacerator was after? Well, I'd deal with that if it happened. It wouldn't be the first time I've had to overpower an assailant. And at least on this occasion I'd been forewarned.

There was a Nando's restaurant a few doors further up the street. It was all a bit amateur but the train crash on Thursday had shown me first-hand what people will do for strangers in trouble and I didn't exactly have time to go into hair and make-up.

I raced into the restaurant and grabbed a bottle of tomato sauce from the selection on the side. I squeezed it over my arm, rubbing the red goo into my shirtsleeve and skin. A couple of diners looked at me quizzically but no one said anything. Another thing about London – people keep their heads down. They don't talk to people they don't know.

I ran back on to the street cradling my arm.

'Are you alright, love?' a driver said, slowing down and leaning out of the window.

'No, I've just been mugged.'

'Mugged?' He looked at me, confused. 'But you've still got your handbag.'

Shit! My cheeks flared.

'I fought him off,' I said quickly. 'But he stabbed me. I don't have a car. Can you give me a lift home? I live by the canal in Little Venice. It's not far from here.'

'Of course.' He smiled. 'Hop in.'

He didn't ask if I'd rather he take me to a hospital and at the time I didn't think it was odd that he hadn't.

It was only as we drove off that I registered the emblem on his steering wheel.

I gripped the door handle, ready to make a quick getaway if I had to, as the silver Honda I was in accelerated up the hill.

CHAPTER 69

It didn't take me long to realise how stupid I was being; a right daftie, Duncan would have said.

The driver of the silver Honda was a man in his seventies with balding hair, chicken arms and a wedding ring cutting into his finger.

There was a Mickey Mouse car seat in the back covered in biscuit crumbs, a photo hanging from his keychain of a smiling young woman in a suit cuddling a toddler, and a kid's book bag in the passenger foot-well with a school logo emblazoned on the front.

This guy wasn't a threat. He was an elderly man, married for years, who was going out of his way to help a stranger in much the same way he must help out with his grandson while his daughter was at work.

He drove along hunched over the steering wheel, shooting glances at me every time we stopped at a red light.

'You okay, love?' he asked for the umpteenth time as we turned on to Avenue Road, 'Chariots of Fire' blasting out of the radio.

The lights changed.

'My arm's really hurting. Could you go a little faster?'

'I'm already going twenty miles an hour.' He checked his rear-view mirror for Black Rats, traffic police.

I made a wincing noise.

'I'll see what I can do,' he said uncertainly, accelerating to twenty-five mph.

If only I had a warrant card I could have requisitioned the vehicle. Of course, I could have used force to get myself behind the wheel but there wasn't really much point. Even in a twin-turbo BMW M6 we were unlikely to garner much speed on these snarled-up one-lane roads.

Getting worked up about a situation I couldn't change was a waste of energy. Better to think through the clues and what they told me about the Lacerator. The picture of the angel on the box. The Cub Scout neckerchief. The 'sleeping' doll.

The angel I got. The scarf I got too, given the Aidan Lynch connection. But how did the doll fit into it all? And what was the link between the three?

'This is Global's Newsroom at six forty-five,' said the radio presenter.

Six forty-five?

I checked my watch with a stab of horror – 18.41. It must be slow. I quickly adjusted it.

> *The London Lacerator has struck a second time in what Scotland Yard has described as yet another brutal attack.*

> *A spokesman for the Metropolitan Police has said more people than previously believed had escaped from the wreckage of Thursday's rail crash.*

> *And Anne Catlin, mother of murdered schoolboy Samuel, renews her appeal for information about her son's killer.*

Samuel Catlin! Could that be it?

I'd found the shoebox on the towpath by Camden Lock, the same place Samuel's body had been discovered. And Jack had said he was part of Aidan Lynch's Scout Group.

Was the Lacerator trying to tell me he'd murdered them both? In which case Samuel, not Aidan, was his first victim.

But how did telling me what he'd done fit with telling me who he was? And how did killing a child tie in with his later targets – grey-haired men who reminded him of the man who'd abused him?

I thought again about the wording of the clue:

The Angel saw and the Angel struck
No more tears, no more bad luck.
On a pillow he rested his head
No more fears of going to bed

I recited the lines in my head over and over until suddenly the haze cleared. The Lacerator *had* killed Samuel first and I knew why.

I also knew it meant he was capable of altering his victim preferences. Which didn't bode at all well for me.

CHAPTER 70

Over the course of the afternoon I'd learned a lot about the Lacerator. Like so many other serial killers, he'd been sexually abused as a child. He attacked men who reminded him of his molester. And although he was responsible for the death of Samuel Catlin, in his mind he'd acted for noble reasons.

It's what we call an 'altruistic homicide' because he believed death to be in his victim's best interests. The Lacerator may have been punishing his other targets, but he believed he was saving Samuel.

The Angel saw and the Angel struck
No more tears, no more bad luck.

It was all there in the clue. The 'Angel' (i.e. the Lacerator) saw something he didn't like and 'struck' so there would be 'no more tears'. In the Lacerator's mind, killing Samuel Catlin ended his suffering.

On a pillow he rested his head
No more fears of going to bed

The language here was tender, conveying caring and compassion. And the Lacerator's perception of the outcome of the murder – that Samuel could now sleep without fear – was a positive one.

Though perhaps the fear of going to bed referred to the Lacerator too. After all, schizophrenics often suffer from insomnia, especially during the onset of psychosis.

When the Lacerator murdered his adult victims he was an avenging archangel but with Samuel Catlin he was an angel of mercy. Or an Angel of Death, as the Holmes typology, which categorises serial killers, puts it.

There are two types of Angels of Death: sadistic killers like Harold Shipman who enjoy the feeling of power they get by ending the life of someone under their care. And mercy killers who believe they're acting in their victims' best interests.

When mercy killers are arrested they nearly always maintain they've done nothing wrong. Typically they claim they were trying to ease their victims' discomfort by 'putting them to sleep'. Even that terminology shows they think they are acting out of kindness, and it's strikingly similar to the language the Lacerator used in his clue.

In the Lacerator's warped mind the murder of Samuel Catlin was an act of benevolence. But why? What made him think Samuel was in trouble? What made him think he needed saving?

Only one thing made sense. It had to have something to do with the Scouts.

I'd already worked out the Lacerator had been abused as a child. Did he find out Samuel was being abused too?

My heart bounced. Aidan Lynch! Did he hurt the child? Is that why the Lacerator killed him? Payback? He identified with Samuel and destroyed the man who was hurting him. As a child he could do nothing about his situation. As an adult, he could fight back.

It would certainly explain why Lynch was so physically different to the later victims. And also the perpetrator's graduation to targeting men who reminded him of his own abuser.

But where did I fit in?

We turned a corner and the canal came into sight; a sparkling ribbon, bright sunlight dancing on the surface.

'I can get out here,' I said to the Honda driver, preparing myself for what was coming next. Either another clue hidden near my favourite bench.

Or a confrontation with a serial killer.

CHAPTER 71

'*In nomine Patris et Filii et Spiritus Sancti,*' whispers Raguel the right number of times, touching his fingertips to the knife hidden beneath his trousers.

Any moment now. The best things come to those who wait.

CHAPTER 72

'I can't possibly leave you on your own in the middle of the street in your condition,' my Good Samaritan said, shaking his head. 'I promised I'd take you home and that's exactly what I'm going to do. Now, where's your place?'

There were no flats or houses for me to claim. The nearest ones were a good five minutes' walk away. I was right where I needed to be and I didn't have the luxury of going 'home' to complete this charade.

'You've been wonderful,' I said, leaping out, my bad arm magically healed.

'What's going on?' He leaned out of his window. 'I don't understand.'

I ran off without answering and a moment later I heard the poor bloke drive away, no doubt wondering what had just happened. I wasn't thinking about him though. I was focused on what was coming next.

I was either walking into a trap or about to find the next clue. Either way, lives depended on me staying frosty.

I scanned the area. Any sign of a hostile? Possible hiding points? Number of people in the vicinity? Best exfil routes? Obstacles?

Out in the open with no back-up, no walls to use as cover and no grenade clipped to my belt, I was about as vulnerable as it was possible to be. All I had to go on were my instincts.

I approached the bench strategically, making sharp turns to the left and right, looking around, eye out for any sudden activity as I'd been taught at Hogan's Alley – the FBI Academy's tactical training facility at Quantico.

I kept my movements as smooth as possible. Smooth equals speed. The faster I was the harder it would be for an assailant to catch me off guard.

There was a narrowing between the trees, a fatal tunnel. Clear the tunnel, don't stop – my instructor's words boomed loud in my head. Stay focused. Move tactically. Silently. And above all, be prepared to react to enemy contact at all times.

I reached the bench. Over-ripe fruit and vinegar. The Lacerator's smell. Was he here?

I spun round; fists clenched, muscles tensed, every fibre primed. Nothing. Was he behind the tree? I took several paces back and executed a search. All clear.

I retreated to the bench and felt around it without looking down. Back, seat, underneath.

What's this?

There was something secured to the bottom of the bench with duct tape. Eight inches long, soft cover. I yanked it off. An appointments diary, a ribbon hanging between the pages.

I withdrew to the canal edge, my back to the water so I couldn't be surprised from behind. I opened the book at the marked section. Today's date was highlighted. There was one name in the box, written in capital letters in black ink and circled seven times. GRANT TAPLOW.

So the Lacerator wasn't coming after me. This was about payback for what had happened to him as a child. Despite my misgivings he'd been true to his word. But then, what did he mean when he'd said, *I spared your life when you sat on your bench, but my knife will be out when you go there again?*

That's when I saw them: two shoe impressions in the wet mud positioned vertically just behind where I'd been sitting.

Had the Lacerator been here this morning? Had he bent over me while I slept, close enough to stab me in the neck? And now was his knife out, ready to kill again as I stood here with his last clue in my hand?

I checked my watch. My stomach dropped. 19.07.

I knew the name of the Lacerator's target. But was I too late to save him?

CHAPTER 73

Raguel smiles. The air tastes sweet. The sky is blue. And even at this hour the birds are singing in the trees.

He was born for this.

CHAPTER 74

I'd lost my car and I couldn't use my phone to gather intel. But there was a way I could get a ride and the information I needed. The minicab place by the Waterside Café.

As I raced over, it occurred to me that although he hadn't given me an address, the Lacerator had made his last clue pretty easy. It was almost like a part of him wanted me to stop him.

Had this whole scavenger hunt been a cry for help? A desperate plea to be understood and saved from impulses he couldn't control?

In his letter he'd said he needed to be sure what God wanted him to do. Clearly the man was torn. In carrying out what he saw as his holy mission he was breaking the Big Man's most sacred rule. For a religious guy in a psychotic break the constant oscillation must have been soul-destroying.

I barged through the doors of the minicab office out of breath, hair gone wild. The woman manning the phones glanced up.

'Can I help you?' she asked, looking me over.

'I need a cab but I have to find an address first. Can I borrow your computer?'

'Well, I'm not—'

'I'll pay,' I said, digging in my bag and whipping out a fifty from my cashpoint haul.

She smiled.

'Be my guest.' She offered me her seat with a fuchsia-lipstick smile.

I pulled up an electoral roll search site I'm registered with and entered *Grant Taplow* and *London* in the search boxes. I couldn't be sure but it seemed most likely that's where he lived given what I'd worked out about the Lacerator.

The screen blinked and a set of results popped up.

GRANT TAPLOW
1975–99: 36 Jamestown Road, London NW1 7BY
Other occupants: Sandra Taplow

1999–2003: 5 Inverness Street, London NW1 7HB
Other occupants: Marcus Lynch, Theresa Lynch

2003–present: The Cedars Care Home, Prince of
Wales Road, London NW5 3AW

Inverness Street? I zeroed in on the middle address. Other occupants: Theresa and Marcus Lynch. Holy shit.

I thought back to the evening I'd spent in the Lynches' living room and how Marcus had told me his wife's father, Grant, had moved in with them for a while after his wife died.

Which meant Grant Taplow was Theresa Lynch's father. And the next name on the Lacerator's hit list.

19.16. Had he stuck his knife in yet or was he playing with his victim? Enjoying his revenge?

I Googled the number of the care home where Taplow lived and asked the minicab woman if I could use the phone.

'Press 9 for an outside line,' she said, pushing it towards me, her long fingernails scraping on the desk.

'Come on, come on,' I muttered, as it rang and rang but wasn't picked up.

A woman answered eventually, a smoker judging by her rasping tones. 'Cedars Care Home, Barbara Burgess speaking.'

'My name's Ziba MacKenzie, I'm with Scotland Yard. I need you to tell me where Grant Taplow is right now,' I said, talking quickly even for me.

'Grant? He's in his room. Why? What's wrong?'

'I need you to listen very carefully and do exactly as I say. Move Mr Taplow into another room on one of the upper floors. Secure the windows and doors. Lock all your entrances and exits. And whatever you do, don't let anyone in to see him.'

'What about the visitor with him now? His grandson. Nice young man. Funny eyes though. Never seen anything like them.'

Funny eyes? My mouth went dry. With two words the whole game had changed.

'Call 999 immediately. Ask for the police and when they arrive take them straight up to Grant Taplow's room.' Then, 'You'd better get an ambulance too.'

CHAPTER 75

Funny eyes. With those two words the picture finally came into focus. CFB. Clear as a fucking bell.

At the beginning of the scavenger hunt my aim had been to save a man's life. Halfway through I'd found evidence suggesting my life was the one at stake. And now, at the end of the trail, I'd found out something else. The Lacerator's identity.

Eyes may be the window to the soul, but in this case that's not all they revealed.

When I checked out the photo of Aidan Lynch the day I interviewed Marcus, I noticed a mark on one of his eyes. A black smudge that looked like the pupil was leaking into his iris.

I'd gone online later and found out it was caused by a defect called a uveal coloboma, a genetic condition that stops a baby's eyes developing properly during pregnancy. It's something that only occurs in around 1 in 10,000 births. So it's incredibly rare.

The Lacerator had said he was Grant Taplow's grandson when he'd pitched up at the care home. I knew Taplow was Theresa Lynch's father. Combine that with the uncommonness of uveal colobomas, the fact most perpetrators of sexual abuse against a child are related to them, and the likely age of the Lacerator's attacker at the time of the abuse and it all slotted into place.

Aidan Lynch wasn't a victim. He was the killer.

He'd been dead for twenty-five years. His corpse had been found in the Lynches' house. The blood type had been a match for Aidan's. And his mother had made a positive identification.

It seemed impossible that he was our perp and yet all the evidence told me it must be him.

'I'll double the fare if you can get me to The Cedars at warp speed,' I said, hopping into the cab I'd ordered.

The driver gave a mock salute and shot away from the kerb so fast I got whiplash.

He may have been feeling jaunty, but I wasn't. I'd been a total idiot, the asshat to top all asshats.

All afternoon I'd been running round London with my head up my arse. How could I ever have thought Fingerling was the Lacerator? How could I have been so stupid?

True, the killer had said he'd watched me at the crime scene and looked deep into my eyes. But the guy was a schizophrenic, for fuck's sake. That meant he was plagued with hallucinations, auditory, visual or both. If he'd watched me and gazed into my peepers it was only in his head. He hadn't been lying when he said it, but he hadn't been telling the whole truth either.

And as for the thing with my hair, Jeez, a two-year-old could have figured that one out quicker than me!

Only a few minutes ago I'd worked out he'd been leaning over me while I slept on the bench earlier on. That must have been when the moon chicken cut my hair, I thought. He probably hacked it off with a knife, so close to my neck he could have stabbed me. Though by not doing so, the maggot reckoned he'd spared my life, hence what he wrote in the final clue.

As for the other things that had suggested Fingerling was the Lacerator, well, they were no more than puffs of smoke. They clouded the picture but were easily dispelled. Possible drug addiction, sugar cravings, exhaustion, black fountain pen – big deal.

If only I'd realised my idiocy sooner and reached out to the team for help, we could have covered more ground and worked out who the next victim was faster. Maybe even in time to save him.

Had it just been stupidity though? Or was it something else?

CHAPTER 76

I'd convinced myself I had to follow the Lacerator's rules and not tell anyone what I was doing. But the truth is, it had suited me to have an excuse not to involve Scotland Yard. Partly because I prefer working on my own but also because I'd wanted to solve the clues by myself. I'd wanted to prove I could.

I was sick of DI Dipstick second-guessing me at every turn. I'd let my feelings about him get in the way of the job.

Nigel Fingerling, always standing an inch too close, always staring at my breasts. I couldn't stand the guy but maybe I was the problem.

I'd told Jack he was a misogynistic gobshite who liked nothing better than to put me down. But I'd put him down too. I'd ridiculed him in public in front of the people he had to work with every day. And then, when he'd tried to put things right between us by suggesting we go out for a drink, I'd shot him down with a Starstreak missile.

I had been meeting Wolfie for dinner that night, but I could have pushed things back by an hour or so, it wouldn't have mattered. And if I had, it would have given Fingerling and me the chance to talk things out. Or at the very least just make nice.

But I hadn't wanted to. I hadn't cared enough. I couldn't be bothered to make the effort to patch things up. It had been much easier, and more fun, to go out with Jack and bitch about him over supper. Because despite all the years and all the training, I'm still the misfit I always was.

Still the girl who talks too fast and says all the wrong things. The teenager more interested in Sufi mysticism than *Mizz* magazine. The kid who never had anyone to play with at breaktime but told herself she didn't care.

I left boarding school nearly fifteen years ago but I'm still the same person I was the day I arrived after my father's funeral in my too-big blazer, itchy round the collar. Part Persian Jew. Part English Protestant. An outsider who doesn't get people despite being an expert in human behaviour.

Ever since the train crash I'd felt I had a purpose, that I'd been given a second chance to do something good with my life. So I'd tended to the wounded in the carriage. I'd tried to honour Theresa Lynch's dying wish. And I'd busted a gut trying to save the capital from an evil man on a holy mission.

In doing all that, I'd managed to sidestep the despair that threatens to engulf me every day. And although I still reached for Duncan across my empty bed every morning, I had something to get up for. A reason to get dressed. A reason to go out and be with people. A reason to live.

For the first time in a long time, I held my head high as I walked down the street. I no longer felt like the walls were closing in on me or that I couldn't breathe. Trite as it sounds, in attempting to save others, I'd ended up saving myself.

But now, thanks to my lack of social skills, hubris and poor judgement, a man had lost his life. How could I live with myself knowing I was to blame?

As I absorbed the implications of my colossal screw-up, the world started collapsing again. My veins filled with sludge. Invisible hands gripped my throat. Outside the cab, the sky turned dark and the birds stopped singing.

Glancing up, I caught my reflection in the rear-view mirror. I looked like a bag of smashed ass. Bone weary and grey with defeat.

I didn't like what I saw. The soldier in me took over.

Snap to, MacKenzie. This isn't the time to wallow in self-pity. You need to un-fuck this situation. Fast.

I pulled my dead mobile, battery and SIM out of my shoulder bag and levered off the phone cover. Adrenaline unsteadied my hands. I slotted the battery in but managed to drop the SIM card into the footwell.

'Broke-dick piece of shit,' I muttered, fumbling about for it.

'You alright, love?' The driver looked round.

'Just dandy,' I said, slotting the SIM into the phone, replacing the cover and powering the device up.

I scrolled through my contacts, already planning what I was going to say.

The line rang once before he picked up.

'Fingerling. This is MacKenzie. We need to talk.'

CHAPTER 77

'MacKenzie? Are you okay?' said Nigel Fingerling, his voice a deluge of relief.

'I'm absolutely fine. I—'

'Where the hell are you then?' he said, the tone changing abruptly. 'I've been trying to reach you for hours. I flagged you as a high-risk misper, for Christ's sake.'

'A missing person?'

'No one could get hold of you. Your phone was off. The Lacerator's letter implied he was stalking you. Certainly he's obsessed. I was worried he'd come after you. I sent officers to your flat. There was no sign of forced entry but your drum looked like it'd been ransacked.

'We started scoping for CCTV and going house to house. Then a call came through to the control room from a toy shop in Brent Cross. A minor shoplifting incident. Security guard said the offender went screaming off in a Porsche 911. The VRN, make and model matched the vehicle we have registered to you in the system. Your car was later spotted on Chalk Farm Road. But the responding officers found no trace of you in the vicinity, though you'd obviously been there. Witnesses said they'd seen a woman matching your description running around the market, highly agitated. POLSA's organising search teams. Your photo's been distributed to the media.'

The trouble I'd caused, the resources I'd wasted. Clusterfuck didn't begin to cover it.

'I'm so sorry, Nigel.'

'I don't want to hear sorry. I want to hear what the hell's been going on with you all afternoon.'

I blew up my cheeks and exhaled slowly. Where to start? Certainly not by saying I'd thought he was a serial killer, that was for sure.

'The Lacerator sent me a second piece of communication. The opening gambit of a scavenger hunt.'

'A scavenger hunt?'

'A series of clues hidden around London. Knowledge of him and his next victim being the prize at the end of the trail.'

'Why the hell would he want to do that?'

'He seems to think the two of us have some sort of connection. He said he wanted me to understand him but needed me to prove I was worthy before he'd reveal himself. It's complicated. Better if I fill you in properly face to face.'

'Okay. But why didn't you call it in? We've talked about your team spirit before.'

My hackles raised but I kept it civil.

'He made me believe he was monitoring me and if I involved the MIT he'd go on a killing spree – starting with me.'

'And you believed him?' Fingerling sounded incredulous, but then he hadn't seen the evidence. Or held it in his hands.

'He sent me a chunk of my hair. He'd managed to cut it off without me noticing. And he knew other things about me too.'

I thought he was you.

'I searched my flat for bugs. I couldn't find anything. But it still seemed like the best thing to do was go off the grid and solve his clues.'

'So why are you calling me now?'

'Because not only have I got to the end of the trail, I've also finally realised he can't make good on his threats. I know now how he got his dick-beaters on my hair. And that there's no way he can have eyes on me.'

I paused, about to tell him the rest, when he jumped in with the one question I was hoping he wouldn't ask.

'You're ex-special forces, MacKenzie. Reconnaissance Regiment. You seriously telling me there was no way you could have got a message to the incident room on the sly? Jesus, even I can think of ways.'

But I thought you were the Lacerator.

'I guess I thought I could handle things myself. I screwed up. I'm sorry.'

'Damn right you screwed up. And another man's just died because of it.'

'You know about Grant Taplow?'

He skipped a beat, surprised, then said, 'I'm with him now. Poor bugger doesn't have much to say for himself though.'

Gallows humour. It would have gone down well with my oppos.

'Presumably there's no sign of his grandson?'

'Grandson?'

'Aye. Aidan Lynch. His visitor.'

'You missing a few screws? Aidan Lynch is dead.'

'I don't think he is. The body at Inverness Street wasn't his. Lynch is the London Lacerator.'

I registered his sharp intake of breath. My afternoon hadn't been completely wasted.

'I'm on my way to The Cedars now. Less than five minutes out. I'll explain everything when I get there.'

CHAPTER 78

'Say thank you nicely to Grandad for taking you out, Aidan,' says the boy's mother. 'I bet you got a lovely surprise when you saw him waiting for you. It was all Dad's idea.'

Dad? the boy thinks, a hard ball of anger growing in his throat.

'Maybe we'll do it again next week. You'd like that, eh kiddo?' says Grandad, ruffling his hair.

The boy's heart beats fast. He turns to his mother, his face desperate.

'Cat got your tongue?' she says. Then: 'What are those marks on your neck, sweetie? Did you get into a fight at school?'

The boy longs to tell her everything. He wants her to make it stop. But Grandad's standing right there, his eyes boring into the boy. And even if he wasn't, he still couldn't tell.

She'd think it was his fault. She'd think he was disgusting.

So he says nothing. Instead, he escapes upstairs where the box of SHIP matches is hiding under his bed.

CHAPTER 79

The train crash set off an explosion inside me, giving me a new sense of purpose. My conversation with Nigel Fingerling set off another. I may not have been able to prevent the Lacerator killing Grant Taplow, but I was sure if we didn't stop him he was going to strike again. Imminently.

The murder of Taplow was the act he'd been building up to all these years. But now he was on a spree and totally out of control. His impulse to kill wouldn't dampen down anytime soon. He'd find another target, I was sure of that. And given the increasingly short time periods between homicides, it was likely to be within a matter of days at the most.

Although we finally had a lead on his true identity we had no idea what name he was going by now. Certainly he wouldn't be calling himself Aidan Lynch. Being a dead man was too good a cover to blow.

Though that begged the question, why had he told the care home people he was Taplow's grandson? Could it have been part of the murderous fantasy he'd created? Had he wanted Taplow to know who he was? Was it central to his idea of vengeance?

But what did that mean for us and how to find him?

Right at the beginning of the investigation, I'd told Falcon we'd have to use proactive techniques to flush the perp out and I was more sure of that than ever now. We'd need bait he couldn't resist. But to find out what worm to put on the hook, I needed to examine his latest work.

'Pull in here,' I said to the cab driver, hand already on the door handle.

'That'll be fifty pounds,' he said, trying to suppress a smirk at ripping me off.

Twat, I thought, handing him a freshly minted note from my haul and jumping out.

We'd pulled in just behind a BMW. There was a Scotland Yard badge issued to Nigel Fingerling in the windscreen.

How did he manage to afford a car like that? I wondered.

Then I remembered his fake TAG Heuer watch. The vehicle was probably leased. All part of his need to keep up appearances.

Instinctively, I glanced in through the passenger window as I walked past. There was a can of Red Bull and a Diet Coke bottle in the drinks holder. King-sized chocolate bar wrappers and empty crisp packets in the footwell. Unopened bills and sports pages with race times circled in red biro on the passenger seat. All in all, his Beemer was about as messy as his desk.

I hurried through The Cedars' big iron gates.

The grounds were teeming with firefighters, CSIs and detectives from the MIT taking statements, all milling around as the sun started to set. I spotted Fingerling straight away.

He was talking to a woman wearing a thigh-length cardigan and Birkenstocks while scribbling in his black flip notebook. She was standing with her arms folded tightly under her ample bosom and her hands tucked in her armpits. Defensive body language.

Must be the care home manager, I thought. Poor cow's probably ass-pissing herself about a lawsuit.

'Would you excuse me?' Fingerling said to her as I came over. 'MacKenzie, let's talk. Over here.'

Before I could say anything his mobile beeped. Eyes narrowed, he pulled it out of his pocket and checked the message. If I hadn't been standing so close I may not have seen it but his face was only inches away from mine. I saw everything.

I saw the way his mouth parted, the way his lower lids tensed and the way his cheeks raised. A second later his face adopted a more neutral expression, a mask. But it didn't matter. I'd seen what I needed to.

The microexpressions gave away his pleasure, as well as his dirty little secret. The secret he was so ashamed of. The secret that made him bad-tempered and snappy. The secret that kept him up all night and left him so exhausted he was on a permanent sugar and caffeine binge.

It was something only an expert in human behaviour could have exposed. Which is of course why he felt so threatened by me.

It's why he ridiculed profiling when we first met. It's why he tried to put things right between us so I wouldn't bear him a grudge. And it's why he was so unpleasant after I rejected him. If anyone was going to figure out what he was hiding it was me.

I looked at him dead on.

'Big win, Fingerling?' I said.

CHAPTER 80

Nigel Fingerling was a gambling addict. I don't know why it had taken me so long to nuke it out but now I had it all made sense.

The anxiety. The jumpiness. The bitten nails and red-raw hands. The tiredness. The sugar cravings. The signs he'd been up all night. They were all indications of an addiction.

So too was the fake watch. He'd probably had to sell his real one to pay off his debts, judging by all the unopened bills I'd noticed on his passenger seat. I was right that it had been to do with keeping up appearances but not about the reason he'd felt the need to have one. Wearing a fake watch wasn't about posing. It was about not being found out by his colleagues.

If he'd always worn a TAG Heuer and then pitched up one day at the Yard wearing a plastic Swatch, people might have started asking questions, especially highly experienced detectives who've been trained to notice such things. Replacing the real thing with a fake would prevent that from happening. It would help keep his secret safe.

And clearly that's something he felt the need to do. His red hands were a sign of over-washing or eczema; both stress related. Either Fingerling had some nasty guys on his back or he was worried his addiction would be found out by the people he worked with.

The latter seemed more likely to me. If anyone discovered he had a serious gambling problem, his position as DI would become compromised. A man like Fingerling, who'd gone to pieces after his girlfriend dumped him, wouldn't have handled losing his job well.

I'd spotted the signs but I hadn't connected them. I'd wondered during the press conference earlier that afternoon whether he had a drug problem but until now I hadn't considered gambling one.

I thought about the sports pages I'd noticed in his car. About how his mobile beeped every two seconds. And how his mood was affected each time it did.

Wherever he was, whoever he was talking to, Nigel Fingerling always checked his phone when it went off, like it was the most important thing in the world – which it would be to a man with a lot of money on the races.

There are plenty of websites that offer live racing results delivered directly to you. And not just results, you can get tips and news too. In fact, you can even place bets straight to and from your mobile. Clearly that's exactly what Fingerling had been doing.

Maybe he felt he could manage the situation and function in his day job while keeping his other life hidden from his colleagues. But then I'd rocked up and changed everything for him. I was a threat and I needed to be contained. That explained both his open hostility towards me and also his attempts to win me over.

What it didn't explain was his concern for my well-being this afternoon. That was genuine. I'd heard it in his voice and it showed me something. It told me that despite all his shittiness and everything he stood to lose if I exposed him, Nigel Fingerling was able to put my welfare above his own.

That meant he was empathetic, unselfish and above all, decent. I may have sussed out his secret but that didn't mean I was going to land him in it. And he needed to know that.

So, 'Big win, Fingerling?' I said.

'I don't know what you're talking about.' He answered too quickly, thereby proving the complete opposite.

'It's alright,' I said, touching his arm. 'It's your business, not mine. We've all got our demons, me included.'

He glanced at his shoes and I ploughed on.

'I may not always say the right thing but I'm not a blabbermouth and you're not on your own. I know what it's like to struggle against something stronger than yourself. So if you want to talk, talk to me. If you want someone to come to a meeting with you, I'll be there. Because I've learned the hard way that going it alone isn't always the best thing to do. Sometimes you have to lean on others for support.'

I thought of the woman on the train, Theresa Lynch. I thought of how I'd profiled her moments before we'd crashed into the freight wagons and how I'd thought she shut herself off from the world because she thought she was safer that way. I thought about myself and how I tend to do the exact same thing. And I thought about what had happened this afternoon when I'd done just that. How it had backfired and got someone killed.

Maybe the best way to protect yourself from the world isn't to close yourself off. Maybe it's actually to open yourself up, I thought, as I stood in front of Nigel Fingerling extending the hand of friendship.

I tilted my head slightly, a deliberately submissive gesture.

For a moment he said nothing. His eyes squinted and his brows turned in. His forehead wrinkled and he pinched his lower lip. He was thinking, weighing up what I was saying, and wondering whether or not to trust me. I waited.

I'd read him. Now it was his turn to read me. I hoped he'd realise I wasn't actually a threat. That I meant what I'd said. And that if we wanted to catch a killer we needed to become a team.

CHAPTER 81

'I appreciate that, Mac,' Fingerling said, meeting my eyes.

I smiled. It was the first time he'd called me by my nickname.

'Now, let's talk about what you said on the phone. What makes you so sure Aidan Lynch is the London Lacerator? The guy's been dead for twenty-five years.'

I started at the beginning. I told him all about the scavenger hunt, the clues I'd found and what I thought they meant. And how I'd worked out the Lacerator's identity and his connection to Grant Taplow.

'Lynch could have faked his death, used a proxy,' I said, winding up. 'It may sound far-fetched but it's not just my gut telling me I'm right. The evidence is telling me too.'

'A detective as well as a profiler.' He smiled. It was patronising but there was no malice in it. 'You may be on to something. We'll share it with the team during the evening briefing. But first I'd like your take on the crime scene.'

'Copy that,' I said, following him to the main building.

He held open the door. 'Youth before beauty.'

'The vic's room's here,' he said as we exited the lift. 'Prepare yourself. I haven't seen anything like this in twenty years on the force.'

He raised the DO NOT CROSS tape. 'Mind giving us the room for a few minutes, people?' he said to the CSIs dusting the place for prints.

We put on protective clothing in the corridor and gave our details to the PC manning the log.

The crime scene manager came out and gave us a whole lecture on where to step and what not to touch. My old drill sergeant couldn't have done a better job.

We walked in. I gagged. Immediately my eyes began to water. The stench was overpowering; rank and pungent with a sickly sweet overlay. The smell of rotting meat mixed with cheap perfume. It got in my throat so I could taste it. I gagged again.

I dug in my bag for my Vicks VapoRub and Altoids – an old trick.

'I'll have some of that when you're done,' said Fingerling as I smeared the ointment round my nostrils.

I stood in the doorway and took in the room, getting a feel for the man who had lived here. A few hours earlier this had been his home. Now it was a crime scene, every smooth surface dusted with a fine film of fingerprint powder.

The place was sparsely furnished, though it had clearly been given a woman's touch. A single bed pushed against the wall with a light-green throw draped over the end. An old-fashioned nightstand with a box of coloured Kleenex. A vase of carnations on the windowsill that had seen better days. The sort of flowers you pick up at the supermarket – probably bought at the same time as the groceries by someone who visited regularly but who hadn't been for a while.

A daughter, most likely. Theresa maybe. Someone who came out of duty, the same person who tried to prettify the room.

An armchair with a patchwork cushion was set by a window looking out on to a playground. Judging by the worn patch on the seat, Grant Taplow spent a lot of his time sitting there admiring the view. I noticed a boy, aged nine or ten, mucking around on a climbing frame and shuddered.

Did he come here often? Did Grant Taplow like to watch him?

I forced my eyes away. Grant Taplow was a victim now, whatever else he might have been.

There was a bible on the bookshelf; not the standard Gideon one you find in hotel rooms but a fancy white-and-gold version with an unmarked spine and a dusty top. So a gift then, and by the looks of it an unwanted one since it had never been opened.

I thought of the big leather-bound bible at the Lynches' house. Had this one been foisted on him by Theresa? I knew she was a fervent Catholic; maybe she was a proselytising one too.

In the middle of the room there was a table. Drag marks on the carpet showed it had been pulled over from by the door. On it lay a naked, severely beaten and mutilated corpse splattered with oil, its face a gory pulp of flesh and sinew.

Gouts of blood from a lesion in the victim's neck dripped on to the carpet, making a soft tapping sound, like a finger on a windowpane, as they hit the floor.

'Sweet mother of dog shit.'

I've seen many things in my time: blown-up bodies, beheadings, torture victims. But this was something else. It wasn't human.

The Lacerator may have thought he was an angel but this was a scene straight out of Hell. I didn't care what Grant Taplow may or may not have done. No one deserved to die like this.

Like last night's victim, he'd been stabbed seven times in the neck and once through each eye. There were multiple contusions and lacerations to his face. And although his genitals had been hacked off in a manner consistent with the other homicides, they'd also been stuffed in his mouth, the word 'guilty' carved into his chest. Covering my mouth and nose, I leaned in for a closer look. There were no hesitation marks.

A fire had been set in a ring on the floor around the table, contained by sand. He improvised that bit, I thought, observing the red fire bucket on the floor next to an upended plant pot. He must have noticed it in the corridor. Probably saw its presence as a sign from God.

I picked some grains off the table – soil, which explained the plant pot but not what the killer was trying to communicate.

'He's definitely evolving,' I said. 'Same signature aspect but the MO's developing.'

'I'll say.'

'Can you believe this guy actually thinks he's doing God's work?'

'Fanaticism's nothing new. Personally I blame organised religion.'

'The distortion of religion maybe. I'm no expert but isn't Christianity all about forgiveness? You know, love thy enemies, turn the other cheek and all that. The Lacerator may think he's a good Catholic but I doubt the Pope gives him a birthday phone call.'

Fingerling laughed through his nose. I smiled and opened up Chrome on my phone.

'This boring you?' he said.

'I've just had a thought about what the Lacerator's trying to convey. Hang on a sec. Ah yes, here we go. Listen to this: "Make an altar of earth for me and sacrifice on it your burnt offerings." Exodus 20:24. We're not just looking at a brutal murder here, Fingerling. We're looking at a human sacrifice.'

'Come again?'

'We know the Lacerator's delusional. He thinks he's the archangel Raguel, also known as the Fire of God. Hence all the flames both here and at the other crime scenes. But what I hadn't realised before is that the most recent victims have been offerings – burnt offerings.

'And the signature fits in well with the theory the offender was abused as a kid. The overkill. The castration. And now the carving on Taplow's chest.'

'I get that but how does the eye stabbing fit in? It's a key element. It must mean something, don't you think?'

'It could be about power and control. Or maybe it has something to do with shame.'

'Shame?'

'The stab wounds on the neck are the first to be administered, and in each case they've been the cause of death. So the ocular stabbing must be symbolic more than anything else. Part of his fantasy is to blind his victims. It's possibly a way of making them feel helpless and lost just like he'd have felt as a child.

'By jamming his blade into his victims' eyes, the Lacerator is metaphorically switching places with his attacker and gaining the control he once exerted over him. He's saying, I'm the last thing you'll ever see. I'm in charge now.'

Fingerling nodded, his lips pressed tight together. 'What would you suggest in terms of media strategy?' he said.

'We should issue an appeal for information. We can get a sketch artist to sit down with the person the offender spoke to when he asked to see Taplow. Then we can share the photofit and the new findings with the press. History of abuse, schizophrenia, OCD, drug habit—'

'Cocaine, to be precise. CSI found traces on the carpet outside your front door.'

So not methamphetamines then. The Lacerator was a coke-head not a tweaker.

'What about the scavenger hunt? Do we tell the media about it?' Fingerling chewed at the sore spot on his lip.

'Yes.' I rubbed my chin between thumb and forefinger, thinking as I spoke. 'Like I said before, the Lacerator wants me to understand him. He thinks if I do I'll be able to protect him. The ass-wipe was probably picking up on what I said at the first press conference. That thing about me wanting to help him but how I needed him to show himself to me so I could.'

'Bit odd, no?'

'I dunno. We're talking about a seriously delusional guy here. Someone who sees signs and meaning in everything. Someone who thinks he's on a divine mission. I empathised with him at the press conference. I told him I understood him and what he was going through.

257

Maybe it's not so surprising he'd think I'd been sent by God to keep him safe.'

'Maybe. But what does that have to do with telling the media about the scavenger hunt?'

'Think about it. The Lacerator believes I can only protect him if I understand him completely. So what do you think would happen if he thought I'd got the wrong idea about him?'

Fingerling scratched his head then smiled.

'He'd get in touch with you again. Put the record straight.'

'Exactly. It's a straightforward proactive technique. We'll feed false information to the media. And if I've read the Lacerator right, he'll react and reveal more about who he is and his agenda. I'm pretty sure he is Aidan Lynch – it all fits, though Lynch is supposed to be dead. So we need something solid to confirm the theory otherwise we risk going off at a tangent, potentially putting more lives at risk.'

I paused, an idea forming. I smiled. Yes, it was perfect.

'I think I know just how to get the Lacerator to give us the proof we need,' I said. 'Bait he won't be able to resist.'

CHAPTER 82

'So you got your bag back, then,' said a DS from the murder investigation team.

We were back at the Yard. I'd given a full debrief, made a televised statement and was now working my way through a Starbucks Dark Roast; extra shot, extra large.

'My bag?' I said, taking a slurp.

'Your handbag.' He gestured to the one slung over my shoulder. 'A call came through for you this afternoon. Some guy said he'd found it down by the canal. Said your name was written on a notebook inside. He recognised the name from the news and got in touch. I wasn't sure when you were coming in so I gave him your mobile number. That way he could get in touch with you directly. I imagined you'd want it back as soon as possible. I know what women are like about their bags. My missus—'

I clenched my jaw. So that's how the shit stain got hold of it.

'You do realise you gave my phone number to a serial killer?'

'What?' he said with a catch in his voice. 'But he described it perfectly. And he said he'd found it in Little Venice. It matched the address we have for you on the system.'

I sighed and dropped my shoulders. The rifle had already been fired. There was no point trying to save the bullet.

'Calls to the Yard get recorded, don't they?'

He nodded.

'Well, perhaps you should see what the tech guys can get off the tapes. You never know, there may be something on them. Perhaps someone out there might recognise his voice. Who knows, this may be the thing that cracks the case.'

'Fingers crossed, eh,' he said, bending to pat me on the shoulder.

'Aye, here's hoping,' I said with a smile that faded too fast. I wasn't counting on anything yet.

As the DS ambled off, Paddy came over to make himself a cuppa. 'Hey, Pad, do you have a sec?'

He still had that faraway look in his eyes and kept twitching and massaging his temples. Something was definitely up with him but I was fairly sure it had nothing to do with a bug or the migraine he'd claimed to have.

'Course. What can I do you for?' he said, unwrapping a sachet of Lipton's and dousing it in boiling water from the machine.

'Tell me to butt out and I will, but I'm worried about you. You don't seem yourself. Is everything alright?'

He chewed his lower lip, a sign of hesitation and discomfort. On instinct I gave him the once-over.

He'd removed his wedding ring recently, judging by the slight indentation on his finger. And now he was rubbing the spot where it used to be.

Something to do with his estranged wife then. A new development in the break-up of their marriage.

There were royal-blue ink stains on the tip of his thumb and forefinger. Ink, not biro. The sort of pen you'd use for something important. The marks were fresh. The pen had been used recently.

'You've just signed your divorce papers, haven't you?'

He started then dropped his shoulders, a gesture of surrender.

'I was served just after you left the Yard, before I came over to your flat. I was thinking about not signing. But then I thought, what's the point, eh? She's obviously not going to change her mind. Though what if there was still a chance we could sort things out? I've been going mad all afternoon trying to decide what to do. Divorce is so final.' He sighed and looked down at his shoes.

His toes were pointing towards the door. His feet were shifting to a starter position. This was a man longing to run away. I recognised the feeling.

'I'm so sorry.'

'Ah, me too.' He paused. 'Look, I know I can trust you, but do me a favour, eh. Don't mention this to anyone else just yet? I know it sounds dead crazy but as soon as it becomes public knowledge, it becomes real.'

'I don't think that sounds crazy at all,' I said, giving his arm a gentle squeeze.

I yawned. It had been a long day. I went over to Fingerling's desk.

'I think I might head on home unless you need me for anything else,' I said.

'No, that's fine. Go get some rest. See you back here at nine for the team briefing.'

'Roger that.' I chucked my coffee cup in the bin and adjusted my bag – the one the Lacerator must have gone through that morning while I dozed on the bench.

'Don't forget your mobile. It's on your desk,' Fingerling said as I started off towards the door. 'Your boyfriend texted to call him.'

'Sod off. You know he's not my boyfriend.'

'But you know exactly who I'm talking about, don't you?'

I flushed.

'No need to get your knickers in a twist, MacKenzie. I'm only toying with you,' he said with a wink.

He was an insensitive ass but he was right about one thing, I did need to lighten up. If I could only rein in the impulse to kick him in the nuts every time he opened his crumb-catcher there was no reason the two of us couldn't work together just fine. At least on this investigation, anyway.

It wasn't until I was walking out the building that it dawned on me how Fingerling had known I'd been at the Camden Brasserie with Wolfie the night of the murder.

Someone in the incident room had moved my phone while I'd been off getting coffee. It must have been him. He must have heard Jack's text come through and read it.

It was out of line. He was a nosy bastard. But there was nothing suspicious in it. And maybe if I could stop seeing hazard signs round every corner I might have realised that sooner.

CHAPTER 83

Raguel is showered and sitting cross-legged on his bed playing cat's cradle in a dressing gown and fresh socks. His clothes from earlier are soaking in bleach; the remains of his supper are on his nightstand. A couple of carrot sticks, toast nibbled to the crusts and a heap of Laughing Cow wrappers.

Only the lamp by Raguel's bed is on, the curtains are drawn tight. Even this high up he hates the idea of anyone looking in.

Sellotaped to the wall is the photo of Ziba Mac he printed out in the computer room at the day centre. He gazes into her eyes as his fingers and thumb tuck and pull at the string.

There's so much sadness in them, he thinks. Just like his first guardian angel. She had sad eyes too.

He takes a sip of water, cloudy from the tap, and turns back to the TV.

The volume's much louder than they had it in the rec room when he was watching the press conference earlier that afternoon with the other outpatients, a vision of Ziba Mac by his side.

'We don't want to disturb the folks who are napping, do we?' the orderly had said when Raguel had asked if they could please turn it up.

He's waiting for the news to come on now, or rather for Ziba Mac to come on the news. She's bound to say something about today. And she's bound to send him a sign to show she finally understands him.

He smiles, thinking how well it all went. The treasure hunt. The unequivocal proof he now has that he's carrying out the Lord's desires and that he need no longer fear his own. Not to mention the punishment of the Devil himself.

His fingers move fast on the string, the patterns morphing like a kaleidoscope.

Everything was perfect today, right down to the bus that was waiting at the stop when he set out on his holy mission.

Your chariot awaits, he'd thought with a secret smile as he hopped on. He'd recognised at once that this was a sign from above that all would be well. So had the voices.

'Trust in the Lord for He delighteth in thee,' they'd whispered.

He took the bus to the demon's dwelling place but walked home afterwards. He always walks home after an execution, the exercise does him good. It allows him to clear his mind and connect with his Maker.

Raguel yawns. He's tired. Today took a lot out of him. He longs to sleep but despite what he'd hoped, he knows sleep will be even more elusive than usual. His body's exhausted but his mind is wired even though his post-kill high receded some time ago.

A memory slices through his skull. The image is so vivid it's as if he's back there again.

'Look at me,' Grandad whispers, the smell of stale tobacco heavy on his breath. 'Look at me while I check you're healthy.'

'Stop!' shouts Raguel, squeezing his eyes shut so tight they hurt.

He'd thought his final confrontation with the Devil would end it all for good, that the memories would release their hold and he'd finally be able to sleep. But seeing his grandad again has done the opposite. He'll get no rest tonight.

Raguel drops the string and grips the side of his head, collapsing into a tight ball on the bed. His body shakes. A sharp pain sears through his brain. For a moment everything goes black then the flashback is over.

The shaking subsides. After a while, Raguel sits up and as he does he hears the voice, the one that whispers louder than all the others, the one that speaks alone: 'Take vengeance on your foes. I am the Lord and you are my servant.'

Just in – following the latest Lacerator murder at a care home in North London, Scotland Yard has issued the following statement about the killer.

Raguel turns the TV volume up. This is what he's been waiting for. He takes up his string again and moves his fingers under and out. A star. A row of diamonds. A spider's web.

He stops. The pattern hangs loose in his hands.

Staring at the television, he screams.

CHAPTER 84

'Why didn't you call me instead of getting a ride from a complete stranger? I'd have come and picked you up,' Jack said, easing his old Range Rover into a spot behind my Porsche, which was still stranded and out of action on Chalk Farm Road. 'As it is, I've been trying to reach you all afternoon. I've been worried sick about you.'

'You don't call. You don't write. Shit, Jack, you sound just like that Jewish mama in the old BT ads.' I rolled my eyes dramatically. 'Anyway, you can't have been worried all afternoon. I happen to know the new Lacerator story didn't come through on the wires more than a few hours ago.'

'I'm not talking about the care home murder. I'm talking about that weird voicemail you left on my phone – which, by the way, wasn't long before I heard the news about you going missing, possibly kidnapped they were saying. And now you're telling me you've been running all over London on some freak-assed treasure hunt. Why didn't you just ring me? You shouldn't have done it on your own. It wasn't safe.'

'Rewind a second. What message?'

He looked confused. 'You don't remember?'

I shook my head. The day had been as long as a year.

'You called my mobile. It went through to the answerphone. You didn't leave a message but you didn't hang up either. So when I checked in there was a recording of things being chucked about and you making funny noises. You were swearing a lot – even more than usual. You sounded scared, Mac. I've never heard you like that,' he said, his voice dropping an octave.

'I tried calling back a number of times but you didn't pick up. Then when I heard you were missing, I went round to your flat but the fuzz wouldn't let me in. So I put a call in to Scotland Yard to see what was going on. I spoke to that Fingerling twat but he wouldn't tell me anything.'

'Well, that's not surprising. He probably thought you were just sniffing for a scoop.'

'Maybe, but you're kind of missing the point here. I was shitting myself that something had happened to you. I don't know what I'd do if it did.' His voice had gone very quiet. He was staring at his hands on the steering wheel.

I touched his forearm. He glanced at my hand then up at my face.

'You don't need to worry so much about me, Jack. I can handle myself. I may be the size of a service pistol but I've been trained in self-defence by the most elite fighting unit on the planet.'

'You can spout that Ninja crap all you want but it's not going to stop me caring about you.'

The colour rose in my cheeks. It was a Freudian slip. Surely he'd meant to say 'worrying about you'. Not 'caring'.

'Jack . . .'

His face was inches from mine, his lips so close I could see the lines. I couldn't draw my eyes away. My mouth parted, the space between us seemed to narrow . . . just as a white van with the green Camden Council logo on its side pulled up next to us.

'Oh,' I said, jerking back, flustered. 'Looks like the clampers have pitched up. About bloody time.'

I jumped out of the car, heart hammering. Flushed with heat. Jack stayed sitting where he was for a moment, his hands at twelve o'clock on the steering wheel, his head bent forwards.

Half an hour later, I unlocked my front door. My Porsche was back in its usual spot, my wallet was a whole lot lighter thanks to the overzealous wardens.

Jack was standing behind me holding a carrier bag bulging with Chinese food.

'You really don't need to stay tonight. I'll be fine.'

'Maybe.' He followed me in. 'But I'd rather not take any chances. This guy knows where you live and he clearly has a thing about you. I'm not letting you stay here by yourself until he's been put behind bars.'

'Another reason to hope he's caught quickly then, eh,' I said as we peeled the cardboard lids off the foil containers and lined them up on the dining table.

He laughed. It sounded forced.

Neither of us had said anything about what had nearly gone down in his car. No doubt we were both thinking the same thing – if we didn't discuss it we could pretend it had never happened. Plausible deniability. Much easier that way.

'Sit yourself down and dig in. I got crispy seaweed. Here, have some.' I passed over one of the boxes.

'Lovely. My favourite.'

'I know. I asked for an extra portion,' I bit into a veggie spring roll; the pastry wrapper shiny with grease, the beansprouts burning hot.

The photo of Duncan in his police uniform bobbed in and out of my sightline each time Jack shifted in his chair. I topped up our wine glasses as we chowed down hungrily.

While the driver of a silver Honda watched us from the road below.

CHAPTER 85

Raguel is in torment. He had to come here but now the Devil drives his claws into his throat while a demonic figure holds him down in a swirling sea of fire and sulphur.

Who is that man with Ziba Mac? And what is he doing in her flat?

CHAPTER 86

I'd laid out bedding on the sofa for Jack before staggering into my room, exhausted and only too ready to doss down for the night. I went over to the window to draw the curtains. And that's when I saw it.

I rubbed my eyes. Was I imagining things? It was late. I was still charged with adrenaline, rattled by everything that had happened that afternoon. I'd be ripped apart as if I were on the stand. Not a reliable witness. Chances were my mind was playing tricks and yet . . .

I switched off the bedroom light so I couldn't be seen from the road and peered out of the window scanning the plates.

It was definitely the silver Honda from before, parked on the opposite side of the street. And the driver was looking up at my apartment through a large pair of binoculars.

Should I say something to Jack? No, I'd never get him off my sofa if I did. But I did need to establish what was going on. Not seeing hazard signs round every corner was all well and good, but that didn't mean being blasé in the face of possible danger. And even if I wasn't in jeopardy, the binoculars showed something was off about this picture.

There are all sorts of innocent explanations as to why someone might spend the evening sitting in a parked car. But spying through people's windows is never a legitimate activity, as my old job goes to show.

I squinted into the night. I didn't have any field glasses of my own, not any more. But my long-sightedness, so often a disadvantage, was now a boon. So too was the fact that the Honda had parked under a lamppost.

I couldn't tell if the person inside it was male or female. He/she was wearing a baseball cap and the binoculars were obscuring his/her face.

However, I could tell something. Although part of the registration plate was hidden, a few letters were visible from my vantage point. LJX. Same as the Honda I'd checked out at Toys 'R' Us.

My arms pimpled with gooseflesh. A tickle ran down my spine.

Was it the Lacerator? Was he back?

I dialled the MIR. I could only see the last three letters but they might be enough to run a trace if combined with the car's make and model, since these letters on a licence plate are randomly selected and therefore the most unique.

The other digits identify where a vehicle was registered and the year it was made. So, a car made in 2002 will have 02 or 52 in its registration. While a car with L and a letter somewhere between A and Y would have been registered in London. It's the sort of random trivia you get to know when your husband's a cop.

'Major incident room.'

I recognised the voice.

'Paddy, it's Mac here. I'm probably overreacting but there's someone sitting in a car outside my apartment block spying on me through a pair of binoculars. Sixth-generation silver Honda Civic. Partial plates. Last three digits LJX. I think I saw the same one in the Toys 'R' Us car park this afternoon, and I've spotted it following me on other occasions. Can you trace it on ANPR?'

'No problem. And I'll send some uniforms over to give the driver a tug. Changed yer mind about a protective detail?'

'No. I'm on the top floor. I'll double lock the doors and set the alarm.'

'Yer sure?'

'Positive. Duncan's best mate's here. He's insisted on keeping guard. He's a big bloke. I'll be fine.'

I didn't add that I keep a Fairbairn–Sykes fighting knife under my bed with a blade capable of slashing a man's throat with a single slice.

'Ah well, alright then. Let me know if you change your mind though.'

'Thanks. But I won't.'

Jack was messing about on his phone as I came out of my room. I fastened the deadbolts, pulling the door chain across for added security, and checked the alarm was set.

'Mind if we keep the windows locked tonight?' I said. 'Just to be extra safe.'

'Not at all. Glad you're taking this seriously now.'

'Actually, I just wanted to make sure nothing happened to you.' I grinned. 'Sleep well.'

As I walked back to my room I felt his eyes on me. Don't turn round, I thought. Don't you dare turn round.

I locked the bedroom door, undressed and flopped into bed. I was asleep the moment my body hit the rack. But I didn't stay asleep for long.

Zero dark thirty. I sat bolt upright, chest heaving, teeth clenched. The knob on my bedroom door was rattling.

Someone was trying to get in.

CHAPTER 87

The blood rushed in my ears – a geyser erupting, a river bursting its banks. My heart was a battering ram trying to break through my chest. Every muscle in me tensed as cortisol flooded my system.

The room was dark except for the luminous red digits on my alarm clock – 02.17. The time respiration and BP drop to their lowest levels. The time most people are in their deepest sleep. The time a person is most likely to die.

The doorknob rattled again. Who was there? What did they want with me?

Seconds became minutes. Time distorted. The world moved in slow motion and yet my body was in overdrive.

I opened my mouth to scream but like in the worst nightmares no sound came out. Though my skin was cool and clammy, my throat was desert dry.

'Ziba. Mac. Let me in.'

Ziba Mac. It was him then. The Lacerator. I'd misjudged things by putting out that statement this evening. I'd pushed him too far. He wasn't going to reveal more about himself. He was going to kill me.

I saw again Grant Taplow tied to the table, stabbed in the eyes and neck, his blood pooling on to the floor. I saw the victim from yesterday morning discarded on the ground like a piece of rubbish, his genitals hacked off and hurled against the wall.

I reached for my F–S fighting knife, a stiletto, some call it, because of its tapered blade. A double-edged dagger with a foil grip. A weapon favoured by the SAS and other specialist units for its thrusting potential.

I slipped out of bed, careful not to make a sound, and positioned myself by the door. Slowly, carefully, silently, I turned the key. Ask any soldier and they'll tell you the same thing – it's always better to play offence than defence.

My left hand on the doorknob, my right hand gripping the knife, arm raised, I readied myself for the attack.

On three . . . Easy does it.

One. Two.

Fuck. BFO. Blinding flash of the obvious.

The thought hit me like a blow to the face. I'd been so focused on myself and my own safety I'd forgotten all about Jack in the room next door, kipping on the sofa.

I may have been trained in close-quarter battle but Wolfie doesn't even know how to kick-box. He'd be no match for a psychopathic killer creeping up on him in the middle of the night with a weapon.

Damn it! Why hadn't he stayed away? I'd told him I could take care of myself. Why did he have to go playing the hero? Why had I let him?

My throat closed up. The old tension built behind my eyes. First Duncan. Now Jack.

I pressed my back against the door. I almost wanted the maggot to finish me off. Put me out of my misery, I thought.

The knob rattled again.

'Ziba. Mac.'

My body took over, my brain fast on its tail. The survival instinct kicking in.

I didn't want to die. I wanted to beat the living shit out of the pox who'd just killed my friend. Standing up, arm raised, dagger at the ready, I flung the door open.

CHAPTER 88

Raguel is in the corner of the room. The voices are loud, the volume in his head turned all the way up.

'Ziba Mac,' he says. 'Ziba Mac.'

CHAPTER 89

I flung the door wide, braced for the assault; jaw clenched, eyes stretched, blood pumping.

'Whoa!' Jack jumped back, his hands raised instinctively to his face. 'It's me. What're you doing? Put the knife down.'

'Jack?' I said, doubting my vision. 'What the fuck?'

'I could say the same to you. What's going on? And would you please put that thing down?'

Scalp prickling, mouth parched, I scanned the room for a man hiding in the shadows, for a smashed window or other signs of forced entry. I sniffed the air for the smell of vinegar and over-ripe fruit – the smell of the Lacerator and of danger. I listened for a floorboard creaking, for a man panting out of sight.

Nothing. Everything was in order. Everything was just as I'd left it. But still . . .

'Ziba. Mac. Look at me.'

Jack's voice was urgent, insistent. Was he trying to tell me something? Was he trying to warn me that the Lacerator was here, concealed in my apartment?

I gave him the once-over. He was standing in front of me in a white T-shirt and a pair of boxers; his hair sticking up, his face rosy from sleep. There were no sweat patches under his arms. He wasn't shaking. His breathing was even. So he wasn't scared then. He wasn't in danger.

And he was alive.

'Thank God,' I gasped.

'I thought you were an atheist.'

I play-punched him on the arm, harder than I meant to.

'Ow. And would you please put that knife down, you're frightening me.'

'I'm frightening *you*? That's rich! What the hell were you doing trying to bust into my room in the middle of the night?'

'I wasn't busting in,' he said in an offended voice. 'I thought he was there.' He didn't need to say who *he* was. 'You were screaming. Really loudly.'

'I was screaming?'

Must have been a nightmare. I get them all the time. Comes with the territory, of course. When you spend your time examining mutilated bodies and trying to see the world through the eyes of society's most evil creations you're going to get the odd bad dream.

The shock of waking the way I had had dislodged last night's particular torments from my mind, but as my heart rate began to slow to normal, snatches came back to me. Being strapped down while my breasts were lacerated with broken glass. Sharp objects being inserted into my rectum, tearing me apart from the inside out. My fingernails being ripped off one by one.

Every killer I'd ever put away had come back to teach me a lesson; to make me their victim; to show me I wasn't as smart as I thought I was.

I knew how they worked. I knew every act of torture was designed to demonstrate their total mastery over me. And I knew the more I screamed, the more I'd excite them.

Yet clearly I'd screamed anyway. So loudly I must have woken Jack, in just the same way I used to wake Duncan. Only when my husband was alive, he held me close, understanding me well enough to know it was best not to say anything. Realising that the warmth of his body and the feel of his arms around me would be enough to chase the monsters away.

But Jack had been on the other side of the door. He hadn't been able to rescue me without scaring me half to death.

CHAPTER 90

'Hey,' Jack said as I stumbled into the living room at 07.00, rubbing sleep out of my eyes and yawning widely. 'Sorry again about earlier. You okay now?'

I was wearing one of Duncan's old pyjama tops. Wolfie was buttoning his shirt by the sofa, his hair damp from the shower. As he moved his arms I caught a glimpse of toned stomach, just visible above his waistband. I felt my cheeks redden.

I turned away before he noticed.

'I'm fine. Just going to fix some coffee. Want one?'

'I've already had. There's a pot in the kitchen,' he said, tucking his shirt into his chinos; the unofficial uniform of the broadsheet reporter.

When I came back he was holding an envelope by the edges. It was addressed to *Ziba Mac*.

'It was on the mat. You think it's from the Lacerator?'

'It's a match to his spider writing,' I said, smiling.

The press statement had obviously done the trick. The killer had taken the bait and got in touch again. Excellent.

I put down my lifer juice, covered the dining table with cling film and snapped on a pair of latex gloves. Then I opened the envelope.

There were two things inside. A letter. And an old train ticket.

It took me a moment to register what I was looking at.

'Shit. This is gold.'

'I was awake all night. Why didn't I hear anything?' Jack said, mashing his forehead. 'He must have been right outside the door. Paddy was right. You should have got a protective detail.'

'Never mind all that. You do realise what this is?'

'What?'

'A return train ticket to Watford. Unstamped.'

'So?'

'Put on some gloves and look at the date. October 1987. Oscar Mike. We are on the move.'

'I still don't get it.'

'7th October 1987. That's the day Samuel Catlin was killed. And this here blows a hole in Lynch's "rock solid" alibi.'

'How d'you figure that?'

'He told the police he'd been on his way to an army physical in Watford at the time of the murder.' I checked my notebook for the details. 'He bought a ticket from Camden Road Station for the 15.09 train. Then he called his mother at 16.30 from Watford to say he'd missed his appointment. He gave his name to the operator. Reversed the charges. The police have the call logs. But he was never there. This ticket was never punched. Lynch can't have been on that train.'

'Could have been an oversight. P'raps the inspector didn't get round to him.'

'The Lacerator sent me this for a reason. He wants me to understand him. It mightn't stand up in a court of law. But he's telling me something. No doubt about it.'

'You're forgetting the phone call.'

'Faked, probably,' I said with a shrug. 'Think about it. All Lynch had to do was get someone else to make the call from Watford. It wouldn't have been difficult. We're not exactly talking *Strangers on a Train* here. All he had to do was drop someone a few quid to do him a favour. Give the operator Lynch's name. Dial the number in Inverness

Street. Easy enough. Then bam, the call would be logged and Lynch would have his alibi.'

Jack scratched his head again. His hair was sticking up even more than usual. 'But his old lady gave a statement to the police. She said she'd spoken to him.'

I glanced at the train ticket in my hand and thought back to my own train journey a week ago. To Theresa Lynch's dying words and my assessment of her before the crash. How I'd deduced she was someone who shut herself off from the world because someone she'd trusted had let her down. Now I knew who that person was. It was Aidan, the son she'd brought up in the ways of the Church but who'd turned to the ways of the Devil.

I looked Jack right in the eye now, the same way Theresa had looked at me just before she died. And then I thought of another look. The one on her face as she grabbed my arm; her face drained white, her eyes stretched wide.

She hadn't been looking at me. She'd been looking into the carriage – at her son, a man she hadn't seen for twenty-five years. A man she alone knew was a killer.

'She knew it wasn't Aidan on the phone and when the police checked out his alibi for Samuel's homicide she must have realised what he'd done,' I said. 'She was covering for him and she kept his secret right up to the moment she was about to face St Peter.

'This was a woman who believed in Heaven, Hell and redemption. She couldn't risk being denied entry through the pearly gates. In her final moments, when she saw her son, she knew she had to confess her sins. It was the only way she could receive the Sacrament of Reconciliation before she met the Angel of Death.'

He did it. You have to tell someone.

'It's taken me this long to figure out what she was confessing to but now I know the answer – not least because the Lacerator seems to have a need to confess too.'

The moment I said the words I knew I was right.

'The Lacerator doesn't just want me to understand him so I'll be able to protect him. Subconsciously he wants absolution too. He may believe in the righteousness of what he's doing but at the same time he's torn – continuously alternating between pride in his actions and the need to atone.

'He's a Catholic,' I said, getting up and pacing the room as it all came together in my head. 'That means he fears eternal damnation. He's revealing all this because deep down he feels guilty and craves forgiveness. Despite all his talk about slaying devils, he knows what he's doing is wrong. This guy could recite the Ten Commandments in his sleep. "Thou shall not kill" figures pretty prominently in the divine list of dos and don'ts. He can try and justify his crimes all he wants but there's no getting away from the fact that murder is a serious no-no in the eyes of God. And that's got to be tearing him apart.'

I paused, an idea growing. I scanned the letter again. Yes, of course! That had to be it! The oil made total sense when you looked at it like that. Why hadn't I thought of it sooner? I'd need to corroborate it, of course. I'm not exactly an expert on these things. But given what I knew about the Lacerator and what he'd written, it did seem to fit.

'Give me a second, Wolfie. I just want to check something out.' I opened my laptop.

My mobile rang just as I entered the search terms.

'MacKenzie,' I said, recognising the number on the screen. 'Excellent. You're kidding! Yes, I do know who that is. Aye, that'd be great, thank you. And thanks so much for keeping me in the loop. By the way, is the boss man in yet? I need to speak to him.'

Fingerling picked up and I gave him the sitrep about the Lacerator's latest package. But I decided to wait till I saw him before telling him my theory about the oil. I wanted to be sure of my facts first; to make sure I wasn't barking at the wrong dog, as my father used to say. He never did get the hang of English idioms.

'The DI's on his way over with Aidan Lynch's murder file,' I said to Jack once I'd hung up. 'But before he gets here you and I need to have a little chat.'

I took a deep breath. How was he going to react when I told him he'd got it wrong, that I really was being followed by the driver of a silver Honda?

I'd thought it was the Lacerator. But now I knew better. The guys at the Yard had run the plates through ANPR and traced it to someone I'd never suspected.

Maisie Turner. Jack's crazy ex.

CHAPTER 91

'You're kidding?' Jack said. 'And she was really following us the other night after we left the restaurant?'

I nodded. 'I saw her tailing me yesterday afternoon too. And then I spotted her parked under my window last night before I hit the sack. Not that I realised it was Crazy M. At the time I thought it might be my other stalker.'

'The Lacerator?'

'Aye, unless you know of anyone else who's got a thing for me.' Bad choice of words, I thought, colouring. 'Anyway, that's why I asked the Yard to check it out. I wanted to be sure,' I added quickly.

Jack shook his head. 'I don't get it. Why would she be following you? It's me she's obsessed with.'

'She must have been tracking you. Online too, probably. Fits the profile and ties in with all those phone calls you've been getting. The girl's clearly fixated. I'm guessing she saw us together and assumed we were dating. It would make sense for her to make a leap like that. Jealousy and obsession go together. So suddenly I'm a threat and she starts following *me*. I don't know. Perhaps she's been building up the courage to bump me off so she can have you all to herself.' I arched an eyebrow.

He looked horrified.

'Only kidding,' I said with a grin. 'More likely she just wants to suss out who she sees as the competition.'

'Shit, Mac. Why didn't you say anything?'

'I did, if you remember. And what was it you told me? Oh yes, that's right. I was overreacting and the world's not as dangerous as I think it is.'

'Christ, I'm so sorry. I feel like a prat.'

I smiled, softening. 'Don't beat yourself up. I do have a tendency to jump to conclusions. And Maisie's going to be given a bit of a talking to by some uniforms, so hopefully that should put an end to it.'

'Wonder if they fancy telling her to stop the phone calls to me while they're at it,' he said, smiling back.

The bell rang. Fingerling had arrived. He came in, wiping his feet several times on the doormat and peering around inside with his usual nosiness. Jack's sheets were still on the sofa. Fingerling looked between us, smirking slightly.

I made a swift introduction. 'This is Jack Wolfe, Duncan's best friend and my self-appointed bodyguard until our Lacerator friend's been caught.'

Scotland Yard's a tinderbox for gossip. Best to quash the rumours before they started.

'Good to meet you,' Jack said, not getting up. His arm was spread over the back of the chair next to him. He was marking his territory, making no move to walk out on the scoop of a lifetime.

I hid my smile and nipped into the kitchen to brew a fresh pot of coffee. When I came back Fingerling was sitting at the head of the table, the Lacerator's latest communiqué in one hand, the old train ticket in the other.

He passed me the murder file I'd asked him to bring and I flicked through it till I got to the bit I was looking for.

'That ticket you're holding reinforces our theory that Lynch is the London Lacerator,' I said when I'd read through it. 'And if he is Aidan, then it explains why he killed again the day of the train crash after such a long cooling-off period.'

'How so?' asked Fingerling.

'We know his mother, Theresa, was killed on the train. It can't be a coincidence that he chose the day of the crash to strike again after all this time. It took days for the papers to publish news of Theresa's death. The only way the Lacerator would have known so soon what had happened to her is if he'd seen her die. That puts them in the same carriage. We know from his behaviour towards me that he's obsessive and compulsive. A stalker personality. I wouldn't be surprised if he'd been following his old lady for years. It'd certainly explain why he was there that evening and how he'd have seen what went down.

'Do you remember me saying at the press conference there would have been some sort of precipitating stressor – a dramatic change or event in his life?'

Fingerling nodded.

'Well, seeing his mother die is pretty big as far as these things go.'

'Mm.' Fingerling massaged the inside of his skinny wrist with his thumb.

'That's not all,' I said, talking even faster than usual. 'If I'm right about Theresa alibiing Aidan out re the collect call from Watford Station, there's a chance she might have done something else as well.'

I opened the file he'd brought, checking my facts as I spoke. 'It's possible Theresa lied when she made the positive ident in eighty-seven. The body was badly burned – almost unrecognisable. The blood type matched Aidan's but it was Type O. That's the most common blood group – 47 per cent of the population are Type O. Apart from the blood work, the other reasons the police concluded the corpse was Lynch's was because of where he was found and because his mother confirmed it was her son.'

'But as you said, she could have given a false ID,' said Fingerling.

'Exactly. The investigating officers didn't do anything wrong. They were simply acting on the information they had at the time. Dental records were out because the vic's teeth were too badly damaged during the attack. And back in 1987, DNA testing was in its infancy, never mind crazy expensive. You didn't use it unless you had to. But the decision not to has meant for a quarter of a century Aidan Lynch has been able to act like a ghost and kill with impunity.'

'It's like something out of a story,' said Jack, clearly thinking of the one he was going to write. I'd gag him later – his scoop would have to wait.

'Truth's stranger than fiction,' I said. 'Something similar happened with Australia's first known serial killer. The police mistakenly thought one of his victims was him. He was only caught in the end because he ran into an ex co-worker in the street five months after everyone thought he'd been bumped off.'

'Plonker,' said Jack with a short laugh.

I smiled but Nigel Fingerling's face was serious. He sighed deeply and dug his phone out of his trouser pocket.

'It all adds up very nicely.' He stroked his chin. 'But there's only one way we're going to know for sure whether we're right.'

'By exhuming the corpse,' I said, making a clucking noise with my tongue.

Fingerling exhaled slowly out of the side of his mouth. No one likes giving an exhumation order – the fall-out's never good.

I glanced at Jack. He was licking his lips, his feet were bouncing. Out of the three of us he was the only one who was excited.

'I realise you've got first dibs on the story of the decade.' I eyeballed him. 'But you're going to have to hold off until I give the go-ahead.

'The Lacerator's toying with us. He has been ever since he butchered the poor sod he passed off as himself twenty-five years ago. And he's been ahead of us this whole time. But the game's just changed in our favour.

'If we play it right, we could finally net this sonofabitch. But to do that we mustn't show our hand. Not least because, if I'm right, he might have just revealed his. And I'm not talking about confirming his identity.'

CHAPTER 92

I read the letter again while Fingerling put a call in to the Yard to get the process moving on securing a Home Office licence for the exhumation. There were seven paragraphs in all, just like the first one.

Dear Ziba Mac,
How could you think I'm a pervert? A paedophile. That's the word you used on the television last night.

You accused me of being a dirty old man touching children where he shouldn't. I am a saviour of children, Ziba Mac, not a destroyer. The enclosed item will prove that.

I need you to understand me otherwise how can I trust you to protect me?

I believed it would end with the Devil in the woods. But the Lord has shown me there is still more work to be done.

The sins of the fathers must be accounted for. The collusion of the guilty must not go unchecked.

I await the time when the sun will be turned to darkness and the moon to blood – and so must you.

In nomine Patris et Filii et Spiritus Sancti,
Raguel.

As Jack shifted position, his arm brushed against my shoulder making my stomach flutter.

Enough with this. I've been carrying on like a teenager ever since that frigging dream, I thought. It's got to stop.

Fingerling hung up the phone and checked his watch.

'Let's finish up here and go brief the team,' he said. 'What's your take on all this, MacKenzie?'

He tilted his head at the letter in my hand.

'Well, our plan worked. He took the bait.'

Fingerling nodded. 'Guess the media has its uses. Putting it out there that our friend's a paedo wasn't a bad call.'

I smiled. That was quite the compliment coming from him.

'Let's go through the letter. There are some telling phrases in here.'

'Go on then, Dr Brussel.'

I smiled again but this time I kept it hidden. Most people have heard of the Mad Bomber, but James Brussel is less widely known. For all his talk the day we met, Fingerling clearly rated profiling more than he let on.

'Okay. First off: *How could you think I'm a pervert?*

'There's real emotion in that line. Calling him a paedophile's the worst thing we could say. And this bit: *a dirty old man touching children where he shouldn't.* Emphasis on "old". He's thinking of his own abuser. Another thing to bolster the theory his grandad molested him and that the previous homicides were about transference. Until yesterday he attacked men who reminded him of Grant Taplow. Until he was ready to go after the true target of his rage.'

'Slow down would you? You're talking faster than I can write.' Fingerling shook out his hand the same way Paddy had done a little over twelve hours ago sitting in the exact same spot.

'*I am a saviour of children, Ziba Mac, not a destroyer,*' I said, watching him write to make sure he was getting it all down. 'Using my name reinforces the connection between us. It also shows how much he wants me to understand him – and how disappointed he is that I don't.

'As well as that, it clarifies his motivation, which up till now we've only been able to guess at. Clearly he believes that by killing supposed paedophiles he's saving kids at risk of assault. While the word "saviour" (which is obviously biblical) ties in with his sense of a higher purpose.'

'Like a calling?'

'Exactly.'

'And the enclosed item he mentions is the train ticket presumably?'

'Aye. He must think that if I knew he killed Samuel I'd understand he was trying to save him. And that he couldn't possibly be a child abuser.'

Fingerling made a face. 'Not sure I follow his logic.'

'Ah well, the guy's got a few screws loose in his noggin.'

Jack caught my eye and grinned. Fingerling's face didn't move. We may have been getting on better but that didn't mean we got each other.

'What's this bit mean?' He leaned over my shoulder. 08.15 in the morning and already his breath smelled stale. *I believed it would end with the Devil in the woods.*'

'It's a reference to the care home where Taplow lived.'

'Huh?'

'The Cedars. Type of tree. Woods.'

'Oh, I get it. Ha ha. Very funny. Not. Anything else?' He checked his watch again.

'Yes.' I paused. 'I think I know why he sprinkles his victims with olive oil.'

Fingerling's face lit up. Flashbulb eyes.

'The devil's in the detail.'

'Go on.' He leaned forward.

Jack looked at us both, confused. Scotland Yard had never shared this aspect of the Lacerator's signature with the media.

'You don't get to use this till I give you the okay,' I said to him. 'Understood?'

'Course.' He was practically drooling. Right now he'd have agreed to anything. This story was going to make his name.

I looked at Fingerling. He gave a nod. I was good to go.

'Olive oil crops up a lot in the Bible. It's a symbol for the Holy Spirit. And it has a special place in the Catholic Church. Priests use it at baptisms, confirmations and to anoint the sick. So for sacramental rituals. But that's not all it's used for.' I paused again. 'It's also used during exorcisms. To cast out the Devil.'

Fingerling's jaw dropped. His head started bobbing up and down like the dog in that insurance ad.

'It isn't enough for the Lacerator to just kill men that remind him of his grandfather. Or to punish them by slicing off their genitals. He also needs to drive out their evil spirit. Which is where the oil comes in.'

'Brilliant,' said Fingerling, clapping his hands together.

Second compliment I'd got out of him. Effusive too.

'That's not all,' I said, pushing the letter closer to him. '*But the Lord has shown me there is still more work to be done. The sins of the fathers must be accounted for. The collusion of the guilty must not go unchecked.*'

'He'll kill again. His spree isn't going to end with Grant Taplow.

'And from what he's written, his next victim will be someone he knows. A "colluder": someone he believes facilitates abuse.'

I looked at Fingerling, right in the eye.

'I think I know when he's going to strike next. We just need to figure out who he's planning to kill.

'And how we're going to stop him.'

CHAPTER 93

Raguel watches from a concealed vantage point across the street as the sinner approaches the front door, takes out his key and puts it in the latch.

The old heat floods through him. His blood begins to sing. But it's not time yet.

Though his muscles strain to act, Raguel must wait until the moon is big in the sky and tinged with red. A sign from the Lord that all will be well, as it was that first time when he threw off the shackles of his former self.

He takes out his loop of string and works it into one shape, then another; his fingers moving fast to slow his thoughts down.

The light from a television flickers in the front window, the silhouette of the sinner visible through the curtains. Raguel's eyes fix on it as he twists and tucks his string, visualising his attack. The voices start to whisper, sibilant and loud. Raguel wraps the string seven times round his forefinger, brings it to his lips and makes the sign of the cross.

Then he goes round to the back and slips inside the house.

CHAPTER 94

The shadowy figure is with him, a spear in his hand. A roaring lion floats in front of them.

Raguel will rescue the world from the domain of darkness and the demons will be cast into the eternal flames.

His vehemence is blazing, his skin hot with it.

'You're so full of rage, it's not good for you,' Katie said that last time. 'You really need to start going to the anger-management programme we signed you up for. I'll have a word with your new care worker when I hand your file over to her.'

'I don't need anger management and I don't want a new care worker. I don't see why you have to leave. I'm used to you now,' he'd said.

Katie had sighed and looked him in the eye, though she'd been careful not to touch him. Touching patients was strictly against Skylark Day Care Centre's policy.

'You'll get used to someone else,' she'd said, speaking slowly, the way she might have if she were talking to a pre-schooler. 'You weren't sure about me at first and look how well we get on now. In the meantime, you must stop missing your programmes. You agreed to the plan in your Community Treatment Order when you sat down with your support team in January. We can't help you on a non-residential basis if you don't meet your obligations.'

Raguel had taken the warning on board. He'd understood the undertone and the threat. He wasn't going to be locked up again. No one was going to clip his wings. So he'd done what he was told and gone to the wretched therapy groups.

Art Group where he was encouraged to 'express his feelings' with glue, tissue paper and paint. Relaxation Group where he lay on a bean-bag listening to pagan music doing breathing exercises. And Talking Group where he sat in a circle and made up stuff about himself.

He'd done what he'd needed to do so he could be free. Free to do the Lord's work: annihilating the wicked, punishing sinners. Ironically though, it hadn't started off with punishment. It had actually all begun with saving a child.

He'd met Samuel Catlin around the time he first started hearing the voices; a couple of months before he failed his army medical and was sent home, branded 'unfit', though he worked out for hours every day.

'Trust in the Lord,' his mother had told him. 'Everything happens for a reason.'

'I'm going to be a soldier like you when I grow up,' Samuel said to Aidan, following him round the hall where the Cub Scouts met.

Aidan was setting out balls and cones for the next game. Samuel was carrying an armful of coloured hoops.

'He worships you, that kid does.' The Den Leader smiled, watching the two of them.

'He's my little helper, aren't you?' Aidan said to Samuel, who grinned at him, poking his tongue through the space where his baby teeth had fallen out.

Aidan smiled back at him. It felt good having someone look up to him, made him feel warm inside. And protective.

'My grandad's taking me camping this weekend,' Samuel told Aidan a week later. 'He's always arranging treats like that for the two of us.' He dug about in his little blue rucksack covered in dinosaur stickers and pulled out a Mars bar with another of his big, gap-toothed grins.

'He gave this to me too. And it's not even a fun-size. He's super cool, my grandad.'

Aidan didn't smile back this time. Under his shirt his belly was filling with worms. That's when the voices started.

To begin with they were mostly soft whispers; more hissing and shushing than actual words. But gradually they became clearer until finally he was able to decipher what they were trying to tell him.

If he hadn't been such a religious man he might have been scared, but his mother had taught him his Bible well. He knew from their nightly readings that all prophets heard God's voice. And some even saw miraculous things. Which is why he wasn't worried when he saw the hedge outside the Scout lodge glowing orange and a voice calling to him from out of it.

'Here I am,' he'd said – the same words Moses had spoken when he'd heard the voice of God calling to him from Mount Horeb.

'I have seen the suffering of my child, Samuel Catlin,' said the Lord. 'His cry has reached me. A demon is coming to him in the dark as one came to you. You must rescue him and bring him up out of his misery. Put your hands around his throat and press hard until his soul returns to me that I may comfort him and keep him safe.'

'I can't,' Aidan said.

He was the Lord's servant but what he was being asked to do broke a sacred law. Cain had been cursed for spilling Abel's blood. How could Aidan end Samuel's life without damning his soul?

'Trust in me. I will send my angel to protect you,' the voice in the burning bush said.

Aidan had walked into the room where the Scouts were gathered and looked at Samuel sitting on the floor with the other boys. He was eating another Mars bar. He brought one every week now.

Aidan had learned the hard way what Mars bars meant. They were a bribe for silence, a payment for services rendered.

Samuel stuffed in the last mouthful of chocolate and grinned at Aidan.

'Can I help you set up for the next session?' he said, hurrying over to his hero.

Sure, he seemed like a happy kid on the outside. He got on with everyone and was always smiling. But Aidan knew all about covering up and making your face unreadable. The voice in the bush was right. Samuel was suffering and Aidan needed to end his pain. He needed to protect him from what was happening to him.

Two days later he helped Samuel's soul find its way to Heaven and afterwards, Aidan's mother protected him from the police. She must have known it wasn't Aidan's voice at the end of the phone from Watford Station. But that's not what she told the cops.

The Lord had sent him a guardian angel just as he'd promised. And his mother had been right, everything does happen for a reason.

After Samuel's spirit had departed on its journey into the next life, Aidan raised his eyes to the dark sky and a shaft of light projected towards him through the clouds. The Almighty was pleased with his work.

He touched his middle finger to his forehead and made the sign of the cross above his eyes, and as he did the voices whispered, 'Thou shalt henceforward be called by a new name. Thou shalt be called Raguel for the Lord delighteth in thee.'

Aidan Lynch was dead. He had transformed into an archangel. And he'd just carried out his first holy mission.

CHAPTER 95

Raguel would stride the earth for another two years carrying out the Lord's vengeance. His mission had changed since Samuel, though. Now he was charged with executing sinners rather than releasing the innocent from the chains of their oppression.

It all began properly on a winter's evening in late December. He found the transgressor in a homosexual bar, searching for young blood to corrupt.

Raguel had known where to go. He knew where perverts spent their time and what the worst of men liked to do to each other.

When Raguel saw the sinner, his soul screamed. He looked just like Grandad.

'Destroy that which hath destroyed the innocent,' whispered the voices. 'Lay waste to those who sin against me.'

Raguel approached the demon and enticed him back to Inverness Street. His parents were away for the weekend so he had the house to himself. Once home, he offered the demon his heathen father's whisky and waited till he'd passed out drunk on the living-room floor. Then he raised his knife. He knew what to do.

'*In nomine Patris et Filii et Spiritus Sancti*,' he said as he drove the blade through the fiend's throat. Except Satan confounded him. Raguel missed his mark, and the demon came to.

His eyes rolled. Horns sprouted from his head and enormous bat wings grew out of his shoulders. The Evil One grappled with Raguel.

'Release me, Serpent. You can't hurt me any more,' he screamed, unleashing a barrage of blows with his knife until the demon fell to the ground, blood gushing from his chest.

Raguel set about trying to remove the instrument of his wickedness. But by now his blade was blunt from the attack. Exhausted and covered in blood, he hacked away at the demon's scrotum for hours before finally collapsing asleep over his work.

The morning light woke him.

'No!' he shouted in a panic.

His parents would be home imminently. There was blood everywhere.

'Loyal servant,' whispered the voices, and the room filled with a bright celestial light. A harp began to play with ten strings. 'It is time for a new song.'

An angel materialised in front of Raguel and beckoned for him to follow her and bring the sinner's body.

'Fire,' whispered the voices. 'Brimstone.'

Raguel hauled the corpse into the bath and ran back downstairs to fetch matches and the can of paint thinner from the utility room cupboard. Aidan Lynch knew all about starting fires. He might be dead but he'd passed his knowledge on to Raguel, though this was the first time either of them had burned a corpse.

Afterwards Raguel fled, consumed again by guilt over what he'd done. The Lord had told him to kill the demon, but the Lord had also written that murder was a sin.

Though that's not the only thing he felt guilty about. There was another, secret reason he couldn't even admit to himself. The voices knew though. And at night they'd torment him about the dark serpent coiled in his heart.

He found the article on a Sunday. God's day. He was sleeping on the streets now, on the other side of town, relying on the kindness of strangers for food.

The newspaper was lying in the gutter, and on the front page, a picture of him in his cadet uniform beneath the headline: *Mutilated Man Named.*

Raguel's mouth dropped open as he read the article. Again, his mother had protected him.

She'd identified the burned corpse in the bath as Aidan, although the man was a good foot shorter than he was. She was his guardian angel. She'd covered for him with Samuel Catlin and she'd covered for him now.

She must be proud of me, he thought, heart swelling.

She was a religious woman. She must realise he was doing the Lord's work and that her role was to keep him safe. It was a sign he must continue with his holy mission.

In time, he returned to Camden to be close to her, safe in the knowledge no one would recognise him now. His long hair, scraggy beard and hollowed-out features were the perfect disguise. The Catacombs, the perfect hideaway.

Hunting demons became a nightly occupation. But Grandad was a slippery snake. Months could go by without finding him. Though when he did, Raguel showed no mercy.

Soon, plunging a blade into an unsuspecting man's eyes became all he could think about. No one would ever tell him again to look at them while they checked he was healthy. He was Raguel now. The Fire of God.

After two years on the streets he was picked up by the police, who told him he was schizophrenic and that the cuts on his body and the blood on his clothes meant he was a danger to himself. They put him in a cell for 'his own protection' until they could find him a bed in a psych ward, which is where he was forced to stay for more than two decades.

But now Raguel is free thanks to his Community Treatment Order. He can live on his own so long as he sticks to his therapeutic programme.

Like the prophets, Raguel never questioned God's will. And he knew that one day he'd annihilate Satan himself. But the Devil had to be his seventh kill: that way it would be perfect and hallowed.

But it isn't over yet, thinks Raguel as he closes the back door of Marcus Lynch's house, which the Lord caused to be unlocked, and slips off his polished Clarks lace-ups.

Raguel hates his father. He's to blame for what happened with Grandad. He arranged that sleepover and so much of what followed. Now it's time for him to pay for the sins he committed.

Because as Jesus said, ignoring the needs of others is the greatest sin of all.

CHAPTER 96

Raguel tiptoes in white-socked feet through the kitchen into the hall where the noise from the television in the living room is blaring, just like it used to when he lived here all those years ago as someone else.

He's performed his rituals. Seven bumps of coke. Seven Our Fathers. Seven signs of the cross from head to chest to shoulders, *In nomine Patris et Filii et Spiritus Sancti.* But he pauses for a moment before entering the room. There's another prayer he needs to say before he can continue. Get anything wrong and all will fail.

'I am your angel, the slayer of the fallen. Rise up in me, O Lord, and deliver them up to the power of my sword.'

He whispers the words, although he knows his father won't hear him. The television's turned up all the way. Marcus Lynch has been hard of hearing for as long as Raguel can remember.

Raguel sidles up to the edge of the living-room door. It's half-open, wide enough for him to see inside without being seen.

His father is still in his work clothes, sitting in an armchair with his back to the door. He's reading the paper. Funny, thinks Raguel, it looks like he's reading a broadsheet. He always used to read the *Daily Mail.*

Raguel pulls out his knife. He unsheathes it slowly so as not to make a sound. The light glints off the blade.

'Do it,' whisper the voices. 'Do it. Do it.'

Raguel closes his eyes for a second and takes a breath, steadying himself. Preparing.

The old excitement bulges in his veins. It feels like a suppressed laugh, like he's swallowed happiness and it's filling him up to bursting point.

This kill will be different, more difficult. Unlike his other victims, Marcus Lynch is not inebriated. But Raguel still has the element of surprise on his side.

'One, two, three, four, five, six, seven.'

He counts in his head then pushes open the door, dagger raised in his right hand, body lifted up on angel wings. He flies at the sinner with a battle cry, an angel's scream, a warrior's roar.

'*Deus Vult!*'

Mid-air, a thought flits into his head. He'd been watching his father for a good few minutes before he pounced. But in that time Marcus Lynch hasn't turned the page of his newspaper once.

CHAPTER 97

It isn't just that Marcus Lynch hasn't turned the page of his newspaper, or that he's reading a paper he's never read before, that's odd. There's also a strange glint of light coming off the pages.

If Raguel hadn't been hurling himself at his father with a raised knife in his hand he might have wondered more about these things. He might have realised something wasn't quite right. But that thought doesn't make it through to his cerebral cortex until Marcus Lynch leaps up and spins round to face him in one fluid movement like an extra from a martial arts movie.

Raguel hasn't seen his father for years. People's faces change over time but unless they've had plastic surgery they look older rather than younger. And the man coming at him now is definitely a lot younger than Marcus Lynch should be.

It happens in freeze-frames. Time has slowed. And yet Raguel still doesn't compute what's actually going on.

The man, who surely can't be his father, is striking him in the face. A left then right hook followed through with a kick to his calf that throws him off balance. Raguel wobbles and tries to stab the man but he drops his front knee on to Raguel's foot and grabs the back of his leg, projecting his weight forwards causing Raguel to tumble to the ground.

Raguel makes another attempt to stab the man but his knee is now on Raguel's stomach, pinning him down so all the avenging archangel can do is flail about like a mewling infant.

Someone leaps out of the shadows and puts their foot on his wrist while another wrestles the knife out of his hand.

'Aidan Lynch, you are under arrest for breaking and entering and for attempted murder,' says the man he tried to kill.

Raguel looks up at him as the handcuffs are snapped on. The man's skin is white and pimply. There are dark circles under his eyes. And despite the muscles in his arms his wrists are as skinny as a girl's.

Raguel's mouth drops open in recognition. He didn't see the detective at the press conferences he watched on the television in the rec room while waiting to be called for his therapy sessions. But he was on the telly the other night, standing just behind Ziba Mac when she told everyone he was a paedophile.

How had he not realised it was an impersonator in his father's chair rather than Marcus Lynch himself? How has this happened?

DI Fingerling is still talking.

'That's just for starters,' he's saying. 'You can be sure we'll be adding a few more charges to your rap sheet when we get you down to the Yard. Now, on your feet, you evil bastard,' he says, hauling Raguel upright.

The prayer forms on Raguel's lips.

Our Father who art in heaven—

The words stop. They dry up, useless and irrelevant. Why has the Lord forsaken him? Why has he broken his covenant, his promise to protect his servant?

Raguel's fingers twitch behind his back. He's counting to seven, seven times while being pushed towards the living-room door. Is this some sort of test?

Job 23:8–10

If I go east, He is not there, and if I go west, I cannot perceive Him. When He is at work to the north, I cannot see Him; when He turns south, I cannot find Him. Yet He knows the way I have taken; when he has tested me, I will emerge as pure gold.

Yes, it must be a test of his faith as Christ himself was tested in the desert. Raguel's shoulders drop. The Lord's Prayer comes easily to him now.

He is in the entranceway by the foot of the stairs, flanked on either side by armed police officers, being frog-marched out of the house.

Thy kingdom come, thy will be done—

'Aidan?' says a voice from the top step. There's a quiver in it. His old name breaks in the speaker's mouth.

Raguel turns his head. It's his father, the foul Judas. And there are tears in his eyes.

'Out, vile Serpent! You betrayer of innocent blood,' Raguel starts to say, his pitch rising with each word as the whispering voices urge him on.

He stops abruptly. Ziba Mac has stepped into view. She puts her hand on his father's arm. She must have been with him this whole time.

'Don't listen to him,' she says, turning her back on Raguel. 'He doesn't know what he's saying.'

A fiend grips Raguel by the throat. His breath turns solid in his lungs.

His guardian angel has forsaken him and sided with the Devil. There's a clock on the wall. The time is 9.13 p.m. Thirteen minutes past the hour. 9+1+3=13.

This moment belongs to Beelzebub. The Evil One is in charge. Raguel has been cast out of Heaven and is falling through the earth. The numbers won't save him now. He isn't even Raguel any more. He isn't the Fire of God.

He's Aidan Lynch again. A little boy all alone and afraid of the dark.

CHAPTER 98

As Aidan Lynch glanced up, I remembered where I'd seen him before. His expression was different but the pleats down his shirtsleeves were as sharp as they had been the day I'd caught him looking at me on the train.

Not that I was the one he'd been looking at. He'd been looking at his mother, Theresa. He hadn't just seen her die. He'd also seen her before the train had crashed – twenty-five years to the day that he'd murdered Samuel Catlin, which, as it turns out, wasn't a mercy killing after all.

Despite what Aidan Lynch may have thought, Samuel had never been abused. Apparently this was an angle the police had explored carefully during the initial investigation. He'd been a happy kid, a golden-haired boy with everything to live for.

I watched the officers lead Lynch out of the door and covered my nose. I could smell the guy from thirty feet away. The smell of vinegar, refuse and over-ripe fruit coming from a chemical in his sweat, as I learned later. TMHA – trans-3-methyl-2-hexenoic acid – a schizophrenic reaction caused by metabolic changes triggered by the disorder.

Nigel Fingerling gave me a salute before following Lynch. I smiled back. We'd got our win in the end.

'I think I know when he's going to strike next,' I'd said to him and Jack at my flat. 'Now we just need to figure out who he's planning to kill. And how we're going to stop him.'

'I'm guessing the timing has something to do with this business about the sun turning to darkness and the moon to blood, whatever the hell that means,' Fingerling had said, referencing the Lacerator's letter.

'I think he's talking about the supermoon lunar eclipse,' I'd said. 'The papers say on Sunday the moon's going to look blood red and much bigger and brighter than normal.'

'Great, another murder in less than two weeks. The DCI's going to love me.'

'He will if we prevent it from happening. But to do that we need to figure out who the next target is.'

It was a puzzle that would take more than one person to solve. I didn't need Nigel Fingerling to make any wisecracks about there being no 'i' in 'team' to work that one out and in the end it really was all down to a group effort.

Jack reminded me what Aidan Lynch's childhood friend had said about him burning down his father's toolshed. The graphologist noticed the extra pressure the Lacerator had applied to the page when he wrote about the 'sins of the fathers'. And my revised profile suggested his next victim would be someone he knew, given he'd finally built up the courage to target his abuser. His subsequent killing would be equally personal – there'd be no going back to strangers and stand-ins.

Despite our concerns, Marcus Lynch didn't need too much persuading to help set the trap once he'd accepted his son was coming after him. Although Aidan had never found out Marcus wasn't his real father, the tension between them cut deep.

'He and his mother were always tight.' Marcus was opening up now there was nothing left to hide. 'She brainwashed him with all that religious claptrap. I was a non-believer and he hated me for it. And if I'm honest, although I tried, I never really bonded with him. Poor kid must have sensed that. Theresa broke it off with her lover and begged my forgiveness. But Aidan was a constant reminder of her betrayal. I couldn't move past it.

'Having said that, I wish to anything that Aidan had told us what his grandfather was doing to him. We could have done something. Christ, how could I not have seen what was going on?'

I thought about Aidan Lynch and I thought about my own dark places. Keeping secrets from the people you're close to is easier than you might think. But some secrets aren't meant to be kept. They can destroy you as much as those you're hiding them from.

'Did you suspect Aidan had been involved in Samuel Catlin's death?' I asked him. 'Is that why you reacted the way you did when I asked if you knew what Theresa had been trying to tell me on the train?'

Marcus looked confused for a moment, then his face cleared in recollection.

'Oh, that. I'm not sure I should say, you being with the police and all.'

'What if I promise to keep it just between us?'

'Well, okay then,' he said in a way that suggested he wanted to unburden himself. 'Look, I'm not proud of this but here it is. Our neighbour up the street has a Maserati. Cost a fortune. He loves it. He's always tinkering about with it. And then I manage to go and ding it the day before Theresa was killed. It was a stupid accident and I didn't say anything. It'd muck up my no-claims bonus if I put a claim in and I couldn't afford to settle up with him directly.

'Theresa kept pushing me to come clean. I realise it sounds stupid now, after everything you've just told me about Aidan, but at the time I thought that's what she was talking about.'

'Your secret's safe with me.' I smiled. 'Though for what it's worth I'd own up if I were you. You'll feel better if you do.'

'Maybe,' he said with a shrug.

'Now, let's recap how things are going to work this evening. We're going to use you as bait and then once you're inside, we'll take over. Still happy with that?'

He nodded.

Fingerling had asked me to go over our plan with Marcus. He'd claimed it'd be best coming from me given how well I understand people. His words, not mine.

I'd smiled. He wouldn't have said that a week ago.

In the end the sting played out like a special ops mission right down to the ruse we used to get our guy.

Fingerling had insisted on playing the part of Marcus.

'I never get to use my jiu-jitsu skills in real-life situations any more,' he said.

'I'd forgotten you were a martial arts expert. Didn't the DCI say you were a black belt or something?'

'Better believe it.' He made a few exaggerated strike movements with his hands.

And so, while armed officers took up strategic positions, he'd sat in the living room disguised as Marcus Lynch with a small mirror carefully positioned inside the pages of his newspaper so he could see the Lacerator sneaking up on him.

I suggested turning the television up high to give the killer a false sense of security. We didn't need to listen out for him slipping into the house. There were hidden cameras set up in every room. When he came, if he came, we'd be ready for him.

And we were.

CHAPTER 99

I didn't get to sit down with Aidan Lynch till after he'd been charged.

'Got him talking in the end,' Fingerling said, coming to find me in the observation room, several files tucked under his arm.

'So I see.' I heaved myself up from behind the TV monitor where I'd been watching the interview play out.

Lynch clearly had a need to offload – not surprising really. It can be a relief for an offender to confess after years hiding from the law. Often, they like to brag too.

But would he talk to me?

He was bound to think I'd betrayed him. The way he saw it, I was part of his holy bloody mission. His guardian angel. And I'd just gone and jammed a blade between his shoulders.

I had to give it a go though.

To fight evil, you have to know how evil thinks. And this was literally a once-in-a-lifetime opportunity. Not just to interview a serial killer – I've done that plenty of times – but to speak to one who felt he shared a special bond with me.

I knew the basics about his background already. The abuse. The feeling he hadn't been protected by his old man. The schizophrenia. And I knew what he'd done.

What I didn't know was why. What had set him off on his initial spree back in eighty-seven after Samuel's murder?

His damaged childhood was a crucible for his future behaviour, but there had to be more to it than that. Sadly, there are plenty of kids who go through the same sort of thing Lynch did. But they don't all grow up to be monsters.

So why had he?

Aidan Lynch was bat-shit crazy. He was hardly going to give me a profound analysis of his thoughts and actions. But talking to him would enable me to see how his mind worked. And get to grips with his inner logic.

I knocked before I went into the interview room. Basic courtesy builds rapport.

'Good evening, Raguel.' I deliberately used the moniker he'd chosen for himself, a way of re-cementing the connection he'd thought we had. 'May I sit down?'

'Ziba Mac?' he said in a wary voice, blinking rapidly.

His head was tilted slightly, as though he were listening to something on the other side of the room. Instinctively, I turned round. There was nothing there.

'I had to see you,' I said, my hands open in a consciously supplicating gesture, trying to spin my betrayal into an act of loyalty. 'Forgive me. This is the only way I could think of.'

'You're a false angel. I saw you. You were there by Satan's side.'

He was talking about Marcus. He'd dispatched his other Satan three days ago.

I had my quote ready, right out of the King James Bible – Lynch's version of choice.

'Let not your heart be troubled. Ye believe in God, believe also in me.'

I could imagine Fingerling next door mouthing, 'What the fuck?' at the TV monitor, but my speech did the trick.

Lynch's shoulders dropped. His face relaxed into a smile.

'John 14:1,' he said, eyes all lit up. 'I am the way, the truth, and the life. No man cometh unto the Father, but by me.'

I smiled. We were in business.

CHAPTER 100

'I need to understand you, Raguel. It's the only way I can protect you. The game you set up for me was so clever,' I said, indulging him, rapport-building again. 'I know how much you suffered as a child; how out of control and alone you must have felt. But I know so little about your work. Will you tell me about it?'

Relating to someone who's committed this level of depraved violence isn't easy. But the empathy's a necessary part of getting them to open up. So is talking their talk.

Lynch glanced down at his hands gripping the edge of the table. The skin on his face was stretched tight across the bones. His eyebrows were thick and angular above his glasses. His blond buzz-cut was starting to grey.

He was wearing a short-sleeved, button-down shirt and a knitted navy tie. His biceps were well defined but not excessively large. His arms were pale and freckled, his fingernails clean and trimmed.

All in all, this wasn't a guy you'd look at twice if you passed him in Costco. Apart from the mark on his iris, his appearance was ordinary in every way. This wasn't Hannibal Lecter or a cartoon-strip villain, but someone real and everyday.

It was clear from his actions we were dealing with a man broken and tormented by his past. But a man nonetheless. A human being with urges that both shamed and drove him.

'I want you to understand me, Ziba Mac.' He raised his eyes to me. 'When I saw you at the top of those stairs, I was so sure you belonged to the Devil. It broke my heart. But I made a mistake. I should have had more faith. Forgive me, Lord.'

He made the sign of the cross seven times then spoke again.

'What do you want to know?'

'Tell me about the first sinner you brought to justice,' I said, deliberately using his language. 'What made you do it?'

He answered without hesitation. 'God spoke to me, of course. Is that a trick question?'

His schizophrenia obviously had a role, but hallucinations were only part of this story. There had to have been a pre-kill stressor. A dramatic event that triggered a deep-seated emotional response, causing him to lash out.

'God works in mysterious ways. I realise he spoke to you. But he'll have done something else too. Something happened before you executed the first sinner. Something that made you angry or upset.'

'Do you mean like the man who mugged me?'

My flesh tingled. That's exactly what I meant.

'Yes. Can you tell me about it?'

'I was walking home. It was dark. The voices were in my head. They'd been there for a while. Though they'd been getting stronger since Samuel. They'd get so loud sometimes, they stopped me sleeping. I tried smoking cannabis to help me relax. But it didn't help. Nothing did.'

The onset of psychosis, I thought. Hitting the hippie lettuce was the very worst thing this guy could have done.

'As I turned onto the street where I lived, a man jumped me. He was big. He had a knife. He held it to my throat and made me give him my wallet. I handed it over but he knocked me to the ground anyway, kicking me hard. Everything was in turmoil. I was shaking all over.'

'That must have been awful for you. Did they catch the guy?'

'The police did nothing.' His eyes dropped to the table. His jaw clenched tight.

'Later that night I went into town. I was so angry. I just needed to blow off steam. And that's when I saw him. A man with glasses and a hideous beard staggering along the road towards me, a beer bottle in his hand. It was Grandad, I knew it. The voices started shouting in my head. Telling me what I had to do. "He drinks the wine of my wrath," they said. "Ungodly. Cast out his iniquity."

'I followed him to a hotel room. The door hadn't been closed properly. A sign of the Lord's favour. The demon was passed out on the bed. I put my hands round his neck and squeezed hard until he was dead.' His hand twitched involuntarily. 'I was Raguel. The Fire of God.'

I looked at Lynch sitting there; his ironed-to-goodness shirt, his worked-up muscles, his OCD behaviour, and I thought about what he'd just said, the words he'd used.

Everything was in turmoil. I was shaking all over. The police did nothing.

And then – *I was Raguel. The Fire of God.*

It all made sense. His screwed-up childhood had created a man with an obsessive need for control. The mugging he talked about had destroyed his sense of order. It had made him vulnerable. And just like when he was a kid, the people who should have rescued him did nothing.

Which is why he'd chosen the night he was attacked to kill his first victim. The mugging had brought his old emotions to the fore. The murder was about reasserting his dominance.

'I found out the demon's name later,' Lynch said. 'Professor Copeland. It was in the papers.'

My blood jolted. So, the man he'd killed at Inverness Street wasn't the first victim? How many more men had he killed that we didn't know about?

And quick on the tail of that thought, another followed. Seven was such an important number to Lynch. And in his letter, he'd told me his grandfather would be his seventh target. But if he'd murdered Copeland too (and possibly more besides) then he'd done the maths wrong, which didn't fit with an obsessive compulsive.

'I thought your grandad was the seventh sinner,' I said, still using his lingo. 'But if you add the professor to the others you executed, that makes him the eighth.'

'Ziba Mac, you understand me so well. But don't worry, the demon in the hotel room doesn't count.'

'Why not?'

'Because I didn't exorcise the evil spirits or remove the source of his iniquity.'

'The source of—?' I stopped, realisation setting in. 'You mean you didn't cut off his penis?'

'Exactly.'

Lynch's hand twitched again. A look of pleasure passed over his face.

My scalp crackled as I made the connection. I'd nailed the profile but I'd missed something out.

This was never about a divine calling. That just gave him the excuse to do what he wanted deep down. Nor was his inner conflict simply about breaking the sixth commandment.

Despite what he wanted to believe, Aidan Lynch killed because murder excited him.

The Bible-basher had a taste for blood. No wonder he felt such a need to atone.

CHAPTER 101

It happened after I got home that evening. I should have known it would.

The Mehr Ensemble was playing in the background; sitars and vocal solos. Heartstring music. Outside the sky was dark and the air was turning cold.

I was curled up on the sofa in my pyjama bottoms and Duncan's old fisherman's sweater. There was a big glass of wine in my hand and a two-thirds-empty bottle of Malibu Estate Merlot on the coffee table. The phone was lying next to me. I'd just hung up with DCI Falcon.

'Duncan would have been proud,' he'd said, his parting words. Shards of glass straight to the heart.

I'd solved a twenty-five-year-old mystery. I'd got a killer off the streets. But my husband's killer has never been caught. His murder has never been solved.

I slumped down deeper into the sofa. The old tightness was back in my throat, a boulder pressed on my shoulders, my blood was turning to mire. The black pit was opening again.

I closed my eyes, inhaled deeply and tried to focus on my breathing the way I've been taught.

I don't know how long my eyes were shut or how long I was breathing in through my nose and out through my mouth trying to dispel the shadows, but I do know what pulled me out of myself and away from the all-too-familiar crevasse.

Saved by the bell, the girls at school used to say at the end of every lesson. It rang again. Ding-dong.

I might have ignored it if he hadn't called to me.

'I know you're in there, Mac. Open up.'

Sighing, I heaved myself off the sofa and padded over to the door.

'It's not a good time, Jack,' I said, opening it a crack, barring his way.

'Rubbish.' He pushed it wide. 'Get out of those old clothes and put your glad rags on. The Lacerator's banged up, the Samuel Catlin murder's been solved and I'm taking you out to celebrate. There's a swish new place just opened up in Notting Hill. I've booked us a table.'

'It's very nice of you but—'

'Hurry up,' he said, shushing me away from the door. 'We need to be there in half an hour or we'll lose our reservation.'

'I really don't feel like going out.'

He gave me a look. He knows my secret – the darkness that draws me in.

'I'm not taking no for an answer, Zeebs. You can sit there and just watch me stuff my face if you want, but you're coming with. Now go and get changed.'

'*The train approaching Platform 1 is the southbound Bakerloo Line service calling at Paddington, Charing Cross and Embankment. In the interests of safety, please stand back from the edge of the platform until your train comes to a complete stop.*'

It was only as the doors opened and we stepped onto the train that I realised Jack's never called me Zeebs before. The only person who ever has was Duncan.

There were plenty of empty seats scattered about. I plonked down at the end of the row and Jack settled next to me, stretching his legs out in front of him. As he did his thigh pressed against mine sending a flush of heat to my cheeks.

I glanced at him out of the corner of my eye. He was twiddling his thumbs and reading an ad for Optrex on the opposite wall. Maybe he hadn't noticed how close we were sitting; maybe he didn't care. I looked at my leg nestled next to his. Oh sod it, I thought, and kept it right where it was.

'*This train is now departing.*'

The doors snapped shut and the engine took a whistling intake of breath as it prepared to accelerate out of the station. We chug-chugged along the track, Jack's thigh warm next to mine.

'You saved me,' I whispered, as we emerged from a tunnel and the train slowed down on its approach to Paddington.

'I know how much you miss Duncan, Mac. But you're not alone,' he said, squeezing the back of my hand. 'I'm here for you. Always.'

I smiled at him, turned my hand over and interlaced my fingers with his. And we stayed like that for the rest of the journey.

EPILOGUE

The boy used to have the face of an angel but now all anyone sees is the Devil. He's spent so long battling demons he's ended up becoming one himself. And the monster the world needs saving from is actually him.

ACKNOWLEDGMENTS

Writing a novel is a bit like bringing up a baby. It really does take a village and I'm so lucky to have such wonderful people in mine.

Thank you to my brilliant agent, Alice Lutyens, whose sharp eye gave this story life and who never stopped pushing for me. I've loved every minute of working with you!

To Melissa Pimentel for your plot suggestions early on and for taking my book overseas. To Martin Toseland who helped me develop Ziba's character and to Helen Bryant from Cornerstones for championing me.

To the fantastic team at Thomas & Mercer, especially Jack Butler, not just for believing in me but also for your perceptive insights, edits and support. You've gone the extra mile for me and I really appreciate it.

To everyone on the Crime Writers' Association judging panel for shortlisting this book for the 2017 Debut Dagger Award; it was such an honour to be chosen out of so many entries.

And to the real criminal profilers, behavioural analysts and serial killer experts who have provided me with inspiration and material, in particular: John Douglas, Robert Keppel, Robert Ressler and Joe Navarro.

Ziba MacKenzie is the hero of this book, but these guys are mine:

My husband, Tim Slotover, who keeps me going; always encouraging me to dream big.

My sons, Max and Joey, who were both published before me. Watch this space!

My friends for putting up with me talking about my book all the time and yet still managing to sound interested. Special thanks to Linda-Jane Buckle (for being my biggest cheerleader), Ali Barr (for Scottish expressions – even the rude ones I couldn't use!), Paddy (for answering all my Scotland Yard questions), and my lovely writer friends Niki Mackay and Polly Philips (for all your support).

My parents, Martin and Carolyn, always so encouraging and enthusiastic about everything I do. And my brother and sister, David and Henrietta.

And finally *you*, my readers, for trusting me with your time.

If you enjoyed this I'd love to hear what you think and keep in touch. Visit me on Twitter **@VictoriaSelman** or at my website, **victoriaselmanauthor.com** for news and giveaways.

READ ON FOR A SAMPLE OF
BOOK TWO IN ZIBA'S
STORY, *NOTHING TO LOSE*

He killed those girls.
I have to tell someone.
Or I'm next.

SATURDAY

CHAPTER 1

Interview Room 3, Scotland Yard, 12.02

My God, how can this be happening? the man thinks, brain spinning out, as the detectives bring him in for interrogation.

The male DS is wearing a waistcoat and pocket square. His face is young but his eyes are hard, not like the female. She looks much softer.

Good cop, bad cop, he thinks. *But both are out to get me.*

'Have a seat,' the female says, gesturing with her hand.

The man sits down, eyes skittering round the room.

There's a white video camera mounted on the wall. A table set with three chairs, all bolted to the floor. A large black recorder tucked into a recess in the wall. And no window.

A low hum's coming from the overhead fluorescent lighting as though an insect's trapped inside the dirty bulb. And there's a lingering smell of cigarettes, despite the big 'No Smoking' sign on the door.

The room's a grey box. A holding pen. A torture chamber for the claustrophobic. The man's mouth is dry. It tastes stale, his tongue's sticking to the inside of his cheeks. It's cold in here but he's sweating like mad. His armpits are damp, his shirt's glued to his back. There's no way the detectives won't have noticed and drawn a conclusion, he thinks. First impressions count, he knows that. He's made his living out of it.

The male unwraps a cassette tape and puts it in the recorder. He clicks a button and the wheels begin to whir.

'I must inform you this interview is being audio recorded and may be used in evidence if your case is brought to court,' he says, shuffling his notes on top of a pile of case files as he goes through the spiel. 'My name is DS Silk. For the benefit of the tape, could you please state your full name and date of birth?'

The man's voice cracks in his throat as he answers, he's not used to sitting on this side of the table. He realises his nerves will be another strike against him. Language is easy to manipulate; he's always been good at reading people and pushing his agenda. But controlling his body is different. Emotions ooze out of our skin. *Even dogs can understand us*, he thinks, remembering an incident not so long ago.

DS Silk is non-confrontational to start with, blatantly trying to lull him into a false sense of security.

Letting me dig a pit for myself, he thinks. *Waiting to shove me in.*

The detective rolls up his sleeves and leans forward, fists on the table. The female is watching the man closely.

They're coming now, the questions he can't answer: *Where is she? What have you done with her?*

THREE DAYS EARLIER: WEDNESDAY

CHAPTER 2

Blomfield Villas, London, 03.00

'Help! Please! Someone!'

My voice came out as a whisper, croaky and weak, though in my head I was screaming. I was short of breath, dizzy and exhausted. My blood pressure was dropping, my pulse thready. I started to shake. My skin felt cold and clammy. I was light-headed and nauseous. My body was going into shock, flooding with epinephrine. A reaction to the blood loss. Without an IV I'd die.

If I hadn't been tied up I could have put pressure on my stab wounds to stem the bleeding. I could have loosened my clothes and elevated my legs. I could have called an ambulance too, I thought, looking over at my mobile phone lying inches out of reach in a spreading pool of blood.

Snap to, MacKenzie. I inhaled deeply from my diaphragm to steady my breathing.

Preserve your strength, that's what they taught us. Don't waste energy on things you can't control. And yet my mind was a kill house; thoughts ricocheting off the walls, firing off in every direction.

Multiple sharp force injuries to the upper torso. Cuts to the breasts and legs. Extreme overkill. This homicide was personal.

How many crime scenes have I attended? How many killers have I profiled based on their handiwork? Except I was the victim now. Someone else would be examining my body and looking for clues. Would they understand what had happened here? Would they see what I would have seen?

As the dull, throbbing pain in my ribs became dagger-sharp, the front door to our apartment block opened and Duncan came out into the street holding a steaming bowl of pasta. I could smell the home-made tomato sauce and freshly grated parmesan from the pavement. It made me want to puke.

I knew what was coming next.

I watched my husband twirl the spaghetti round his fork and bring it to his lips. My heart squeezed. The panic rose as bile in my oesophagus. In the distance there was a buzzing noise, loud and insistent. I tried to shout, to warn him what was about to happen. But my voice was locked in my throat.

He must have sensed me though, because at that moment he looked right where I was lying, my body bound, my flesh punctured with open-mouthed lesions. And yet he didn't react. Why isn't he moving out of the way?

'Duncan, get down!'

Nothing.

Despite all my training and years of experience, there wasn't a single damn thing I could do to save him.

The bullet came then, the bullet I knew would come, the bullet I couldn't stop. Fired from an unmarked VW Crafter with no plates. An execution shot which blasted my husband's forehead, leaving a deep circular wound with seared edges and heavy tattooing. His knees buckled. His body tilted forward. And he collapsed on to the concrete, the poppy in his buttonhole sprayed with arterial blood.

I screamed again and this time the sound came out so loudly it woke me up. My heart was clobbering, the sheets soaked in sweat, my husband's spot cold as a grave.

My mobile was vibrating on the nightstand next to the device I'd found only hours earlier.

Backlit on the screen were three words: SCOTLAND YARD HOMICIDE

CHAPTER 3

I fumbled for the switch on my bedside lamp and answered the phone in a sleep-furred voice. Since quitting the SF and going freelance, there have been plenty of late-night briefings, critical updates and pre-dawn crime scene visits. But a zero-dark-thirty call from Scotland Yard when I wasn't part of an investigation? That was new.

Whatever this was about, it wasn't going to be a beach barbeque, that's for sure.

'Ziba MacKenzie.' I reached for a biro and pad of paper, my brain already shifting into first.

'Mac, DCI Falcon here. Apologies for the ungodly hour. But we need your help. We have . . .' He hesitated. 'A situation.'

He was rattled. This was serious then. Falcon's been on the job since Jesus was a corporal. Like me he's seen more than his fair share of guts and gore. And also like me, he's become habituated to the sort of violence that would send Joe Public into a lifetime of therapy. So, what could have shaken him now?

'What's going on, sir?'

'The homicide in Primrose Hill. You know the one?'

'Aye, of course.'

The papers had been full of it. No surprises there. That level of violence, never mind depravity, always shifts copies. On top of which the victim was a pretty, young mother. The police still had no leads and the discovery site was slap-bang in the middle of Celebrity Central, home to the sort of A-listers even I've heard of. It was Christmas and Chanukah rolled into one for the news boys. They'd be pumping the story until there was no juice left.

I always take a professional interest in murder cases, even when I'm not on the investigation team. But this one was different. This time the victim looked a lot like me.

'Yasmin Pejman. Nasty business,' I said to Falcon now.

'Yep.'

And there it was again, another pause. My stomach tripped. So much of communication is non-verbal. I didn't need him to say what he did next. It wasn't just his speech patterns that gave it away. I've been round the block long enough to know the way killers work, and the way Yasmin Pejman's body had been posed hinted at what was to come. I'd almost been waiting for it.

'The perp's struck again,' he said. 'Same MO. Same victimology. Found in the same area as the last dump site.'

'And the positioning of the corpse?'

'Like before. Legs splayed. Skirt up. Womb ripped out.'

So, the signature was the same too. Contrary to what most law enforcement bods will tell you, signature, not MO, is the critical component when it comes to profiling offenders and linking crimes. It's the combination of ritual and method and is as unique as a set of fingerprints. Understand the signature and you understand the perp.

'Two murders in little over a week. You know what that means?

'We're dealing with a serial killer. And he's just warming up.'

Nothing to Lose will be published in Spring 2019

ABOUT THE AUTHOR

Photo © 2018 Andrew Marshall

After graduating from Oxford University, Victoria Selman studied Creative Writing at the City Lit and wrote for the *Ham & High* and *Daily Express* newspapers. In 2013 she won the Full Stop Short Story Prize and her first novel, *Blood For Blood*, was shortlisted for the 2017 Debut Dagger Award. Victoria lives in London with her husband and two sons.